Blue

LISA GLASS

Quercus

New York • London

Quercus

New York • London

ISBN 978-1-62365-414-6

Library of Congress Control Number: 2015933389

Distributed in the United States and Canada by
Hachette Book Group
1290 Avenue of the Americas
New York, NY 10104

Manufactured in the United States

10 9 8 7 6 5 4 3 2 1

www.quercus.com

For Amelie, Alyssa,
Laura and Eve

"There's beauty in the deep;
the wave is bluer than the sky"
                         John G. C. Brainard, 1795–1828

Chapter One

We stared up at the twinkling lights on the ceiling. In the quiet ballroom, I could hear his deep breathing as if it was my own. If I just reached out my arm, my fingers would graze his chest. I moved my head a fraction of an inch to see him better. A couple of years older than me, he had longish brown hair, sun-streaked and wet, and a tattoo down his right forearm that said *Surf or Die*. I had no idea who he was.

This was not what I'd had in mind when I'd finally given in to Kelly's nagging and agreed to come to the yoga class at Hotel Serenity. I hadn't even bothered to put on make-up; I was expecting a handful of yummy mommies and some bendy old ladies because, well, yoga was for sophisticated ladies, right? Not in this class. Crammed into the hotel ballroom there were at least a dozen very hot guys, and the hottest one of them all had put his yoga mat right next to mine.

I looked over to my best friend, who turned up late. Kelly was in the row opposite me, grinning her head off. She'd been coming to this yoga class for a while, but she hadn't warned me. After everything that had happened with Daniel, I had barely gone anywhere or seen anyone for months. This was Kelly's way of getting me back in the dating game, I guessed.

Keep cool, I told myself. I was so busy telling myself to keep cool that I totally lost track of what the teacher—a skinny blond woman called Natasha, who was in her mid-twenties and wearing nothing but a bikini top and some yellow board shorts—was going on about.

She smiled over at me and said, "Yoga is perfect for you teenage girls. It will encourage you to be strong, brave, open to change and, most important of all: to live in the moment."

When she turned away, I shook my head very slightly at Kelly and mouthed the words, "Is she for real?"

Kelly nodded, and mouthed back what looked like, "Trust me."

People were moving to sit in a cross-legged position and doing something crazy with their breathing. I'd missed the instructions and sat there like an idiot.

The surfer dude turned to me and smiled. His face was a bit sunburned and, what with the wet hair and still-damp T-shirt, I knew he'd come straight from the sea, probably not even stopping for food or a rest. He was swigging from a bottle of water and he had that surfed-out, super-contented look that shredheads get after a decent session. It was the weirdest thing, but he gave off this vibe of total confidence.

"It's like this: you're sitting up really straight, taking a big breath, then slamming the air out of your lungs using your core.

Your belly is coming back to meet your spine, OK? And it's a count of eight. So—" He took a really deep breath and then let his breath out in eight sharp exhalations. I had to look away when he was doing it, because the exercise was basically really loud panting, which is not exactly a normal thing to practice with a guy you've only known for twenty seconds.

"Chick in the bikini says we'll feel it in our abs tomorrow," he said. I detected an accent. American? Yeah, but not strong, and different somehow. Other stuff was in there too. South African or Kiwi, maybe. If he was American, then he had traveled away from home, definitely. Probably lived abroad for a while.

"Wanna try?"

"Is this right?" I said, trying to squeeze the air out of my chest without making any kind of porny sound.

"Yeah, but you need to do it harder. Watch out, it'll give you a real headrush the first few times."

I did what he said. He was right about the headrush. I was seeing stars.

"That's it," he whispered, giving me a fist bump.

"I've never done it before. Er, *yoga*, I mean."

I hadn't done the other thing either, but he didn't need to know that. And anyway, that was the last thing I wanted rushing around my head as I talked to this guy. I was already about two seconds from going red.

The teacher went to fiddle with her iPod, trying to find the right hippie soundtrack for background music, so we had a few moments to chat.

"You'll get the hang of it. I'm Zeke, by the way."

"Iris," I said, smiling back at him and wishing I had a cooler name. I also wished I'd dressed in something nicer than a faded Maroon 5 T-shirt and my old blue running shorts. In an ideal world I'd have also shaved my cactus legs that morning and maybe put on some mascara.

"Pretty name," he said. "I used to really dig that song 'Iris' by the Goo Goo Dolls."

"I think I was named after the blue flower, not the song or, y'know, the colorful bit of your eye."

"It's kinda cool any way you look at it."

He liked my name? Even Daniel thought it was weird.

"So, if I'm remembering my Classics right, Iris was the Greek goddess of the rainbow?"

"Yeah," I said, impressed. I only knew that because it was on a fridge magnet my mom bought me when I was eight. "You had Classics lessons at your school?"

"We were mostly home-schooled by our mom."

Lucky boy. More time for surfing.

The teacher's voice rang out again, and I locked eyes with Kelly, who was completely lit up with excitement. Her eyes darted to Zeke and she blatantly mouthed the word "phwoar."

"Now if you could all move to the front of your mats, we'll begin the first round of our sun salutations. Firm your feet down into the mat, take an inhalation and reach up to the sky . . ."

The teacher's voice droned on and I tried to concentrate on her instructions as best as I could, but I kept getting distracted by the sound of Zeke moving to my left and the flashes of him I could see through the curtain of my hair, which I'd forgotten to tie up.

In many ways, yoga was a lot like surfing; it used the same muscles, required lots of strength, coordination and balance, and, just like surfing, yoga looked super-easy but was absolutely exhausting.

It would have been a lot easier to concentrate without the mirrored walls opposite us. I couldn't stop taking sly glances at Zeke. But he was totally absorbed in what he was doing, and I didn't see him look at the mirrors once.

"Now it's that time of the class when we get into pairs for assisted inversions. Today we're doing handstands! You know you love them . . ."

I turned to Kelly but she was looking at the blond boy next to her, rocking with laughter, and then the next thing I knew the yoga teacher had paired me with Zeke.

I had to turn to face him. He turned at the same moment and suddenly I was looking up into his face, all fierce blue eyes and high cheekbones.

There was a moment of silence, which I ended by saying, "How do we do it?"

He cocked an eyebrow at me and smiled, but didn't make any jokes. He was wearing a blue T-shirt and some gray baggies, hanging low on his hips, and I watched as he dragged his yoga mat toward the wall.

"Stretch into a downward dog," he said.

Downward dog is basically making a big triangle with your body, with your hands and feet on the ground and your butt as high in the air as it will go. I had to do this facing *away* from Zeke.

I could feel the heat come into my face. Kelly caught my eye again, flashing me a funny look where she simultaneously went cross-eyed and touched the tip of her nose with her tongue. She did things like this when she thought I was acting too serious. Message received. I would just have to get this over and done with. I bent right over in front of Zeke, put my hands on the ground and made a triangle with my body.

"OK," I said, between my own ankles, noticing that Zeke had a couple of long thin scars on his shins, where he'd probably been caught by his surfboard fins. "Now what do I do?"

"Put all your weight into your left leg. Make it really heavy because I'm gonna hold it."

"What do you mean, 'hold it'?" I mumbled.

Before I could say anything else, he had taken hold of my left leg, one of his hands strong on my calf and the other around my thigh. My right foot swung up and touched the wall, and he guided my left leg up after it. So there I was, doing my first ever yoga handstand.

"Now flex your toes, and squeeze your legs against my fist."

My arms began to shake, though I wasn't sure whether that was because of the strain on them or because there was a strange boy's fist between my thighs.

All I could think was: Oh my God, a totally gorgeous surfer dude has his hand three inches from my pants. Do not faint, sneeze, puke, fart, burp or make any other mortifying noise AT ALL.

At the same time though, and as sad as it was to admit, it was kind of nice to be touched by another human being, especially a hot male human being. I realized that since it had all gone bat-shit crazy with Daniel, I was seriously low on human contact. Sometimes my mom or Kelly would grab me for a hug, but apart from that, day in, day out, I was flying solo.

"The more you squeeze your legs together, the more strength you can draw on in your core, and the more stable you'll be. Feel it? Deep in your abdominals, yeah? Now bring your toes away from the wall and just balance on your hands."

Somehow I managed to squeeze my thighs against his fist, balance for ten seconds, and then my feet went sailing to the floor with a bang.

"Aced it," he said.

"I s'pose you don't need me to get you up?"

Honestly, it was like I could not stop saying the most embarrassing things.

Before he got a chance to reply, the yoga teacher's voice boomed: "Assisted backbends. Get into threes."

Kelly sauntered over and was followed by the teacher.

"Zeke, will you demonstrate, honey?"

"Sure thing."

"OK. Could you assist Zeke?" she said to me. I nodded, even though I had literally no idea what I was doing.

"Kelly, could you come around to the other side?"

"Sure."

"Now, Zeke, turn to face the wall, please, and the girls will stand on either side of you," she said, nodding at me.

I moved to stand opposite Kelly, just a few inches from Zeke.

"You grab each other's wrists and hold on tight so you're like two arms attached to two bodies, OK? Right, you're going to move one of your arms to the imaginary bra line. Not that Zeke is wearing a bra, of course."

Kelly gave me her "you never know" look, but at least didn't say it.

"And the other arm goes to the base of the spine."

At this point the yoga teacher shoved our wrists into the top of Zeke's butt, which I could totally feel under my hand. Kelly winked across at me and I knew my face was burning up.

"Zeke, put your hands into prayer position, that's it. So, we are going to concentrate on our man 100 hundred percent. Spread your legs and bend your knees a little, darling, so you have a nice stable base. Great. Now, with you supporting him, Zeke is going to lean backward. He's going to think length, stretch up and then back. That's it. When Zeke sees the floor, he's going to release his arms from prayer position until he can touch the ground, and then you'll leave him in wheel pose until he's ready to come back up."

Zeke did this with no problem and held the wheel pose for ages. My legs were trembling from being crouched for so long with my arms beneath his back. I couldn't even risk looking at Kelly, so I stared at Zeke's feet, which had serious knots on them from hardcore surfboard action. When he'd had enough, the teacher counted to three and we whipped Zeke back up to standing.

Before anyone else could try the backbend, the teacher said to Zeke, "Let's try one more thing. Could you demonstrate scorpion pose, just to give the rest of the class something to aim for? You do know scorpion, I take it?"

"Nope. Always wanna learn though."

The teacher loved that and said she'd instruct him every step of the way, of course she would, and there was no need to worry because he was in safe hands.

Scorpion pose, it seemed, was like a headstand, but instead of balancing on his head, Zeke had to balance only on his forearms, arching his torso with his legs held still in the air.

It looked ridiculously difficult.

"Perfect," the yoga teacher said, grinning from ear to ear, when Zeke held the pose.

The veins in Zeke's forearms were bulging. The fabric of his T-shirt was stretched tight across his shoulders, and the bottom of it had slipped up toward his ribcage, so that everyone could see his taut stomach. Standing to the side of him, I could also see that he had a tribal tattoo curling up his back and I caught a glimpse of a weird word.

YOLO

I knew what that meant. Boys who had that tattooed on to their bodies were macho, risk-taking adrenalin junkies. It meant they lived on the edge, that they preferred stroking out to a killer wave and dying in a blaze of glory, to dying old in bed. You Only Live Once.

At least it was better than Daniel's tattoo, which was inked as a tramp stamp across the top of his butt, just above the tan line, with the hardened stokehead slogan: *Eddie Would Go*. The Eddie in question was Eddie Aikau, the Hawaiian surfer who was known for paddling out to the craziest waves on the planet. When working out if the surf was too big and gnarly for a surf contest, someone had once replied, "Eddie would go," and the phrase was sucked into surf culture. Eddie died a hero after disappearing at sea, at age thirty-one. Still, I always thought it was a stupid thing to have tattooed on your ass. But that was

Daniel. Not the greatest thinker in the world. His other tattoo was a swirling black script written up his forearm, which said, *"If it ain't got fins, boobs or sparkplugs, I ain't interested."*

The rest of the class looked pretty awed at Zeke's strength and balance, especially Kelly, who gave me a few vigorous nods that quite clearly told me, "If this guy is single, you are asking him out."

The teacher gave Zeke a little round of applause, as he came up red-faced and panting.

I smiled at Zeke, and was debating whether or not to go for a high-five when the teacher boomed in my ear, "Now back to our assisted backbends. Iris, is it? It's your turn."

I thought about Zeke's hand on my ass, panicked and said, "Um, I'll sit this one out. Think I tweaked my back in that handstand."

Kelly looked concerned and gave my back a quick rub. She was only six months older than me, but she was like my big sister. We had grown up together on Fistral Beach, bodysurfing when we were really little. I was a crazy kid with no fear. The beach lifeguards had to rescue me about once a week. They'd call my mom and say, "Your girl is a total nuisance. She got caught in a rip current again," and my mom would say, "No, not Iris, she's doing her homework in her bedroom," but of course I wasn't in my bedroom. When the surf was up, I was out and, short of chaining me up, there was not much my mom could do about it. My dad had gone, Kelly's dad too, and our moms were working more than one job each. In fact, my mom was working three, so she could afford to pay the bills while getting her teaching qualification. So Kelly and me made a new family down the beach. The silver surfers checked in on us, and Kelly tried her best to stop me from doing the potentially deadly stuff like high cliff-jumping, or lilo-surfing storm waves. And, when I wouldn't listen, she'd stick around so that if I got smashed, the lifeguards would know where to look.

"No way am I doing that backbend either," Kelly said. "My spine's had enough of a beating already from three hours of kayaking."

"Oh no, time's up. Savasana," the teacher said, gazing at Zeke.

"Chill-out time," he translated for me.

"Time to get your socks and sweaters as the body will get very cold very quickly once the muscles are inactive," the teacher went on. She didn't bother getting dressed though, I noticed, wondering again why anyone in their right mind would choose to do yoga wearing a bikini top.

I didn't have socks or a sweater, but I didn't care because, lying next to Zeke, I was red hot.

The teacher lit an incense stick and a candle, and then she turned off the lights.

For a moment the room was absolutely silent, and then people began to breathe deeply as the teacher went through every area of our bodies, getting us to focus on the muscles that she wanted us to relax. Zeke was breathing really loudly next to me, much louder than I was. All of the boys were. Did boys have bigger, stronger lungs than girls? Or was that totally crazy? Yep, I had gone crazy. Fantasizing about a boy's lungs was a new low.

Just relax, Iris, relax, I told myself.

"Breathe into any areas of tension. Breathe out any stress. Be at one with the universe."

I messed this up totally. I was incapable of being at one with the universe. I wasn't even capable of being at one with my yoga mat. I kept shifting, wriggling to get comfortable. All I could concentrate on was the fact that the first boy I had liked in ages was lying next to me. When do you get to lie on the floor, in the dark, with a cute boy?

When it counts, that's when.

Kelly skipped out in the middle of the relaxation segment of the class, as she always had a cleaning shift on Friday evenings, but she made the phone sign, so I knew I'd be hearing from her before too long. Seeing Kelly get up, another girl also took the opportunity to leave early. That girl had seriously long legs, red hair tied in a bun at the nape of her neck like a ballet dancer and the sort of curves that Daniel would call "pure filth." I didn't get a look at her face from my position sprawled on the floor but, as she padded quietly past me, I heard her whisper, "Bye, Zeke. See you tomorrow, darling." Even from her whisper I could tell she was posh. She had that confident public-schoolgirl drawl, like Liz Hurley chatting up Nate Archibald in *Gossip Girl*. Uggh.

Who was she? More important, who was she to Zeke?

Finally the class ended and I started to roll up my mat, keeping my eyes firmly on the ground in case Zeke caught me staring, but also because it was hard to look straight at him: something about him was a bit blinding. I was just putting the mat in the big cardboard box at the back of the ballroom when I felt a hand on my shoulder.

"You surf?" he said.

Chapter Two

The Earth is constantly battered by waves. Sound waves, light waves, heat waves, radio waves, but the waves of the ocean are the only ones I care about. When you step into the ocean you are stepping off the everyday solid world and entering something that has way more power than anything you will ever encounter on land, and it is awesome.

Yeah, I surfed, but I was so startled by his question that it took me a moment to answer. There's surfing for fun, which I did, and then there's radical skills surfing, which I didn't do. So I went with, "Um, a bit."

"Knew it."

"Sure you did," I said, smiling.

"You've totally got the surfer shoulders."

"Oh," I said, not sure if I liked the sound of that.

"And, y'know the incredible poise," he added, trying to dig himself out of the hole. He caught my gaze and looked at me dead-on, making my mind go totally blank again. "There's a big swell coming in. Sets building at the north end of the beach. Wanna go catch a few?"

"Haven't you already been out today?" I said, looking up at his still-damp hair.

"Yeah, but only like four or five hours. Can fit in another two hours, easy, before sundown."

After five hours of surfing I would be dead, that much I knew. This boy surfed seven hours a day? That was insane. Or at least a serious addiction. No wonder he was a pro at yoga. He must have been all muscle.

All these thoughts flooded through my head in a split second, but my brain caught on the image of Zeke in scorpion pose and his T-shirt riding up and I couldn't think of anything to say except, "The lifeguards will have gone home."

"We can take care of each other."

"It's not that," I said. "The lifeguard flags will be gone, so everyone will be mixed in. These conditions? It'll be packed out there until the sky turns pitch black. We'll have to watch out for kooks and speed bumps."

Kooks are novice surfers and they are a pain in the ass to more advanced surfers. They get in the way, they don't know how to handle their boards and what's worse is that they roam in packs of hundreds, which is why the lifeguards normally cram them into a little space down the south end of the beach, between the black-and-white flags, where they can't cause too much trouble to real surfers. They're always injuring each other though, because they're show-off menaces with no proper train-ing and a minimal understanding of the sea's power.

"Speed bumps?" he said, frowning.

"You know—bodyboarders."

He smiled. "I never heard that before. Harsh, but kind of accurate, I guess. Back home they call them dick-draggers. Or shark biscuits."

You'd think that stand-up surfers and bodyboarders could be friends, but it never seemed to work out like that. There was this rivalry that didn't go away. It could be funny but it was also a shame, because almost all stand-up surfers started out bodyboarding as kids.

But why would you stick with a bodyboard when you had the option of a real surfboard? Something that took real skills and paid off with real thrills. I didn't get it.

"So you gonna come hang? You can use one of my spare boards if you can't be assed going to get yours."

I looked at my watch, not because I was particularly inter-ested that it was 7:35 p.m., but because I needed a moment to think. He wasn't actually asking me out, was he? Me, with my ancient shorts and make-up-free face?

As I told Kelly later, I'd have much rather gone home and watched *EastEnders* than gone surfing with this gorgeous boy. *Even though I really liked him.* That was how scared I'd become in the few months since Daniel, suspicious of everything outside my own bedroom.

But something the yoga teacher had said came back to me. During relaxation she'd been banging on about the importance of being open to new experiences, to new adventures and to new people, telling us how saying yes, instead of no, could change our lives for the better. It sounded a million miles away from the boring person I'd become.

What's the worst that can happen? I thought.

"OK. You're on."

I put on my flip-flops, grabbed my skateboard and followed him out of the ballroom, through the hotel's bar and down to the esplanade.

"Boards are on my van," he said, nodding at a retro VW camper which was gleaming silver in the evening sunlight and looked as if it had been refurbed to mint condition. He had his own ride, so he was at least seventeen, then. A year older than me. The same age as Daniel.

I looked out to the bay and saw set after set lining up; pure corduroy.

"Definitely OK for me to borrow one?"

"Sure."

"What if I ding it?" Nightmare. Damaged surfboards were tricky and expensive to fix, but if you didn't bother, the board would get waterlogged and have to be chucked in the bin.

"You won't. I trust ya. Even if you do, who cares?"

He trusted me. I'd known him less than one hour. I didn't even trust me and I'd known me for sixteen years.

"Can I leave my skateboard in your van? Don't want it to get stolen."

"No problem. Sling it wherever."

I slid it in front of two of his skateboards, a regular-sized one and a much longer carveboard. It made sense. Skateboarding is basically land-surfing, or "sidewalk surfing" as they call it in America.

He had five surfboards on the roof rack of his van, including two seriously fancy high-performance longboards. Just those two boards alone would have cost him a couple of grand.

Zeke stood behind me as I examined all this, and I eventually picked out a seven-foot-six mini-Malibu, which I knew I'd be able to catch at least a few waves on.

Surfers say you are what you ride. In which case, that would make me a pretty sturdy, pretty easy pig board.

"OK if I nab the mini-Mal?"

As I said it, my eyes dropped to the inside of his van again and I noticed he had a rolled-up duvet and some pillows stashed near the back. Home-from-home or shag wag? A lot of the dopehead surfers who lived in their vans at the South Fistral esplanade were total douches when it came to surf groupies. There were always girls angling to get into a surfer's wagon, even if only for a half-hour, and there were plenty of guys that let them. In the years I'd spent hanging out at the esplanade, I'd seen some of the worst offenders have five or six girls going through their vans in one *afternoon*. I really hoped that wasn't the case with Zeke.

"Good choice," he said. "You'll get some great rides on that."

"Hope so. I guess it's the safe choice really. The easiest board to ride . . ."

"Nothin' about surfing is easy. Or safe."

"Yeah, but these waves are, what, four or five feet?"

He stared at the break, this heavy look in his eyes. "I know this French guy. Great surfer. Rode huge waves at Teahupo'o in Tahiti. He comes back to his home break in Biarritz. Shoulder-high waves that day, nothing special at all, but he falls, and he hits the bottom. With his head."

"Shit. What happened? Is he OK?"

"That was his last surf. He broke a cervical vertebra and severed his spinal cord. He's in a wheelchair now, paralyzed from the neck down. No reef there, and he didn't even cop a boulder. The bottom was sand. The force of the wave closing out on his back slammed his head into the sand hard enough to snap his neck."

"Shit," I said again. I didn't know what else to say.

"So yeah, surfing's always dangerous, whatever you ride, wherever you ride it. And no board is harder or easier than another. They're all just instruments with their own music."

I noticed how much Zeke used his hands when he talked about surfing, how he couldn't seem to keep still, not even for a moment, which was weird after seeing him so still and composed in yoga class.

With every passing minute, I was liking him more. He was just so totally himself. No front, no bull. And he was freakishly chilled out.

Zeke looked over his remaining boards and eventually picked up a red-and-white longboard that looked like it should have been in the Surfing Hall of Fame. It was heavily glassed, single fin and shaped in a retro sixties design.

"It was my grandfather's," he went on, as if reading my thoughts. "Pop used to shape his own boards. Made some money. Taught my mom too. Later my pa bought into the business, once my mom taught him how to surf."

Zeke was obviously from surfing royalty, then. His parents were surfers, so was his granddad, and I'd bet if Zeke ever had a kid, the kid would surf too. It was in the genes.

"She taught *him* to surf?"

"Yeah, he'd hardly been in the water until he met her. She was a natural. Like a young Rell Sunn. She looked like Rell too. Just beautiful. Their board business is still going strong, though someone else owns it."

Rell Sunn was Hawaiian. A legendary waterwoman and a world surfing champion. So was Zeke's mother Hawaiian too? Or some other kind of foreign? It would explain Zeke's good looks. Those high cheekbones.

"Oh, right," I said, hoping he would tell me more, but not wanting to ask any personal questions about his family. Being with Daniel had made me sensitive to those particular pitfalls. Zeke seemed to have no such hang-ups though, and carried on like it was normal to talk about your folks to a complete stranger, "I'm a bit of a mutt. My mom's Hawaiian and my pa's from Newquay, but he only just moved back here. Before that he was doing his paramedic thing someplace called Ex . . . Exeter, I think?"

"So you're just visiting?"

"Yeah. Pa's about to turn fifty and is having a huge party. Plus Nanna—Pa's mom—is pretty sick with her heart, so I wanna stick around as long as I can."

"Oh, I'm sorry. That must be really rough for your dad."

"It is. I say 'Pa,' but he's actually my stepfather. My biological father is some Danish guy, but, after having three sons with my mom, he figured family life wasn't for him. He bailed when I was five months old. Haven't seen the loser since."

"It's OK, you don't have to tell me about it, if you'd rather not."

"Nah, it's no secret. Pa adopted me and my brothers, and we had this amazing childhood. But he and Mom split up, what, three years ago, when I was, like, fifteen. It's all good though. They're still friends."

So Zeke was eighteen.

"Sucks when that happens," I said, thinking of my own parents.

"Pa wanted to move back to England permanently. Mom didn't. She's in love with Hawaii. She got a boyfriend pretty soon after my pa left. She's a big personality, you know?"

I nodded, although clearly I didn't know.

"So what do you think of Fistral?" Safest to change the subject.

"What's not to like? The surf's clean, so is the beach. I've never actually been here before, as Nanna only recently switched nursing homes. Before that she was in, um, Exeter, but she wanted to come back here, as it's where she lived when she was young, so Pa changed his job to be with her. Had a short gap in my planner, so I thought I'd stick around for my family. Stoked I did."

He gave me this really pointed look. Did he mean he was happy because of me? Nah, that was ridiculous. We'd only just met.

"It's looked pretty solid for the last week," I said.

"Yeah, it's been great out there. Just the best fun, and I've scored plenty."

"Yeah?" I said, my heart freezing.

"Of waves, I mean."

I was glad he cleared that up. He was right about the surf. We both turned to look at the beach. The waves were totally clean with no wind chop, and I was actually starting to look forward to an evening surf session. I hadn't been out for ages. I hadn't wanted to do anything except watch crummy TV, eat Cheerios straight from the box and obsessively listen to the song "Daniel" by Dia Frampton on my iPod.

Once upon a time nothing had made me happier than surfing. How could I have given up something I loved so much? Just because I was worried about bumping into a stupid boy?

"Wow, the sky is pretty here," Zeke said. "One of the great things about living near the sea is that you can really relax your eyes. In the city, your eyes never really look into the distance. They're always being caught by something in the foreground. But if you come out here at dusk or dawn, you can stand on the cliff and look out and the light is soft enough for you to not get dazzled and you can really look into the distance. Your eyes can just let go and soar."

Looking out over the ocean then, with Zeke next to me, felt a lot like soaring.

"My wetsuits are gonna be way too big for you," he said, breaking the silence. He was a lot taller than me, and though he had that surfer narrowness around the waist, he also had the typical surfer barrel chest.

I couldn't go home to get my own, because as soon as I was through my front door, I'd lose my nerve and not come back.

"It's all right," I said.

The board-rental shack was about to close, but I ran up to a dreadlocked guy who was hosing down the wetsuits.

"Hey, Denny, any chance I could grab a suit?"

"No worries, Iris. Take whatever you want. Just chuck it in the big yellow bucket around the back when you're finished. Promise you won't pee in it, huh? No wettie warmers."

I laughed. What happened in the ocean stayed in the ocean. Except in the case of wetsuits.

"I promise. Actually, I'd better use your toilet before I get into it."

I came out carrying the cold wetsuit over one arm, and saw that Zeke had changed his mind about the old longboard and put a shortboard on the pavement instead.

He was busy wriggling into his own wetsuit and I saw his baggies crumpled on the pavement, so he was obviously old school and went naked underneath. I quite often did that too. There's nothing worse than a bikini getting jammed in some unspeakable place underneath a wetsuit and you not being able to move it. I grabbed a beach towel from the van and began the undignified process of squeezing myself into the suit while trying not to flash any passers-by; not an easy task.

Eventually the suit was over my legs and I was grabbing the neoprene on my hips and tugging it up, while holding on to the towel with my chin and jumping down deeper into the suit. Zeke was trying not to watch this, but I could tell he was amused.

"Need a hand?" he said.

I forced my arms into the damp fabric, dropped the towel and turned my back to him. "Yeah. Thank you."

He grabbed the zip and I could feel his fingers on my back, giving me goosebumps. He zipped me up slowly so as not to catch any skin and I turned back around to do the same for him, when I noticed a jagged scar running between his shoulder blades up to his neck.

"What's with the *Jaws* scar?" I said.

"Coral reef tattoo."

I zipped him up and was going to ask him more when a car with some crazy heavy-metal tune pumping came tearing down the road. As the car slowed behind me, I realized the track was "Killing in the Name" by Rage Against the Machine, and then I saw the blue VW Beetle with a black shark painted on the hood. Daniel. Next to him was his new girlfriend.

Chapter Three

"Yo, Iris!" Daniel shouted, waving. He dropped his hand and looked at Zeke.

I walked over to the car, and he turned down the volume of his stereo for the last part of the track, the main sentiment of which was probably his personal anthem.

"All right, Daniel," I said, my heart sinking down to the pit of my stomach at the sight of my ex-friend Cass sitting there, all straightened blond hair and red lipstick. Daniel was wearing the gray Vans cap I had bought him on our trip to Bude. Back when he had promised me we'd be together forever.

"We're gonna park up and watch the sun go down. It's supposed to be amazing tonight." As Daniel said this, he looked slightly apologetic. Cass smirked. Watching the sun go down. Yeah, right. And the rest.

I turned to Zeke, who looked up and gave me a big smile.

"Who's the new kid?"

"Hardly a kid. He's a year older than you, Daniel. And taller."

"Skinnier though."

"More like fitter."

Daniel was muscly, not fat, but he had that thick, bull-necked build. He was five foot nine to Zeke's six foot one. Like most surfers, Daniel was constantly eating, or drinking protein shakes. You could pretty much eat what you wanted when you surfed.

"New boyfriend?" Cass said, nodding toward Zeke. I ignored her, something I intended to do for the rest of my life.

I looked at Daniel. "No."

"Who is he, then?" Cass asked.

I spoke to Daniel again.

"I just met him and we're going surfing. He's not my boyfriend."

"No wonder," said Cass. "Premier league, that one. Would you look at the shoulders on him. Good arms too, perfect V torso, fab butt." Zeke turned toward us. "*Amazing* eyes." Jesus, Cass was annoying. She was worse than boys for perving. I honestly didn't know how Daniel could stand her.

Daniel was still eyeballing Zeke with a grim look on his face—not that he had the right to say anything about who I spent time with. Not anymore.

"I know that dude," Daniel said.

"No, you don't."

"Not *know him*, know him. I mean I, like, recognize him."

"So who is he?"

"Dunno. But I seen him somewhere. I don't forget faces."

"I'll never forget that face. In fact, let me get a photo," Cass said, smirking. I shot her a pissed-off look, but she didn't put her phone down.

"You don't know what you're talking about," I said to Daniel. "He's new here. Just arrived last week."

"New from where?"

"Hawaii, I think."

"Just what Fistral needs. Another foreigner thinking he owns the place, disrespecting the locals and scratching for every wave out there. Be two minutes before he gets a slap off one of the tribe."

Zeke was busy waxing the boards and was totally ignoring Daniel, although he must have heard Daniel talking stink about him.

"He's cool, Daniel. Just leave him alone, OK? You not going out for the glass-off?"

A glass-off is the early evening when the sea is calm, the wind drops and the breaking waves are smooth as glass.

"Nah, the plans with the missus gotta come first, eh? Check out the quiver of boards on that van. You'll have fun keeping up with him, dear," Daniel said, turning to nod at the breakers coming in thick and fast.

Daniel had spent the past two summers as a surf instructor for Ocean Ride Surf School, which is when he'd started saying things like "a quiver of boards." Waves were no longer good, they were "porno," "crippler" or "super-epic."

In fact, since Daniel started working there, he'd begun acting like he owned the beach, dropping in on the waves of other surfers if he thought they weren't good enough to ride them properly. The more I thought about it, the more I realized that

Daniel had become a total tool in the past year: ultra-competitive and selfish. No wonder he didn't like the look of Zeke. God help a guy that Daniel thought might surf better than he did.

Cass piped up with, "Keeping up with that dude? She *wishes*," which annoyed Daniel even more.

"Shut up, Cass," he said, "you're really starting to give me a headache."

Ha. Good. They deserved each other.

"I've gotta split," I said, seeing that Zeke had almost finished waxing the boards and was looking over at me. There wasn't that much time until nightfall.

Daniel couldn't resist one parting shot. "Don't waste your time, Iris. You know he'll end up with a Barbie on his arm."

"Yeah, you'd know all about that," I shot back.

"Well, don't blame me when he breaks your heart."

I walked back to Zeke, still sick at the thought of Cass and Daniel all cozied up together and having the nerve to take a shot at me.

"Sorry," I said to Zeke, shaking my head.

"Friends of yours?"

"No."

"Used to be, huh?"

"I guess not," I said.

Zeke gave me a look like he knew a thing or two about people letting you down and breaking your heart, but he changed the subject.

"So let's go surfing already," Zeke said. He locked his van, stashed his keys on a magnet under the wheel arch and then picked up his board.

But it was as if all the courage had drained out of my feet, because all I wanted to do was turn back and go home. In the end, I made myself go.

Walking down to the beach, I could tell that other people were staring at Zeke, most likely wondering what he was doing with me in my horrible rented wetsuit and easy board.

We were wading through the ankle busters when, at the worst moment possible, just when I had dropped my board leash and was bending over to get it, three tweeny girls came up to Zeke and took pictures of him on their mobiles. They tried to do this slyly, but the flashes from their camera phones lit up the evening beach.

Zeke didn't say anything. It seemed like he was embarrassed. Still, they were just kids and probably went around taking photos of all the hot surfers on the beach.

Zeke started limbering up and, as he tossed his board on to the water, I was glad to see that he wasn't moaning about needing boots or a hood, or complaining about the coldness of the water. Some foreign surfers would just not quit going on about how cold it was, or how much better it was to surf free, without a wetsuit cramping their style. I thought the cold was a small price to pay for surfing the most stunning beach break in Europe.

It was low tide and it was breaking clean, the waves peeling off perfectly. We paddled out, and Zeke was off, much faster and stronger through the water than I was. He made the line-up, which is where surfers wait to catch a wave, while I was still battling the impact zone. Finally outside, paddling through the pack of hunched surfers, I tried to find my sweet spot by checking the markers on land that I always used to position myself at the best sandbar location. Today, though, the current was zippy and I had to paddle just to maintain position. I was too far outside and I missed a few sick waves.

Zeke got them.

He had some killer moves. I watched him shoot across the wave face, then turn the board 180 degrees and back again for a perfect cutback. On his next wave, he really embraced the speed, and when I saw how fast his board was moving across the water, I knew what he was going to do. He accelerated toward the crest of the wave, where his board lost all contact with the water to score him some serious air on an aerial 360-degree turn. He must have been six feet above the water.

Not many surfers could do that. Hucking air was the sort of thing you'd have to do thousands of times before you got any good at it. And Zeke was really good, with his own loose, super-graceful style. I'd never seen anyone surf Fistral like that. Zeke was slipping across the waves like a skater, light-footed, as if he and his board weighed nothing. He must have spent most of his life in the water.

There was so much I could learn from him. If he wanted to teach me, that was, but I knew that not many surfers of his ability were bothered about teaching other surfers. They were just out to do what they loved as well as they could, as often as they could, and wanted everyone else to get out of the way. Zeke had total control, total power, total grace.

Basically, his style of surfing couldn't have been more different from Daniel's.

Daniel only taught people to surf for a living because it paid really well. He resented the time away from his own surfing.

He'd get so frustrated with his students' lack of talent that when it came to his own sessions he'd psycho-surf. Even his riding stance looked like a fighting stance. He pushed it too far. Taking off too late, charging hard, then riding in so far at Little Fistral that he almost ate the rocks. And he was always breaking boards in insane wipeouts, which was not funny as surfboards cost hundreds. He'd perforated his eardrums, slashed his hands on rocks and he'd lost three teeth, although he wore a partial bridge so you couldn't tell.

It was like he wanted to prove something. I don't know what, or even who he was trying to prove it to. The whole world, maybe.

I sighed, as if I could sigh Daniel out of my mind, and my eyes settled back on Zeke, which was when he did this incredibly sexy thing. He was up and charging, when the lip of the curling wave started falling on his face, and he did this head-flick. It should have looked cheesy because it was just to get his hair out of his face without using his hands, which would affect his balance. But it was just gorgeous. It was like I was there under that waterfall with him. I could feel the phenomenal weight of that water crashing down on to his broad shoulders and jerking his head forward. By rights he should have wiped out. But he didn't. His spine bent forward under the immense pressure of the breaking wave, but somehow he managed to stay vertical, that head-flick getting the hair out of his eyes and righting his balance at the same time.

He was amazing. I let myself feel the weight of his amazingness and suddenly I felt this strange kind of hunger, a cold ache in my belly. Right there, in that moment, I would have willingly got on the floor, forehead to the tile, and bowed at his altar.

I was never like this about boys I'd just met. It took me a while to get a feel for them and let them in. Even with Daniel, who I ended up falling head over heels for. But Zeke was something different altogether. I didn't know exactly what kind of person he was, but I knew what he wasn't. He wasn't ordinary. He was different from any of the guys in Newquay.

I slid down on my board and went for a wave of my own, my tail spun out, and I got nailed. I ended up on the bottom, with a sand facial and a belly full of Neptune's cocktail. When I paddled back out to the line-up, I couldn't see Zeke. I wasn't worried though. I had just lost him in the mass of black-suited surfers. It's like that out there, with the strong longshore drift current and so many surfers in the water. Unless you keep your eye on someone constantly, which would be creepy and would mean you couldn't surf yourself, you soon lose your friends.

With Zeke out of sight, and some of the best waves I'd seen in ages, I just gave myself up to the moment and paddled and popped up like my life depended on it.

I caught a few envious looks and heard a few hoots and whistles as I grabbed some nice long rides. Other surfers moved out of my way and only a few douches dropped in on my waves, trying to block me out. On any given day there were at least a dozen sexist pigs riding Fistral who could be relied upon to say something gross. Something along the lines of, "Don't come back until your boobs are bigger," or, "Get out of my way, muff-rider." Mind you, those were the guys who were pretty jerky to everyone.

Most of the guys were cool, though, and knew me well enough to leave me alone, and sometimes gave me a whistle like they did for their friends when I caught a glory ride.

It was always a great feeling to catch any wave, but that evening I caught one of the primo rides of my life. I could see the waves were starting to hollow out. I'd managed to position myself well in the takeoff zone, close to the peak of the wave, so I stroked like hell.

Those cylindrical waves are the nirvana of surfing. Glassy green walls all around, the lip curling over and locking you in the green room. You never know if you're going to ride out the other side or if the wave is going to stomp down on your head like a giant's foot, but air builds up inside the barrel, and there's this vacuum effect, so that when you're about to come out of it, you feel this pop of air and you know you've made it. It is the coolest thing ever. Like total Zen concentration and total exhilaration at the same time. Adrenalin pouring out of your ears, but freaky calm too.

Just as I was charging for that perfect trippy wave, out of the corner of my eye I saw another surfer going for it too on the other side of the wave peak. I expected a paddle battle as we were both equally close to the peak, but then he swung his board around to paddle wide on the wave shoulder, which was my cue. I went for it. Only after I was up did I realize that I'd seen a flash of green on the surfer's shoulder. It was Zeke.

He could have taken that epic wave right from me, but didn't. No surfer in his right mind would have backed off that perfect wave, which meant that Zeke was mad, ultra-polite or . . . he liked me. And, oh God, I really hoped he liked me.

I felt the bite as I was caught by the wave's momentum. The water was moving super-fast under the board, so that I was streaming along, the most intense endorphin rush charging through my body. There was so much spray in the water that it was chucking up mini-rainbows. When I finished, my first thought was: *Wow, did Zeke see that?* and my second thought was: *I need another one.* The addiction kicks in so hard, so fierce, that your brain joneses for more. Catching your first real wave is pretty much sticking a needleful of drugs in your arm, because after one insane hit of surf stoke you'll spend the rest of your life craving it.

I caught another seven or eight waves and I stayed on one too long, so that by the time I hopped off my board, I was knee-deep in whitewater slop.

I started paddling back out, but the sets were close together without much of a break and I was really getting pounded in the impact zone. A couple of times I was pinned down in the gray darkness and, even though I made myself flow not fight, it was exhausting to be shaken like that, with my lungs screaming for air.

I had a crazy ice-cream headache and my arms felt like spaghetti from all the paddling. I gave up trying to reach the line-up and bodysurfed the inside whitewater back to the beach. I padded through the pools, which felt unbelievably warm compared to the chilly sea, and sank down on the sand.

I thought I'd take a quick break to catch my breath. Killer. I let myself feel tired and that was it. I was done.

I checked my watch again and saw that we had been in the water for nearly two hours.

It was getting cold, my mouth was parched and I was starving.

I got up and walked around, searching the water for a glimpse of Zeke, when it occurred to me that I didn't have to wait for him to finish his session; I knew where he'd left his van keys, so I could stash his board and go home, without prolonging the awkwardness any longer.

I was just sliding the board into the van, when I heard someone shouting my name.

Zeke must have been keeping an eye on me after all, because there he was behind me, looking surprised that I hadn't waited for him.

He high-fived me and said, "You scored some epic rides. That first tube? If you'd spent any longer in there you'd have had to pay rent, huh?"

I smiled.

"Everything OK?" he said.

"Long day," I said, feeling some serious bed gravity. "A few nasty wipeouts. Swallowed a bit of water."

"Me too."

He didn't look like he'd swallowed a load of seawater. He looked great and he was glowing from the exertion.

"Yeah? You looked like a pro out there."

He grimaced a bit. "I always swallow some water when I'm duck-diving."

I nodded. It happened. Normally went up your nose.

"Deliberately. It's almost a superstition now. I figure if I get a little of the sea in me right at the start, then my body will know how to handle this stuff all around it, or something. So I drink a little before every session. For luck, I guess."

That was crazy. There was no other way of putting it. You did not go around swallowing seawater if you could possibly help it. Seawater was horrendous on the kidneys. Even with a light surf session, I'd have to drink a ton of water afterward.

I looked at him and there was something so serious in his eyes that I didn't want to mock him. I wanted to be there with him, believing that a mouthful of saltwater could educate your body, keep you lucky.

The light was failing, the sky overhead changing from deepest blue to silver, the horizon taking on a hint of the coming sunset. The wash of the sea was loud in my ears, even with the wind that had begun to swirl across the cliffs.

"I could coach you, you know. If you like."

I didn't know what to say to that, other than, "Why?"

"Why not? You charge real hard. You've got something."

"Me? I only learned to surf three summers ago."

"Seriously? I started on a stand-up when I was four."

"Ah, so that's why you're so good," I said, without thinking. He gave me this big smile, but I wasn't buttering him up, I was just being honest. Anyone with eyes could see he was the best surfer out there.

Zeke grabbed a towel and started stripping off. He turned toward the van, working his way out of his wetsuit and pulling on his shorts. I did the same. For a split second, as the wind caught his towel, I saw a flash of butt.

"Come on," he said, turning back to me, "let's go grab some coffee."

"That sounds good, but honestly, I am so exhausted."

With the cliff wind whipping my wet hair against my neck I was also so cold that it hurt. I went to stash the wetsuit for Denny and when I got back to Zeke, I said, "It's been great tonight, but I really should get home. I have work first thing in the morning and it'll be dark in an hour."

"We only live once, right?"

I thought about his tattoo and could feel myself wavering.

"Come on," he said. "We need to talk about my plan to get you competing in the Wavemasters' Girls' Junior Open, which just so happens to be held in this little town in September."

"Funny," I said.

"I'm not kidding."

I thought about my job selling surf clothes in the Billabong concept store on Fistral Beach, and then I thought about how amazing it would feel to stride down the beach in front of a crowd and compete in a surf contest. If there was even a 1 percent chance of that happening, it was worth a late night.

The hungover tourists wanting to buy board shorts, bikinis and strings of beads would just have to make do with the bleary-eyed version of me.

"Where are we going?" I said.

"The hottest joint in town. My house."

"Don't you live in your van? I saw a duvet."

Plenty of surfers did. The NO OVERNIGHT SLEEPING signs dotted along the esplanade were a total joke. Those surfers weren't necessarily slumming it either, because if they didn't like Fistral's rank public toilets, or washing with a bar of soap in the sea, they could pay forty bucks a month for gym membership of Hotel Serenity. That way, they could use the hotel's fancy gym showers and bathrooms, and get a decent workout whenever they wanted.

"I have a slightly nicer place."

Good to know.

"I do crash out in my van sometimes though. If I'm surfing late."

Or when a girl wants to see the sun rise over the sea, I thought.

"Well, I can't go to your house because I don't really know you and, no offense, you could be some murderous psychopath. My judgment is not the greatest when it comes to boys. Not lately anyway."

"Where then?"

"Fistral Blu?"

"That place right at the other end of the beach, with the bartender who's like seven feet tall?"

"Yeah, Fistral Blu Beach Bar."

"That's quite a walk."

"So lend me your jacket."

Chapter Four

Surfing brings people together. No matter where you're from, no matter what your race or background, no matter what your beliefs, the waves are waiting. We are one tribe. Some of us ride ocean swells that break over beaches, headlands or reefs; others ride the wind-swells of inland lakes or the mega-waves made by collapsing glaciers. We ride on our feet, our knees, our fronts, our backs, sometimes even on our heads. We leave our land lives behind and come together in the ocean, under one big sky, to play.

Zeke was in the tribe. Always would be. I could see that from the first moment I met him. He was a surfer from the top of his head to the tips of his toes.

From his van he handed me a jacket, which had green and blue checks in the classic surf style and heavy padding. I zipped it up and it came nearly to my knees. But it was warm and soft and the smell of it, when I nestled my nose into the collar, was pure ocean.

We never got to the bar. The surfrats of North Fistral were having a party on the beach. A few of the guys down there were backstreet surf trolls who lived out of their cars, and had only a board, wetsuit and pair of shorts to their name. Loads of car headlights from the beachside parking lot were trained on the beach, lighting up a soccer-field-sized area of sand. The blare of a dozen car stereos replaying a Radio 1 Ben Howard concert drowned out the surf, and at least fifty guys and a handful of girls were playing around on the sand, some swigging from bottles of beer but most just enjoying the music and the vibe.

Zeke's face lit up when he saw the beach ranger, but he must have been feeling the cold because he put up his hood and pulled it down tight around his face. The sun bobbed for a moment on the horizon and then disappeared.

"Should we stay here?" I said, noticing a few of the guys I knew from the line-up. Nice guys who didn't think it was OK to block girls from waves or drop in on them. Guys who realized surfer girls and water-women had as much right as boys to surf a break.

One of them, Caleb, caught my eye and waved. Caleb was a great surfer, one of the young guns who had masses of talent but none of the ego. Those guys were into saving the environment, picking up plastic bags from the beach so that they wouldn't choke out sea life and campaigning to stop the hideousness that is shark-finning, which is where millions of sharks are caught every year and get all their fins chopped off while they're still alive, before being chucked back in the sea to die an agonizing death. All because some people like to eat bland, status-symbol shark-fin soup. Caleb and his crew didn't care about looking cool; they just wanted to drop out of mainstream values, out of capitalism and into Mother Nature.

"Yeah, yeah, sure," Zeke said, smiling. He pulled out some sunglasses from his jacket pocket, which seemed like overkill. True, the sunset was still pretty dazzling on the horizon, but it was almost like Zeke didn't want to be seen or something. I really hoped that wasn't because he was worried about bumping into his surf-bunny one-night stands. Horrible thought.

Caleb came over and I introduced him to Zeke.

"Nice to meet you, man," Zeke said, and Caleb shot him a funny look and mumbled something polite. Then he turned to me and whispered, "He's here."

"Who?"

"Daniel."

I hadn't noticed them, but there they were down at the water's edge, ankle-deep in the ocean. Daniel and Cass wrapped up in each other, tongues in the wrong mouths. It made me want to puke.

I took Zeke's arm and pulled him up toward the dunes where someone was spraying deodorant on to a T-shirt and trying to light it to make a fire. Zeke went over to ask if they needed help, and like a perfect boy scout he got some pieces of driftwood and kindled them until he had a real blaze going.

I just sat there, knees up to my chest, and watched him work. I did not turn to the shoreline to see Cass and Daniel. I was so sick of them and everything they stood for. Stupid sheep, the both of them. The only person stupider than them was me, for not seeing what was going on right under my nose.

Zeke was obviously a pretty friendly dude, as guys were coming up to him and chatting away. I liked to see that. It was nice spending time with someone happy and positive, someone who liked people. I wondered if any of the guys had spotted Zeke surfing earlier. They'd want to know where his home break was, if he'd been to Indo, Java or Tahiti.

I realized then that even I didn't know where Zeke's home break was.

"Zeke," I called out to him. "Where exactly are you from?"

"We traveled all the time. I was born in Oahu, but we followed the waves to Kauai, then Maui, then the North Shore of Oahu again. For a while we just lived off the fat of the land."

"What, like camping out?"

"Yeah, then later in a beach hut. Climbing trees for coconuts, spear-fishing. Endless summer and all that. My folks had hardly any money at first, but they lived the dream their way."

"Where does your mom live now?"

"All over. She spends a few months of the year in South Africa. Her boyfriend is from there. She still keeps our place in Oahu. It's this geodesic dome, just off the beach. It's so cool. But I've spent a lot of time with her in South Africa too."

"Do you surf there?"

"Sure."

"Don't they have white sharks there that *eat* surfers?"

"I mean, it happens, and it sucks, but it's so, so rare. And it's not the sharks' fault; they're just doing what comes natural to them: feeding when they're hungry."

Caleb piped up with, "Sharks kill maybe five people a year. We kill eighty *million* of them. Every single year. They have way more to fear from us than we do from them."

"I guess . . ." I said, unconvinced.

"Look, I'm in the ocean pretty much every day of my life," Zeke said. "Yeah, I might be in the wrong place at the wrong time one day and get chewed up by a shark, but it's a risk I'm willing to take. Mostly, sharks stay offshore and give us a wide berth."

He raised an eyebrow at me, and added, "When you make the ASP World Qualifying Series you'll have to surf super-sharky waters. And, you know, you won't even care. You'll just be like, 'Let's go surfing already.'"

Ha. As if I would ever in a million years be good enough for the QS.

Right then, two guys came jogging through the dusk. One of them had long brown hair that was hanging around his shoulders in wet squiggles like seaweed. The other was slightly taller and had cropped white-blond hair, also wet. Something about them seemed vaguely familiar.

"Hey!" Zeke shouted. I was surprised to hear him hollering like that. As a visitor to Newquay I hadn't expected him to bump into friends of his own. As it happened, they weren't friends.

"Garrett, Wes! Dudes! Come join us!"

They came loping up, both of them smiling and looking dead pleased to have found Zeke.

"Iris, these guys are my brothers."

Even if he hadn't told me, it would have been obvious. There were the same half-Danish, half-Hawaiian good looks, same fierce blue eyes, same broad shoulders, same strong jaw, and something else, if it didn't sound nuts to say it: they moved in the same kind of super-relaxed way.

Zeke went over to them and they all did this forearm-to-forearm handshake, then turned to me.

"Really nice to meet you," I said, putting out my right hand. Wes shook it very solemnly and gave Zeke a cryptic look.

Garrett was asking Zeke something, and Wes said to me, "So how do you know Zeke?"

"I literally just met him tonight during yoga class."

"Yeah? Which class?"

"The one at Hotel Serenity."

"Zeke goes to that?"

"Yep. Have you been? It was my first time."

"No."

Garrett interrupted, squeezing in front of Wes to shake my left hand and kiss it. I laughed, handed him a can of some cheapo lager from Lidl, and he said, *"Mahalo,"* which I knew was Hawaiian for thanks, and then shook and kissed my right hand too.

For a second Zeke looked mildly annoyed and then Garrett cuffed him around the head and they started a play fight, which Wes joined, and soon the three of them were wrestling and rolling around the beach like primary-school kids. I had to smile. It was cool to see a boy so happy around his family.

A group of boys had started up a game of rugby, and a second group was kicking a soccer ball around. The Fistral surfrats could be surprising like that. People expected them to be totally lazy beach bums, but to me it seemed like they all had some kind of hyperactivity disorder. They could not sit still.

Girls and some older women in their twenties were starting to trickle toward our fire from the beach bar, lured by the macho display and the hope of bagging a summer romance with a surfer on their seven-day vacation. These were the girls that went to the beach to sunbathe, and they wore wedged heels rather than flip-flops, and lipgloss that would get covered in sand with every breath of wind. You'd hear them at the water's edge, screaming when a three-inch musher washed over their ankles, because, "Omigod, I forgot about my fake tan! It'll go all streaky!"

Girls with no bottle. Girls like Cass. Some of the boys liked these ultra-wimpy girlie girls, found them cute. I didn't care about them as long as they kept out of my way and didn't decide to come swimming just when I'd taken off on a wave. The worst thing ever was when their new surfer boyfriends tried to give them surf lessons, taking them out too far and too deep, just to prove how macho and talented they themselves were. It was way dangerous, and I'd had to help out these clueless girls and their arrogant boyfriends three or four times since I'd started surfing.

Whitewater. Everyone knows that. When you start surfing, you only surf the whitewater. Straight back to shore and then repeat until you've done it hundreds, if not thousands, of times. After six months of that, maybe, just maybe, we'll talk about riding the curl of a breaking wave.

People were pulling steaming burgers off disposable barbecues and throwing them into bread rolls. Some tanorexic surf groupie in a short skirt came up and offered one to Zeke.

"There you go, babe," she said.

"No, thanks," he said.

"Do you want something else then? Someone's doing steaks."

"I don't eat meat," he said, all of a sudden very serious.

"You're one of those vegans, are you then?" she asked, like veganism was a terrible disease.

"No, I'm vegetarian." I thought about Daniel scarfing down his three Big Macs a day, and his extreme fishing weekenders where he'd camp out on the rocks without any food and only eat if he caught, killed and gutted a fish. Daniel loved the macho bull.

"Oh," she said. "Is that different?"

"Kinda," Zeke said, giving her a look that said, *How stupid are you?*

The girl was still clutching the burger as if she didn't know what to do with it. Eventually one of the other surfrats came over and plucked it out of her hands, and she drifted off.

Wes and Garrett rolled their eyes, although I wasn't sure if this was because they thought being vegetarian was pathetic or the burger-toting girl was.

Soon enough the sky was full of stars, and a puffed-out Zeke came and sat next to me. I could feel the warmth of him through our clothes. He yawned and, since it was dark, I snuggled next to him and put my head on his shoulder. I felt him sigh in this really nice contented way, and I realized in that moment that I was totally calm and happy.

Zeke's brothers had come over too and they were chatting. Zeke was saying something about big waves thundering along like freight trains, and Wes was pointing out that fewer people had surfed the planet's giant waves than had been to outer space. That Zeke was kind of a pioneer, if you thought about it.

So Zeke had surfed giant waves too? Had he been there with his friend at Teahupo'o in Tahiti? He hadn't said that. But if he had surfed that mega-scary reef break, then not telling me about it was freakishly modest.

Then Zeke said, "Once, during this epic storm swell at Maverick's, in California, I fell on to my board, landed on my chest and had the wind knocked out of me and I swear I thought I was dead. I had no breath. And I was so far under, just pinned down in the dark, with tons of water pushing on my back. Thought I was gonna pass out from oxygen deprivation. I could feel myself going through all the stages of hypoxia: the mental thrashing around, the throat spasming, the bright stars, and then it all went black."

"Sounds way intense," Garrett said.

I could hear in Garrett's voice how he felt about his little brother. It didn't seem to be an act just to do Zeke a favor with me and the other girls that were listening. Wes and Garrett actually respected him.

Then Wes said it: "We're so proud of you, bro. What you do is next-level brave."

"I don't feel brave. When those big waves close out, they explode like bombs, bro, and when I wipe out then, I feel like I'm six inches tall. I don't think, '*Wow, this is the most radical wave ever.*' I think, '*SHIT, please don't kill me, wave.*'"

"Well, that's fair enough, brah, 'cause those bombs totally could kill you." This was Garrett.

"They probably won't though. They'll keep kicking my ass, yeah, but I don't care. Just so long as I only get injuries I can recover from."

"Well, I think you're a nut for riding super-heavies."

"Yeah, sure. No doubt. But I love it. You're in the middle of a huge tornado, just chaos and heavy water all around, but in the center there's this pocket of total calm. So long as you come out clean, it's fine."

"Why risk it?"

"Just for the smile. I always get out of the water happier than I went in. Literally always."

"Just don't tell Mom, eh? She has no idea what you're doing out there. She still thinks you're taking on clean little five-footers. Lucky for you she doesn't have the Internet, 'cause you'd be shipped off to a psych ward. She'd think you were suicidal."

"I'm not. And I'm not stupid. I know that any wave could kill me, and especially the big ones, just like that." I heard the snap of his fingers. "But that knowledge that you're real close to death? It makes you feel totally alive."

Adrenalin junkie. No doubt about it.

Then my eyes settled on Cass, who was running up the beach, shrieking, with Daniel chasing her in an attention-seeking way. In five or six steps he caught her and swept her up in his arms. It was one of his old moves. He was super-charming when he wanted to be. It had made me ache the first time he'd done it to me. I thought I was lucky to be with someone who had that much swagger.

Always be suspicious of a person who doesn't question any of their own beliefs, my mom says. They think they know it all and that makes them dangerous to be around.

Oh yeah, Daniel had all the answers. I should have known to beware.

My teeth had begun to chatter in the cold sea air and Zeke put his arm around me. Suddenly Daniel was looking right at me. Slowly he shook his head.

I checked my watch and saw it was way past my curfew.

Crap.

"I gotta take off," I said to Zeke.

"Yeah, no problem."

We walked to Zeke's van so he could give me my skateboard, and I saw that someone had left a note pinned to his windshield.

He read it, crumpled it up and tossed it in the back of the van.

"What was that?"

"Just some punk kid."

"What's it say?"

"Huh? Oh, that some dude is gonna mess me up and telling me to beat it. I dunno. It happens. Just your run-of-the-mill localism."

"Jesus, surfers can be such assholes."

"Don't sweat it. People get the wrong idea sometimes. Assume stuff, you know?"

Yeah, I knew all about that. But what had Zeke done to piss people off? He'd only been in town a week.

Chapter Five

The next morning my shift started at 8:30 and I paced around tidying up the shop and sipping at a monster cup of coffee for at least an hour. My hands were busy, but all my brain could do was relive the events of the night before.

It was the kind of thing that Kelly liked to say could happen to a girl like me, especially in the months after Daniel, but I never believed it. But then, I'd never met anyone like Zeke before.

There were only two customers and neither of them bought anything. As I pointlessly said thanks to the second of them, the shop phone rang. It was my boss, Billy, in a total panic.

"I'll be there in twenty minutes," he said.

"It's Saturday. Shouldn't you be relaxing with the wife and kids?" I said.

"The damn press is coming. The *Cornish Guardian*, can you believe? The shop needs to be shipshape and Bristol fashion."

"OK . . ." I said, not entirely sure what he was talking about. Probably another Billabong promo gimmick. I tossed my empty cardboard coffee cup into the wastepaper basket and began flicking a duster around the till.

"Do I need to do anything else?" I asked.

"Tie your hair back. You'll want to look presentable for the paper."

"They won't want me in any pictures," I said. "I'm nobody."

"Not true, my dear."

"What's happening anyway?" I said, but he had already put the phone down.

I slipped away from the shop floor to tidy myself up. I kept a kit of toiletries in my locker and I found an old lipstick in there. I slathered it on. It was bright red and reminded me of Cass. I rubbed it off, but it still left a pink stain.

The shop door opened and a girl dressed in a black pencil skirt and a vintage-style blouse walked in. Her sky-high Mary Jane shoes smashed against the stripped wooden floor of the shop. She turned to me and I was dazzled by wide green eyes and shiny red hair.

Hot on her heels was Zeke. As he came through the door, the red-haired girl turned to him and kissed him on both cheeks. She reeked of money. It wasn't just her clothes; it was the way she moved and how she held her head. It had to be the girl I'd seen at yoga. You could tell she had a trust fund as big as the entire GDP of Cornwall.

"Hello, beautiful," she said to Zeke, batting her eyelashes. "I can't believe you're here already. Not like you to be so punctual! I wonder what could have brought you here on time . . ."

Her voice was really something. The most plummy Home Counties accent that I had ever heard in real life.

Zeke gave me a quick salute and then started talking to the girl in a low voice. She looked over at me with a surprised expression, which didn't make me feel paranoid at all.

I shuffled around tidying handbags and wallets and then took a deep breath and went over to Zeke, who was looking out the window toward some fishing boats sitting in the bay. His hands were shaking a little, so he was either nervous or hungover, and he definitely hadn't drunk more than one can of lager when he was with me, so . . .

The girl was talking loudly on her cell phone. Giving directions to Fistral Beach.

"Hi there," I said. "How's it going?"

"OK. I guess I didn't sleep much last night."

"No?" After yoga, surfing and the beach party, I'd slept like the dead. I wondered what had kept him awake.

He looked back out at the sea again and I said, "I had fun last night."

"Me too."

He gave me a big smile. I'd said the right thing for once. Technically the night hadn't been that amazing, as I'd been so nervous to be out with someone other than Daniel that I hadn't been able to totally relax for more than two minutes at a time. First impressions were so important; what if I screwed it up and said something that offended Zeke, or something he thought was stupid? And Daniel shaking his head at me had killed my buzz.

"Who's the city chick?" I said.

"Oh, that's just Saskia."

Just Saskia. What was he doing here anyway? My early-morning brain couldn't put it all together.

At that moment Billy came in and bustled over to me.

"Iris dear, I see you've met our star. The press will be here shortly. I've brought some chocolate cookies, so could you arrange them pleasingly on a plate and put on the kettle?"

Zeke gave me a sympathetic grimace, and then the door opened to reveal a stream of young girls clutching posters of Zeke.

I read over one of their shoulders:

Zeke Francis. Hawaiian Champion, 2013.

I knew he was a good surfer, but this was ridiculous. Hawaii had some of the best waves and surfers on the planet, and Zeke was Hawaiian Champion in the Junior Men's category. He hadn't said a word to me about it and we'd spent the whole of the previous evening together. Well, this explained the stream of star-struck teeny-boppers taking pictures. I'd just thought they were acting so giddy around Zeke because of his looks. Apparently I was wrong. In the surf-contest world, Zeke was a megastar.

It made things less complicated for me. There was no way someone like Zeke would stick around in Newquay. He'd have places to go, people to see, contests to surf. He was probably on the Association of Surfing Professionals world tour, in which case his schedule would be brutal: traveling from ocean to ocean, beach to beach. In a few days he'd be gone and everything would go back to its old boring sameness. And I'd go back to watching garbage TV and eating dry cereal.

Over the course of the morning, the shop filled until there was a line out of the door. Zeke kept checking in with me every so often, and even bought me a cappuccino and a cookie from the cafe downstairs. It was hilarious really, all his polite attentions, because he still hadn't said a word to me about his status as a renowned surf champion. Not one word.

In arranging the signing at my shop, was this his way of telling me? I didn't get it. Did he think that would impress me? It didn't seem like him at all. But then how well did I actually know him?

I guessed he could also just have been embarrassed—having to tell a girl something like that would be pretty major. Like saying, "Listen to how cool I am." It would sound show-offy, to say the least. Then I figured out that actually Zeke probably didn't have anything to do with choosing the venue at all. He was on the Billabong Surf Team and I worked in the Billabong concept store. Where else in Newquay would one of their champion surfers hold a meet-and-greet signing event?

Twelve o'clock came and I couldn't wait to ditch the shop for lunch break. It was boiling in there, with the hot breath and body heat of tourists and Zeke's adoring fans. I grabbed my spare kit from the storeroom and went down to the beach for a surf.

I only caught two waves, as the wind was blowing the surf out and making it choppy, but when I was up I pulled a few head dips, which is where you lean over and stick the top of your head right into the wave face. It sounds stupid, but it's actually pretty lush.

There is something healing about the ocean. I'd always known about it, ever since I was a little kid when I'd go open-water swimming out past the breakers after a bad day at school. I had known it even through all the pain and hassle with Daniel, but I didn't want to be healed then. I just wanted to keep picking at the scab, making myself feel worse and worse until even Kelly despaired of me.

I looked to the north end of the beach and I saw a jet ski and behind it a surfer who appeared to be flying above the water. I paddled a bit closer and spotted another one. It was Zeke and his brothers, surfing hydrofoil boards, which were unheard of in Newquay. Hydrofoils were a Hawaiian invention and were ridable in even the choppiest conditions, as the board was suspended two feet above the water, with a strut attached to a small plane beneath, so that they harnessed the energy of the deeper part of the wave and the rider didn't get affected by any choppiness on the surface. It looked impossible. Four long lenses were trained on the Francis brothers, and I knew the photos would be all over the newspapers the next day.

I caught a wave to shore, sat on the beach and looked out to sea.

The surf was junky, but thousands of people were in the water. After five minutes or so, I saw a big crowd of people and cameras gathered around a surfer who was walking out of the mush and on to the beach, with a hydrofoil board slung under his arm. Zeke. So now he was doing a photo shoot.

I had to get back to work, so I tried to box around the crowd but Zeke spotted me.

"Iris!" he shouted.

The red-haired girl, Saskia, was there in bare feet, high heels poking out of a designer handbag. Perhaps she was his girlfriend.

She was definitely into him. She kept looking at him adoringly. But then if he had a girlfriend, wasn't he way out of line for taking an interest in me? Maybe he wasn't interested in me. He might have just wanted to be friendly. After all, it wasn't as if he'd made a move on me.

Saskia walked over to me and said, "Do get in the picture, babe."

A) I hate being called babe, and B) I hate having my photograph taken.

"I'm sopping wet," I said. "Anyway, nobody cares about me."

"You'd be surprised."

What was that supposed to mean? Had Zeke said something to her?

Zeke came and put his arm around my shoulders, then smiled to the camera in a total cheesefest. The photographer from the paper was at least sixty, and he had the smarmiest face I'd ever seen.

Saskia went around to the other side of Zeke and slipped her arm across his lower back.

After a few more clicks of the camera, I turned to Zeke. "I've really gotta get back."

He took my hand and another flash went off.

"See you tonight?" he said.

"I don't know. I'm supposed to be seeing Kelly. We're going out for a drink."

"So bring her along too. We're having a party to celebrate a new board that my sponsors have brought out. I have to promote it as part of my deal."

"Where's the party?"

"Up at the Headland Hotel. It could be fun."

"I'll ask Kelly what she wants to do."

"Go out with the boy," the newspaper photographer shouted. "Look at him—he's living the dream!"

Wasn't he just? Zeke was living every surfer's dream, I thought grumpily. But some of us were in the real world and were paid by the hour.

I swung back to the shop, stripped off my wetsuit, got dressed and got back to work. No one except a handful of tourists came back into the shop that day, and I had no idea what Zeke and Saskia were up to, or why Zeke seemed so keen for me to go to this party.

I thought about Saskia and the way that she seemed so full of herself and confident. Oh well, those types of girls could never surf, and Zeke obviously liked being around other surfers. Whoever she was, Saskia couldn't be Zeke's type and he couldn't be hers. She'd have her eye on an investment banker with a sports car and a pension plan. Surely.

Chapter Six

Kelly called my home phone about three seconds after I'd gotten in the door from work. I slung my skateboard against the wall and picked up.

"We still on for today? And before you say no, you'd better say yes because I've washed my hair especially, shaved my legs *and* done a face mask."

"Yeah, I guess so. I mean, I dunno. The thing is, I've been invited to this party."

"You're ditching me?"

"No way. It's not like that at all. You're invited too. We don't have to go. I just thought I'd mention it in case you wanted to do something a bit different."

"Different. What sort of party is this?" she asked, suspicious. She still hadn't forgiven me for the time I took her to my mother's Tupperware party. She said she had never been so bored in her entire life, or learned so much about plastic food-storage containers.

"It's a surfboard launch."

"I saw that on Facebook. How did you score an invite?"

Facebook. That was a point. I opened the app on my phone and typed Zeke's name into the search bar. No personal profile but one fan page. With 121,000 likes.

My brain helpfully reminded me that I'd barely scraped five hundred Facebook friends.

"Zeke asked me to come."

"Zeke?"

"The guy from yoga I was talking to."

"Whoa . . . back up! You've been seeing that hot dude from yoga on the sly? Go Iris!"

"It's not like that. We're just friends."

"Friends with benefits, ha."

"No. Well, I suppose getting an invite to a swanky surf party is a benefit, but nothing else has happened."

"How come he could get you an invitation? Friends in high places?"

"He *is* the high places. He's a surf superstar."

"You're not serious."

"He's the Junior Men's Champion of Hawaii."

"Score!"

"Oh yeah, he's a big deal."

"You don't sound all that happy about it, Iris . . ."

"I'm plenty happy for him."

There was an awkward silence.

"You're going out with an uber-cool surf champ! This is legend."

"He's hardly my boyfriend. We've only just met."

"He's kissed you though."

"Nope. And PS, are you blind? Why would he kiss me? Have you not seen him? He's prettier than I am. Much prettier."

"I saw the way he was looking at you. Every time you smiled at him he went all sparkly."

"You've been reading *way* too much *Twilight*."

"Not actually sparkly. But his face lit up. Honestly. I'm not messing with you, girl, I promise."

"Well, he hasn't made a move on me yet, so he can't be that interested, can he?"

"He will kiss you though. At the party, I bet."

"I don't even want a boyfriend."

"Everyone wants a boyfriend."

"Not me. I've had enough boyfriends to last me a lifetime."

"You've had three."

"Exactly. That's two, maybe three, too many."

Kelly sighed. Then she had a thought. "What exactly are you planning to wear?"

"My new Roxy jeans and that black sleeveless top."

"I'm coming over."

Fifteen minutes later Kelly pulled up in a taxi with an armful of glittery dresses and a pile of shoeboxes almost as tall as her.

"We have like one hour before we have to get there," I said. "I don't think we've got enough time for you to turn me into a full-on drag queen."

"Oh shush, and move your butt, girl!"

I had to laugh. Kelly was rarely this girly. My PG-rated relationship with a top surfer was obviously bringing out her romantic side.

My mom was at the library overseeing a book launch by someone from Newquay's Historical Society, so we had the house to ourselves. My mom's a teacher; not one of the nice, generous kind, who believe in the goodness of all children. She's one of the harsh ones who gets through the boredom of invigilating three-hour GCSE exams by playing games with other teachers at the expense of the pupils. Like the one where they walk around the room and the mission is to find the ugliest kid, who they then go and stand next to. Or in round two maybe it's the boy most likely to commit a violent crime. Or the girl most likely to get pregnant before her next birthday. And then they just stand next to that poor kid who's scribbling away, and smirk at each other. My mom's proud of the way she is. She thinks there are too many artistic, sensitive types in the world. My dad was one of those.

The first thing Kelly did was brush my hair so that it was really shiny. Then she sprayed it with water from my mom's plant mister, then hairspray, and then she wrapped a thin headband over my head, cutting across my forehead. Starting from the front, she wound small sections over and under the band until my whole hair was done. I looked like some forties reject. It was the sort of hairdo someone like Saskia would have.

"Don't worry," she said. "It's not going to stay like that. But when you shake out your hair before we leave, you are going to have the most gorgeous curls. I saw a YouTube tutorial for heatless curls. I swear it works."

"If you say so."

"I do. Right. Make-up."

Kelly was a great painter, which is what made her so good at make-up. Basically, she painted on a more obvious version of her face every morning. She didn't use loads of make-up on me but she had all sorts of tricks for making my eyes look bluer and my mouth look poutier. She had a shedload of products in one of the shoeboxes. Things with names like "Moonbeam Cheek Highlighter" and "Liar Lips Mouth Stain." Her mother worked on the make-up counter at Boots, so Kelly got all the best samples for free.

I had to admit that I did look all right when she'd finished.

"That isn't just pretty," Kelly said. "That is practically Model Pretty."

"Yeah, right. Don't overdo it, friend."

Kelly smiled.

"What about you?" I said.

"What about me? This isn't my date. Quick swipe of mascara and lipgloss and I'm done. Anyway, nobody's going to be looking at me with you looking like that."

Talk about overkill. I looked good for me but I wasn't going to be stopping any traffic.

"What about the guy from yoga that you were laughing with? He might be there," I said, remembering the cute guy with the fluffy blond hair that she'd been chatting to.

"He might be. But I'm not interested."

"No?"

"Or rather, he isn't. He's 100 percent gay."

"Really? How can you tell?"

"I can always tell. Especially when they mention that after class they're going over to their boyfriend's house."

"Oh. Sorry."

"It's OK. The best ones are always gay."

I didn't know about that, but I let it go.

"So what am I wearing?" I said, looking through her dresses, which were all from fancy shops in Truro and Plymouth.

"Try them on and we'll see."

"All of them? The taxi will be here in ten minutes."

"Dammit. OK, go for that strapless one."

It was a clingy pink number that screamed hooch.

"I don't wear pink."

"It's actually fuchsia."

"Pink."

"That purple rockabilly one, then. It's short though, so wear leggings maybe? And you can't wear a bra with the halter-neck."

I looked at it. It had little black skulls printed on the fabric and black net hanging down from under the skirt. It was pretty awesome.

"I'll wear my Docs with it."

"Uh, no you won't."

"Docs are perfect with those kinds of dresses. Without Doc Martens they're just sad."

"I wear it with stilettos."

"Yeah, but you're a total slut."

Kelly rolled up a *Cosmo* mag and hit me on the head with it.

"Dressing like a slut doesn't make me a slut," she corrected me. She looked up at the clock. "Five minutes, Iris."

I peeled off my work clothes. Kelly had seen me naked plenty of times, as we'd pretty much grown up together, so I threw all my clothes into a heap on the floor and stepped into her dress. It was a bit tight around the waist, but OK if I held my stomach in. Kelly was busy stepping into the pink dress, which looked surprisingly good against her dark hair and olive skin. She loosened the band around my head and my hair came tumbling out in perfect curls. Kelly gave it a quick misting with a shine spray and it was done.

The beep of the taxi sent us running down the stairs to get our shoes. By the time I'd laced up my Docs, Kelly was already in the front seat chatting away to the cab driver.

"Headland Hotel," I said, sitting down on the back seat with a big swish of my skirt.

Kelly turned to me and said, "This is going to be a big night for you, Iris. I just know it."

"Feel it in your waters, can you, dear?" This was the cab driver.

"Just look how beautiful she is. Her new boy is going to be falling over himself to show her a good time."

"Oh God," I said.

"What?"

"You've made me really nervous now. I'm bound to say or do something stupid."

"Confidence, girl. You're going to rock his world."

Basically, we had no idea what we were walking into.

Chapter Seven

We walked through the antique revolving doors of the Headland Hotel and into the lobby. The music from the live band was thumping, even from there. I stopped to catch my breath for a moment before walking the long corridor to the function room.

Kelly looked at me. "You OK? You've gone really pale."

"What am I doing here? I'm still not over Daniel."

"You're over him. You are. You just don't want to be. Because that'd mean you'd have to get off your butt and take a chance on someone else."

There wasn't much I could say to that, so I just stood there until Kelly leaned forward and gave me a big hug.

"I love you," she said. "You know that, Iris, don't you?"

I nodded, so she continued.

"Then trust me. You're going to be all right again. This is the first step. It's time."

I jumped as I heard a loud voice beside me, "What's up, laydeeez?"

My heart sank.

Daniel.

Kelly gave him a fearsome glare and said, "What do you want?"

"Don't," I said to her under my breath. Even after all these months I still couldn't bear seeing my best friend and Daniel at each other's throats. Not when we'd all once been so close. Back before everything went to crap.

"Just being polite and saying hey. Is that a crime?"

"No, but that doesn't mean we want to talk to you." Kelly was determined to have the last word. "How did you even get a ticket to this?"

"If you did the beach clean this morning, your name was put on the guest list."

"*You* did a beach clean?" Kelly's mouth was practically hanging open.

"Well, yeah, it was a bargain. Forty minutes' work and they gave you a ticket for this party, plus a free Billabong swag bag. It's all good."

Daniel looked at me and for a minute I thought he was going to do something mortifying like kiss me on the cheek, granny-style, and pat my back. He'd put wax in his dark hair, and his eyes were sparkling the way they did when he was happy, or when he'd had three cans of lager.

"You're both looking lovely tonight," he said, looking at me.

"Well, you're a dick and I just boregasmed. So fuck off." Kelly again. She gave everyone a lot of chances, but once you'd crossed her line, she was stone. If she'd written you off, that was it. She didn't forgive. Neither did I, really, but I was a lot more subtle in my grudges.

"Where's Cass?" I said. A shadow crossed Daniel's face. I'd hit home with that one. Subtle is sometimes harsher than blatant. Kelly had yet to work that out.

"I'm here with the boys. Cass's family is doing some saddo intervention thing tonight because of her bulimia. I bailed. Said I had to work."

"Oh, ever the charmer," Kelly said.

"I don't want her hatin' me. She's going to feel very betrayed after tonight. I'll go around when her folks have gone to bed."

I nodded. Just the idea of Daniel creeping into Cass's bedroom at night was totally sickening.

"Screw this for a laugh," Kelly said. "Let's go get drinks."

She hooked her arm in mine and dragged me off to the free bar. We picked up a couple of half-filled glasses of white-wine spritzer before the bar staff could get a good look at us.

There was no sign of Zeke but Saskia was there, ordering a barman around like he was her personal slave. She was wearing a floor-length black dress with a nipple-grazing neckline and a slit up one leg. It made Kelly and me look like we were on the way to a seven-year-old's birthday party. Though I guessed Saskia wasn't much older than me. Two, maybe three years.

I rolled my eyes.

"Foe?" Kelly said.

"Don't know her."

"You don't like her though."

"She's friends with Zeke. She's called, get this . . . *Saskia*."

"Posh girl, then."

"Not just posh. London posh."

"Interesting. Let's go talk to her."

"Nah, you're all right."

"Come on, she might know stuff about Zeke."

Kelly clattered off toward Saskia and I could either follow her or stand on my own. At least that's what I thought.

I felt a hand on my lower back and turned around to see a man smiling at me. He was skinny, late twenties or early thirties, with brown hair that was already greying, and really hyper body language.

"You must be Iris. Nice to meet you, darlin'."

He was the other type of Londoner: the cockney type, which suited me fine.

"How'd you know?"

"Local surfer girl fitting the description Zeke gave me. I'm Anders."

"OK." The memory banks were coming up blank. I had definitely never met or heard of anyone called Anders. And how exactly had Zeke described me to this man? And were the words "distinctly average-looking" in there?

"I'm Zeke's agent. Didn't he mention me?"

"No."

"The lowlife. Well, Golden Boy's not here yet. He's still working out at the beach. He said you can meet him in his room, if you like? Billabong's sprung for a suite for him tonight. He won't be long, and you can order drinks and snacks from room service. I have a spare key card for you."

He held out the card in two fingers and I took it and clasped my hand around it, one edge digging into my palm, not ready for Kelly or anyone else to see.

"Third floor. Room 1."

Kelly was giggling at something that Saskia was saying, and I turned on my heel, walked out of the bar area and straight into the elevator.

What was I doing? Why did he want to meet me in his room? What was he expecting from me?

The elevator doors pinged open and I padded along the thickly carpeted hall until I was standing outside Room 1. I knocked just in case, but as expected no one answered.

I slid the key card into the slot and opened the door. The front of the room was all windows, giving the most incredible view of the bay, which was dotted with the lights of marker buoys and moored fishing boats. It wasn't just a suite; it was the penthouse suite.

I kept still for a second and listened in case Zeke was in the shower, but the room was silent apart from faint thudding music from the party downstairs.

The room was pretty tidy, with only a couple of surfboards leaning against a wardrobe, a crumpled T-shirt on the bed and a Billabong messenger bag by the window as evidence that anyone was staying there at all.

I picked up the phone, pressed 0 for room service and ordered two Coronas and a plate of mixed sandwiches, since I was starving, and I knew Zeke was bound to be too after a beach workout.

I had a look at the fancy bathroom, which had a separate wet-room shower on one side, done out in sandstone, and a full hot tub on the other. I dipped my hand into the water. It was still lukewarm.

That's when I saw that Zeke's iPhone was lying on the far side rim of the tub. Maybe he'd been texting someone while he was in there.

Don't pick it up. Don't invade his privacy.

I walked around to the other side of the tub and looked at his phone in my hand. When I pressed the On button, I saw that it had been left open on his Contacts page. Apart from an Andy, an Arron and Anders, it was all girls.

Abigail, Agnes, Aimee, Alice, Amelia, Anabel, Angelina, Annemarie, Arianna . . . The list went on and on. Who were all these girls? What did they mean to Zeke?

Suddenly I had a cold, sick feeling in my stomach. What was I doing? Just because Daniel had cheated on me, that didn't mean I had the right to go snooping through Zeke's phone. It was gross.

The door clicked open and I slammed the phone down where I'd found it. It slid across the dewy surface of the hot tub and dropped into the water with a tiny *plink*.

Oh crap.

Panicking, I went straight to the toilet and flushed, so whoever had come in would think I was taking a leak, rather than being a psycho stalker. I walked out of the bathroom, where Zeke was beaming at me. He was wearing gray sweat pants, his feet were caked in sand and his chest was glistening with sweat.

"You came? Awesome." He kissed me on the cheek. "I thought you'd dig the view up here. Pretty nice, huh?"

All I could think was, I've totaled your iPhone. I owe you about four-hundred fifty.

But how could I tell him that? How could I admit that I was being Jealous Stalker Girl?

A loud knock on the door made me jump, and Zeke gave me a curious look, probably wondering if I'd invited a load of local girls to check out his suite.

"It's room service. I ordered us some sandwiches and beers."

"Cool. My blood-sugar level is through the floor. Mega-hungry."

"Thought you might be."

He opened the door and the room-service guy wheeled in a trolley with a huge platter of triangular sandwiches, two frosty beers and two half-pint glasses.

Zeke signed for it, showed the guy out and turned back to me. "I'll just grab a quick shower and be right with you. Help yourself."

He went into the bathroom, not bothering to close the door, and I heard the shower running. This lack of shyness didn't surprise me particularly, as most surfers weren't fussed about being naked. We're constantly getting in and out of clothes in public and trying to towel-dry ourselves in strong sea breezes, and most of us have surfed naked at least once. So I guess you could say we're pretty comfortable in our own skins. My legs were having a battle about whether to go check him out, but my brain kicked in and stopped me. What would I do if he saw me? Jump in the shower with him? No way.

I sat on the bed and ate a ham sandwich. Then I remembered that Zeke was vegetarian. I peeled apart all the sandwiches to look at their fillings and there were only two cheese ones on the whole platter, so I figured I'd have to eat all the meat and tuna ones before he got out of the shower.

By the time Zeke came into the room a few minutes later with a beach towel around his waist, I had downed six sandwiches, including the crusts. Only the cheese ones remained on the platter. Zeke was holding a small hand towel and rubbing his hair with it, leaving it sticking up at crazy angles. He looked at me with my mouth full of bread, then at the platter, then back to me.

"Wow," he said, and then added, "Impressive."

"Missed lunch," I said. "There's some cheese ones for you."

"Sweet." He pulled on some checked boxers, dropped his towel and then went to a chest of drawers and found some loose jeans. I thought about all those girls in his phone; wondered how many of them had been in my shoes, watching him get dressed.

He pulled on a gray vest, cut deep across his shoulder blades, and then he fished a blue and white Hawaiian print shirt out of a plastic bag. He used his teeth to pull off the tags and I noticed the shirt was really creased from sitting in the bag. I could see him looking around for an iron.

"Wardrobe?" I said.

I watched as he set up the ironing board, peering beneath it to look for the little lever that released the catch. He dragged it over to a socket by the dressing table and plugged in the iron.

"I've actually never seen a boy iron something before," I said.

"Anders says I gotta wear a shirt tonight and not look like a surf troll. Oh crap," he said, "I was supposed to shave too. Wait a minute."

He went into the bathroom and came out holding an electric shaver. He switched it on and raked it against the stubble of his cheek, the hair disappearing in clean little patches until his face was totally smooth. He looked different. Younger.

The iron was hissing away, steam pouring out of the front, and Zeke still hadn't eaten a thing.

"I'll iron your shirt," I said. "Eat your sandwiches."

"No way, you don't have to do that."

I took the iron out of his hand and said, "Go eat."

My mom had taught me to iron at the age of eight, and I'd been doing my school uniform and my mom's work clothes ever since, so ironing one boy's shirt was hardly going to break my back.

He scarfed down the sandwiches like he hadn't eaten in days.

"Anders has got me doing all this extra prep. He wants me to be at my strongest this season. Some of the workout sessions are insane. Plus, he has me doing like a hundred push-ups every morning and night. I'd better do the night ones in a minute actually."

"Anders seems like quite a character."

"Yeah, he's nuts, but real good at his job. I'm stoked you came, Iris."

"Kelly kind of dragged me here. Not that I didn't want to come. It's just, I had work all day, and I couldn't face a big night."

"Remind me to buy Kelly a drink. So I guess you know I've been telling Anders all about you?"

"Me? Why are you telling him about me?"

"You've got real quality. The way you were ripping Fistral . . . That tube you caught was a perfect ten. Cool dress, by the way. I should have already said that."

"It's Kelly's. I was going to wear jeans, but she thought I should dress up."

"You look crazy hot."

If it's possible for a whole body to blush, then mine did. Zeke, a pro-surfer with an international reputation, had said that I looked crazy hot. I glanced at the glitzy mirror hanging over the fireplace just to check my head hadn't been swapped with someone else's. Nope. All I saw when I looked in the mirror was someone average with a bit of a tan. Nothing special; just me.

Zeke guzzled from a bottle of water and jumped on to the floor to do his press-ups. I finished the shirt, hooked it over the end of the ironing board and sat on the bed to watch him.

I took a swig from my bottle of Corona and said, "So I left a note telling my mom I was staying over at Kelly's house tonight."

"Uh-huh."

He was breathing hard.

"Must be fun to sleep in a penthouse though. Watch the sun come up in the morning."

Where had that come from? Had I just been possessed by the ghost of a slutty chambermaid?

He waited for a few seconds and then said in his lovely accent, "You wanna stay here?"

Oh God. Didn't he want me to?

"Well, I mean, it *is* nicer than Kelly's room. Have you lost count?"

"Nope. Sixty-nine, seventy, seventy-one, seventy-two . . ."

"It was just an idea. Doesn't matter, I'll stay at Kelly's."

"No . . . Stay here."

"That OK?"

"Yeah."

"Cool."

He hesitated again, like he was going to say something else but changed his mind.

"Cool."

What am I doing? Am I drunk on half a glass of wine and two sips of beer?

No, you're drunk on him.

When he finished his press-ups, he rolled over and said, "Anchor me?"

"Er, sorry?"

"Gotta do stomach crunches."

"Right."

"Sit on my feet?"

He sat back and I squatted down, awkward in my super-short rockabilly dress, and eased myself on to his ankles. His skin felt warm against the cool of my bare thighs.

I looked at the hair falling around his face, as he came forward with his palms bracing the sides of his head. His eyes were locked in concentration. I stared at him, looked straight at those sea-blue eyes, bluer even than the sky, and caught a glimpse of the competitive, totally driven pro-surfer that lurked behind the chilled-out exterior. Behind all the hippy dippy stuff was a boy who was absolutely going to win.

He looked across and caught my gaze. His eyes were bright and his face flushed, but he hadn't broken a sweat. He was crazily fit.

"Done. Just need to find my cell phone and we can party."

Oh dear.

He looked around his room for the phone but of course he couldn't find it.

"I guess I had it in my pocket when I went to the beach. Some local kid's probably listing it on eBay right now. I'll have to pick up another one tomorrow. You have an Apple Store here?"

"No, but Truro does. You're not bummed about losing your phone?"

"Yeah, it's too bad; I had some nice pictures of Fistral on there. But, no worries, I'm always losing cells. I have my planner and contacts backed up to iCloud, so I won't lose anything important."

So the numbers of the eight million girls on his old iPhone would just be transferred over to his new iPhone. It figured.

He scooped the shirt off the ironing board, buttoned it and tried to straighten out his hair without even bothering to look in the mirror. Then he put his wallet and room key card into his back pocket, grabbed his bottle of Corona and opened the door for me.

"After you," he said.

"Do you want your room card back?"

There was a moment thick with stuff neither of us was saying, before he said, "Hold on to it."

I stood next to him in the elevator and my head was a jumble of thoughts: busted iPhones, Hawaiian shirts, Zeke doing sit-ups, the fact that I had just invited myself to stay over in his penthouse suite . . .

We walked into the blare of the Headland's function room.

"Anders! Come talk to my girl Iris."

Chapter Eight

My girl?

"Golden Boy tells me you're a natural. Shredding Fistral, so he says," Anders said, handing Zeke what looked like a pint of some rank real ale.

"Wouldn't go that far."

"Zeke only tells the truth. This I know. So if Zeke tells me you've got something, then you've got something. Mind you, all surfers are narcissistic suicidal jerks with a chip the size of Mars on their shoulder, me included. It's just the cloth we're cut from, sweetheart, so being a natural surfer isn't necessarily a compliment."

He talked like he was being paid by the word. It was difficult to keep up with him. What he said was pretty offensive, but he said it with enough charm to be able to get away with it.

"I don't have a death wish," I pointed out. "I'm just in it for the stoke. Plus I only surf when I can handle the conditions."

This comment made Anders talk even faster.

"Handle the conditions? The ocean is a bitch that will suckle you at her tit or dash your brains out on a rock, like dear old Lady Macbeth. And she can change in seconds. Don't tell me you haven't been caught out? Course you have. We all have. One mistake can result in death—that's why surfing is classed as an extreme sport. Oh, it's the best rush you'll ever have in your life, but every wave could be your last, and if you don't admit that it's a potentially lethal way to spend an afternoon, you shouldn't be out there. For the ultimate thrill, you've got to be willing to pay the ultimate price. Are you willing?"

"Er, I, um . . ." I mumbled, feeling pretty sure that the guy had been smoking something not available in stores.

"He has a point," Zeke said. "The beach in Morocco where I train during the spring? A surfer dies there every month, and the waves aren't even that gnarly."

"I'll just have to take my chances," I said, trying to sound more confident than I was.

"Atta girl. Well, darlin', it just so happens that Billabong is looking to sign a hot young female charger from Britain. They want an unknown. Someone who hasn't been sponsored before, someone they can build up from scratch and claim credit for. Zeke says you've never even gone semi-pro, not even for free wetsuits. That right?"

"Yeah, my mom would've never let me try for sponsorship, even if I really wanted it."

"Old-school hippie type? Despises the commercialization of surfing?"

I didn't want to tell him that my mom wasn't a hippie at all; she just hated the risks of surfing; constantly worried about me breaking my neck, or drowning.

"So, are you interested?"

"For real?"

"Yep. It's going to be a big deal. They're looking for ten girls internationally, one from each participating country. Five grand check, magazine coverage, entry to a series of new girls' contests that will run parallel to ASP Qualifying Series events—same locations and dates as the main events, to guarantee the biggest audience. It's gonna rival Rip Curl's 'Gromsearch,' but this is just for girls under eighteen. Billabong is spending a lot of money on this, really investing in the future of women's surfing."

"That sounds awesome," I said, which was an understatement. All the surf magazines wrote articles about the sexism in pro-surfing: how hardly any money was spent on women's surfing, compared to men's; on how women surfers were objectified and judged mostly on their ability to look hot in a bikini. Those same magazines would run pictures of female pro-surfers posing in their underwear, whereas the men were almost always pictured actually surfing. They didn't seem to see the irony.

Anders continued. "The girl's gotta have the attitude, the ability and total courage, because the waves you'll be riding won't be 'bitchen' or 'sweet rides'; they'll be killers. Can you handle that?"

Zeke interrupted him. "Iris will give any girl a run for her money. You should see her, Anders. She's a wave magnet. She has great instincts and no fear."

Well, that was a laugh. If only he knew just how much fear I had in me. I'd been afraid of everything for months on end. Surfing was different though. You could lose yourself in the surf. Or find yourself. Or something.

"How about we try you out tomorrow morning?"

"Are you serious?" I said. "Is it even good tomorrow?"

I hadn't checked the surf report and you could never bank on the surf being good from one day to the next. Beach breaks weren't as predictable as reef or point breaks. The swells came from storms deep in the Atlantic and you never knew exactly when one would arrive and how it would work against the beach.

Zeke turned to me and took my hand. "He's serious. He'll see what I saw."

"Well, you've got my hopes up now, Zeke, so she'd better not disappoint. Let's hope she's the next Stephanie Gilmore."

Gilmore was incredible. I wasn't fit to surf the same waves as someone like that. It was ridiculous to compare us, but it was exciting to think of what could happen if by some miracle I managed to impress Anders.

I looked over to Kelly, who was listening, slack-jawed. Saskia was standing next to her with a weird smug look on her face. She was expecting me to bottle it. To say I couldn't possibly do something like that. Well, screw it. Why couldn't I at least try? What kind of girl wouldn't even try something because she was worried about losing? A gutless wonder.

"I'll be there," I said. It would be super nerve-wracking and it was bound to end in hideous, embarrassing failure, but I had half a white-wine spritzer and three sips of beer inside me, and that was apparently all it took for me to get some guts.

Someone else caught Anders's attention and he moseyed off. My head was reeling. What had happened to my life in the past day? It was crazy. To think I'd been in my pajamas stuffing ice cream for pretty much all of Thursday and now this! I actually had the chance to surf in front of a big kahuna surf agent. What a difference a day could make. The yoga woman had said saying yes could change your life. Maybe she was right.

Kelly was on the verge of doing cartwheels. "Oh my God oh my God oh my God, Iris!"

"Good luck to you," Saskia said. "This could be the big time, princess. Don't cock it up."

What can you say to that? *I won't?* Pointless when you know you will.

Zeke was staring into his glass when he suddenly looked up and said, "Iris, come outside with me. I wanna show you something."

We walked across the heaving dance floor, through some double doors and out on to a terrace which had steps leading down to the grass. The sea wind sent clouds racing past the stars, and I felt goosebumps come up on my arms.

There was a strange noise out there, a deep punchy boom that almost seemed to rock the headland itself.

Zeke pointed to out to the dark water, where an arc of white was racing toward the cliff beneath us.

"Wow," I said. "I've lived here all my life and I've hardly ever seen it. I can't believe it's happening tonight."

"Yep, the swell's hit just right and the Cribbar's going off. What do you think? The faces of those waves are, what, twenty feet high?"

The Cribbar is a rocky underwater reef just off Towan Headland, and when conditions are right, with a low tide and a huge swell, the reef sends massive waves surging toward the shore. Cribbar waves are between fifteen feet and fifty feet in height. The sort of waves they get in the winter in Hawaii.

"Yeah, eighteen to twenty. Not the biggest ever, and it probably won't double up with the tide coming in, but seriously cool," I said, thinking the night was getting stranger and more magical by the hour.

The Cribbar only worked for a few hours and most surfers—sane surfers—steered clear, although one or two might give it a try, if they'd surfed big waves abroad. But it was serious shit. It wasn't called the Widow Maker for nothing. You didn't mess around with power like that unless you absolutely knew you could handle it.

Zeke was watching the waves, mesmerized. He wouldn't even look at me when he was talking. I could feel the lure of the water on him. He was itching to get in there. Even alone; even in the dark.

"You ever surf a big wave, Iris?"

"Five to six foot . . ." Which seemed big enough.

I sat down on a bench and pulled my skirt down over my knees to keep warm.

Startled as if he'd been sleepwalking, Zeke turned and stood in front of the bench, looking down at me.

"I wanna stick around longer."

"In Newquay?"

"Yeah."

"Can you?"

"Don't know. I'll work on Anders."

"You think he'll let you stay?"

"Maybe. Nanna has this enlarged heart thing. It's getting worse and I wanna be around for the end."

"Really sorry. That's so sad."

"It's OK. She's ready. She says she's lived a 'completed life'; seen her children grow up and have their own, which is all she ever wanted. But if she dies it's gonna hit my pa like a fifty-five-gallon drum."

I thought about the weeks after my own grandma had died, and how shattered my mother had been. How the tears kept ambushing her. How she'd told me that, even though she was forty, losing her mother made her feel like some orphan kid.

"When were you supposed to be going home?"

"Next Monday. I start contest training in Portugal on the Tuesday. Then the week after, I'm in Utah for a base-jumping and slacklining trip with some guys from home. First vacation I've had in two years."

Some vacation.

He couldn't go so soon. I needed more time with him. This amazing boy couldn't come into my life only to leave it again almost right away.

"But even if I do have to leave then, I gotta come back to Newquay next month for the Saltwater Contest."

"OK."

A month was forever. In a month he could meet a hundred girls that were cooler, prettier and nicer than me. Girls who knew how to do things like base-jumping and slacklining.

Zeke sat down beside me, putting his arm around my shoulders. I could feel the warmth of his body, so much warmer than mine. I rested my head against his shoulder and looked up at the night gulls wheeling in the wind.

Was he going to kiss me?

I never found out the answer to that question as, coming around the corner of the hotel, cigarettes hanging out of their mouths, were Daniel and his crew. I say crew, but their private little surf club was more like a gang.

Daniel was doing this aggressive walk where his feet were slightly turned out to the sides, and it looked like he had an invisible roll of carpet under each arm.

Just turn into the hotel and don't look back, Daniel.

Daniel looked up at us. The laugh died on his lips and he stared hard at me and then Zeke. He said something to his friends and then suddenly me and Zeke were faced with six boys.

"All right, Iris?" Daniel said, like it was a threat, not a question.

I could see that he had been drinking. His face was flushed and his eyes were definitely glazed.

"Yeah, peachy," I said, in my most formal accent. "You?"

"Having a kiss and a cuddle with the new boyfriend, are you?"

"I told you, he's not my boyfriend, and even if he was, that'd have nothing to do with you."

"We just came out to look at the Cribbar waves, dude. They're breaking clean." Zeke said this in a friendly way, trying to defuse the tension, I guessed.

"We're not fucken blind."

"Didn't say you were, brah."

"You need to watch the way you're talking to me. *Brah.*"

"Chill out, yeah?" I said to Daniel. His attitude was violent; I had never seen him so aggressive. Like he was juiced on steroids or something.

"Very cozy you look out here, under the stars. Very romantic."

"Oh, fuck off, Daniel."

"What did you say to me? *Slut*."

That was it. Zeke had been all politeness until he heard that word. He jumped up and got right into Daniel's face and said, "Don't talk to her like that." His voice sounded weird, really serious and low.

"And what are you gonna do about it? You overrated. Piss-ball. Yank."

"Cool it," I said. "You're drunk, Daniel."

"He thinks he's the big man," Daniel went on, "but he's a total pussy."

"I'm the pussy? Yeah, keep surfing your two-foot waves, dude."

"You don't even paddle out. You get towed by a jet ski. Afraid to mess up your pretty hair? Pussy."

"You can't catch a train with a skateboard. It's about speed, not balls. And you really don't wanna call me a pussy again."

"Come on," Daniel was saying, "how hard is tow-in surfing?"

"Pretty fucking hard actually," Zeke said. "Unless you think surfing a super-fast wave with a sixty-foot face is easy. But then you wouldn't know anything about that, would you? Stick to the little kid stuff and I'll be out there with the men catching the real waves."

I cut in.

"Zeke has done nothing to you, Daniel. You're just talking crap. Go home. See Cass."

"Oh, here she goes. Wetting her underpants over some fuckin' twinkletoes poser. He's not even English, let alone Cornish. Don't know what you're thinking, shacking up with that. It's embarrassing. Thought more of you, girl."

"Oh, racism too. You're delightful tonight, Daniel. Just go home and take your psycho friends with you."

"Yeah, that sounds like a great idea," Zeke said. Then added, "*Aloha.*"

Daniel punched Zeke.

Chapter Nine

Zeke took the punch like it was nothing, then slapped Daniel around the back of the head really hard, which was a move I'd seen other surfers do in the water when someone dropped in on their waves. It hurt like hell but it wasn't a real punch. It was a warning.

Daniel looked a bit stunned and then caught Zeke with a glancing blow to the jaw. Zeke spat out a bit of blood where his teeth must have snagged his tongue, and it was on. He swung back and hit Daniel square in the nose, which sprayed blood over Zeke's Hawaiian shirt. I was shouting for Daniel to stop, but it was as if he couldn't hear my voice at all, as if I didn't even exist.

Daniel went for Zeke again, but he was so drunk and giddy that he staggered to the side and his fist hit nothing but air. He tumbled on to hands and one knee and scrambled to get back to his feet.

Angry now, Zeke held Daniel down with one hand. With his other hand he hammered Daniel's head with punches.

Daniel's friend Sammy hit Zeke from behind with a beer bottle to the head, and another friend quickly kicked Zeke three or four times in the kidneys, then went for the lowest kick. Zeke doubled up and dropped to the grass, and Daniel, out of control and his face a gory pulp, just raging like a wild animal, tried to kick Zeke in the ribs, but I got in the way and Daniel ended up kicking the bench instead. He swore and swung for Zeke again, but ended up hitting too low and catching Zeke's leg.

I looked around, desperately hoping someone was coming to break up the fight, but there was no one.

Another of Daniel's friends, Matthew—who was basically the only sensible one out of the bunch of them—tried to hold Daniel back, but Daniel snaked around and punched Matthew too. Matthew retaliated, and it was a brawl between all of them. Zeke was down and not moving. I grabbed his arm, got him to his feet and began dragging him toward the double doors. Something was wrong, because Zeke wasn't saying a thing.

After a few steps Zeke seemed to revive a bit, but I could tell he was hurt by the way he was breathing. A dark patch was growing on his thigh. I put my hand to it and my fingers were bright red in seconds.

Oh my God.

Zeke was a pro-surfer with an international rep and he'd been knifed in Newquay, by my ex, right in front of me. This was breaking very, very bad.

"We're nearly there," I said.

We got into the hotel. As I pushed open the doors with my back, I saw that Daniel had got away from his friends and was walking unsteadily after me, carrying something in his hand.

The hotel residents' bar was empty except for two old dudes sipping beers and picking at bags of chips. I heard a door slam in the wind and I pushed through another door and on to the heaving dance floor, where we stood gasping for breath.

Garrett looked across and saw us, slammed his drink back down on the bar in an eruption of froth and pushed through the crowd to reach us. Wes followed Garrett with his eyes and then saw us too. A couple of boys I didn't recognize, but who were obviously friends of theirs, were close behind.

Garrett arrived first.

He took one look, undid his shirt and used it as a tourniquet around Zeke's leg.

Something inside me had seized up and I couldn't even move my own body. I was just frozen by the sight of the blood. So much blood.

"What the hell?" Garrett said. "Would someone call a fucking ambulance?"

"Negative. Anders'll drive me. Don't need an ambulance, just a second to think. Figure out how I'm gonna explain this. Fuck. Other dude had a flick knife."

"Yeah, brah, I see that. Don't look like he caught an artery though." Garrett touched Zeke gingerly on the chest, and Zeke winced. "Couple ribs broken too maybe," Garrett said, his face going tight with anger. "You k'den? Not gonna croak?"

"Not today."

"I can leave you with Iris?"

"Don't do anything stupid," Zeke said, trying to disguise the pain in his voice.

"You think? Those punks are dead. Where?"

"Just like three feet outside the door," I said. And then added, "*Mahalo*." I hoped that Garrett would kick Daniel's ass. Daniel had crossed the line, gone full-on psycho and tried to kill someone. If he wasn't put in his place now, what else could happen?

Without another word Garrett was out the door, and Wes and the others followed him.

For ten seconds, which felt like forever, I looked at Zeke and I could feel the pressure building up behind my eyes, but I couldn't cry. Not now. Now when it was all my fault.

Zeke was covered in dirt, with his shirt ripped and smeared with blood. His mouth was bleeding and he had a few nasty cuts on the back of his head where the bottle had broken. I looked down at the leg of his jeans, soaked with blood. I still couldn't believe it. Daniel had done that? He'd never carried a knife before. He'd use his own fists or nothing.

Zeke had a hand across his chest and was grimacing with the pain of breathing. I had my arm around him, trying to support his weight and keep him steady. He was much heavier than me though, and I couldn't move him.

Kelly rushed over, came out with the most colorful bunch of swear words I'd ever heard and used her weight to prop up Zeke on the other side. We limped over to a booth, where Zeke slumped down and tried to breathe.

"Get Anders," I said to Kelly, who turned on her heel and ran.

"S'OK," Zeke said. "Gotten better beatings off of the ocean."

I held his hand tight and stroked it with my other hand. His gorgeous eyes had laughter in them, even then, when he was in so much pain.

Anders ran over, took one look at Zeke and made a call on his phone.

"You didn't call an ambulance, man?" Zeke said to him, through a rasping breath.

"You're damn right I did, and I'm about two seconds away from calling the fuzz."

"You can't. If this gets out, I'll lose my sponsorship. Out in the boondocks, fighting with locals? Looks great, huh?"

"Have you taken anything?" Anders said.

"Nothin'. Come on. Don't ask me that."

A weird question, I thought. Zeke didn't seem like the type to mess around with drugs.

"How much have you had to drink?"

"I don't know. Two beers. You can't call it in, dude. We just need to get out of here before anyone else sees me like this. If this makes the news, it's gonna be messy. Just take me to my pa's place."

"Fuck. OK, I'm gonna cancel the ambulance, but I'm taking you to A&E under a fake name, OK?"

Zeke looked at his leg, and the blood pooling around his foot.

"OK. Guess I am gonna need some stitches. Maybe a pint of blood too."

Anders gave me a look like he was really pissed with me, and for a moment I thought he was going to take it out on me, but Zeke shook his head and Anders stopped himself.

After everything that had happened, Zeke turned to me and said, "I'm sorry. Shoulda walked away."

"Don't," I said. "It's all my fault."

"I've messed up your big chance."

"Huh?"

"Your try-out tomorrow. I'll make it right, I promise."

How could he even think about me having some stupid surf try-out at a time like this? If he had any serious injuries, he'd be out of the competitive surf scene for the rest of the season, if not forever. I could have ruined his whole life.

I let go of Zeke's hand, and Anders led him away. Kelly and I followed at a distance, not sure what to do or where to go. Saskia appeared out of the powder room, where she'd obviously been applying make-up with a shovel, and said, "Everything all right, girls?"

"Not exactly . . ." I replied, tailing off.

Saskia followed my eyes to Zeke who was leaning heavily on Anders as they limped out of the fire exit. "Oh my goodness!" she said, and ran after them without another word to us.

I turned to Kelly and said, "Never gonna forgive myself for this."

"It's not your fault."

"Never forgiving Daniel either."

Kelly gave me a grim smile. "You will. You always do."

"Not this time. He went totally crazy out there."

"Have you asked yourself why?"

"Doesn't like seeing another boy with me. Probably thinks it's disrespecting his male code or something. He's crazy."

"Yeah, for you."

"He's with Cass."

"Because you said no to him."

"Hello? I was fifteen. What was I supposed to say? What did he expect?"

"He expected you to say yes. He doesn't care about Cass. He's just with her to hurt you."

"Thank God I said no. Look what he's turned into. Just because he didn't get what he wanted from me. He could've killed Zeke out there."

"Yeah, well, what goes around comes around. He'll get his."

"Good."

"He thinks you belong with him. He doesn't want to lose you to anyone else. Especially not someone like Zeke. He knows that if you hook up with Zeke you'll never come back to Newquay. That's why he's going so nuts. What is it they say? Wider horizons. If you get with Zeke, the world will be your oyster. You'll be gone."

"You're trippin'," I said.

"No, I'm not. I get it. I don't want to lose you either. But I know you've got to do what makes *you* happy, not anyone else."

"I'm not going anywhere. Jesus. I only met Zeke yesterday. You're all crazy."

"OK, OK. Let's stop talking about it."

Kelly got out her phone and called a cab. I sat down in the lobby, shaking. I'd done nothing much for three months and now it seemed like three years' worth of drama had been crammed into twenty-four hours.

I didn't speak to Kelly in the cab home. All I could focus on was getting my key in the door, getting into my bedroom and getting under the covers of my bed.

Kelly grabbed my wrist as I was getting out of the car and said, "I got Zeke's business card off Saskia. Just in case you don't have his cell phone number."

I took the card and typed the number into my phone. I'd never thought to get his number. I don't know why. Maybe we'd both just figured that we'd keep running into each other if we were meant to. But then it dawned on me. I couldn't phone him to check how he was, because I'd dropped his phone into a hot tub.

How had it come to this? How had it all gone so wrong, so quickly?

I thought back to the previous evening. Zeke had the most gorgeous laugh; I kept noticing that. We stayed out for two hours past my curfew, before we rode our skateboards back to my house. If I hadn't liked him so much, it might have occurred to me that I could talk to him as easily as I could talk to Kelly, which was saying something, as Kelly was pretty much the only person in the world who got me. My mom had been waiting for me on the garden bench with a lecture, so I never got to find out if Zeke was going to kiss me goodnight. As soon as I spotted my mom, I handed Zeke his jacket and told him to split while he could. My mom would tell off anybody, even Zeke Francis.

I took Zeke's room key card out of my ancient Rip Curl wallet and let myself think about what might have happened if Daniel hadn't gone out for that cigarette with his friends. Would I have bottled it, or would I have ended up going back with Zeke to his room?

I didn't know. All I wanted was for Zeke to be all right again, like he was before he came to Newquay; before he met me.

I could hear my mom coming up the stairs, so I shoved the key card under my pillow and switched off my lamp so that she would think I was already asleep. I heard my door open a crack and then close again. I reached for my phone.

It rang three times before he answered.

"Didn't mean to cut him, did I? Just wanted to scare the prick," he said.

"You're dead to me," I said. "Don't ever contact me again." Then I put down the phone and let out the tears that had been burning the backs of my eyes for an hour.

Chapter Ten

Monday was school. Exams were finished but we were all supposed to go in for some crappy farewell day where we'd sign everyone's shirts, write in each other's yearbooks and make a film of ourselves playing around, so that we could look back on it in the future, when we were old and past it. In the afternoon, a few of the jocks and nerds were going to get awards and the rest of us would get to sit in the sweltering assembly hall and clap. It was going to suck.

On Sunday I'd called Zeke's cell phone a bunch of times, hoping he was out of the hospital with a new iPhone, but all I got was his mailbox. I couldn't call the hospital because I didn't know what name he'd used. I was seriously considering ditching school and taking the bus to Treliske in Truro to scour the wards and see if he was there.

On the other hand, would he even want to see me? In the cold light of day, perhaps he'd come to his senses and realized that I was more trouble than I was worth. His agent would be telling him that.

I didn't particularly want to see Kelly and listen to her be nice to me, but without her I was so alone. Where was my family? There they were, their smiling faces in the huge collage of photos around my bedroom mirror.

Lily, my older sister, was at art college (my dad was so proud; my mom not so much) and she was a total scene kid. She would quite often leave the house wearing one red Converse high-top sneaker and one blue one. She had a different hair color every month, different colored contact lenses every week, and she changed her sexual orientation every couple of days. She'd called to say she was working as a stewardess at various music festivals over the summer vacations. She was a free spirit, she said, and couldn't be brought low with regular jobs, like shop work. That was aimed at me, I guessed, but my shop was three seconds from Fistral Beach, so what did I care? I could surf in my lunch hour, which was the main thing.

My sweet grandmother's face was there, smiling through her wrinkles like she knew the answers to all the questions in the universe. She had walked the continents, sailed the seas. She'd fallen in love a hundred times, with adolescents, men in their twenties, thirties, every decade up to old men in their nineties. My grandfather was lost in the war and my grandmother spent the rest of her life living it to the full, with no regrets, no guilt and no looking back. She'd rubbed shoulders, to put it politely, with millionaires, aristocrats, vicars, politicians and her own share of surfers.

I missed her so much that the pain caught in my throat like a lump of stale bread.

She would know what to say now. She would say the perfect thing to make it feel better. But she was out of my reach.

With Zeke in the hospital, I let my mind wander. It wandered back to the day Lily and her friends took me out in a twelve-foot boat; a piece of crap from the seventies that belonged to my uncle. It was supposed to be a fishing trip, we were after mackerel and bass, and I was adamant I wanted to go, even though it was before I had my sea legs and I couldn't stand the smell of fish.

But Lily did her good deed and brought me along. There was some beer drinking, some smoking of weed, a bit of serious rowing and then we got out by the Zorba reef and things got rough. Turn-your-skull-into-a-blender rough. After puking my guts out over the side of the boat, I looked up and saw this huge thing coming toward me, with its mouth open and its massive black fin shooting into the air. Cody sprayed his mouthful of beer right over Alfie's lap, and I was laughing and terrified at the same time, but Kai kicked back and said not to sweat it, it was only a basking shark. It was humongous, bigger than the boat. It could have capsized us, swallowed the five of us whole and still had room for plankton.

So many times I remembered that boiling-hot day on the sea with them. Maybe there's something about kids' brains that makes color brighter, heat hotter and smells stronger, because when I remember it, it's like spinning through some Van Gogh world.

I missed Lily and her friends. I did. If they had been at the Headland Hotel with me, Daniel and his moron friends couldn't have done that to Zeke, because Lily and her crew would have stepped in, held Daniel's arms by his side, pushed him to the ground if he kept struggling and held him there until he calmed down.

But they were all long gone.

I got into my uniform, tied up my hair and walked to school. I passed Kelly's house and she came running out behind me. Her shirt was hanging out of her pants and she hadn't done her hair.

"Hey, how ya doing?" she said.

"I'm super. It's Zeke I'm worried about."

"Can you wait a minute and I'll walk with you?"

"OK, whatever."

"Come inside if you want."

"Rather wait out here."

I leaned against a lamppost and watched the sets roll into Fistral. Just looking at the waves made me feel calmer.

I thought back to the fork in the road. To the question that had started the madness. It was because of Daniel's insane plan.

It was too difficult to get a good enough job to pay for a house, he said, and we'd be thirty by the time we saved up a deposit. Apartments in Newquay were sky-high, way out of our league. What we had to do, he said, was simple when you thought about it.

I disagreed.

Daniel wanted us to have a baby, so that we could get a local-authority apartment.

"'Cause of these scuzzy second-homers we're not gonna be able to afford our own apartment so we'll have to live with our moms forever. No thanks, and anyway my mom's told me she's kicking me out on my eighteenth birthday. So if we can't afford to live in Newquay, we'll have to move to Plymouth or Exeter to find some crappy job in a factory. Ten hours a day on a production line, or a life on the beach? What sounds better to you, Ris? Because I don't wanna leave Newquay for anywhere else."

It would be paradise, he told me.

"For you," I'd explained to him gently. "What is it for me? Knocked up, labor, childbirth, everlasting responsibility. At the age of fifteen? Uh, no thanks."

I just couldn't seem to explain it in any way that made sense to him. Babies are cute and everything, and my cousin Cara was adorable, but there was no way I wanted to get pregnant at fifteen. Or seventeen. Or twenty, for that matter. I wanted to live a bit, see the world, and not only the places with good surf. I wanted to see it all, in my own way, on my own terms. I didn't intend to be stuck on the beach looking after babies while my boyfriend surfed for six hours a day.

Down on his knees, with a small black box in his hand containing a ring with a tiny diamond, Daniel couldn't believe that I was saying no to this glistening life that he was offering me.

"Why not though?" he said, over and over, like I was the most unreasonable person in the world.

And now look what he'd done.

But Zeke would get better. He had to. He would get back into the ocean because he was born to it. All he needed was time to heal.

I was still choked up and couldn't talk much to Kelly on the walk to school. As soon as it got to lunch, I skipped out. I ignored a dinner lady who was asking me if I had a home lunch pass, walked through the school gates and turned left. A hundred yards down the road, I heard a noisy engine and a beep.

Pulling up on the curb beside me was Saskia, in a red convertible. She waved me over and I walked to the driver's side window.

"Zeke's asking for you."

"How is he?"

"So-so. Get in."

She looked over her shoulder and pulled into the road, forgetting to indicate and causing one of my teachers to swerve. I sank down a bit lower in my seat.

"I'll give it to you straight, Iris," she said. "Zeke has a cracked rib and a deep cut in his thigh. If that knife had gone two millimeters deeper it would have caught the artery and he'd have bled to death in that lousy hotel. He is lucky to be alive."

I felt my stomach grip with the shock of what she was saying. Lucky to be alive?

"He was in a lot of pain, but here he is today sitting up and asking to speak to the girl who some people might consider responsible for this nightmare."

"All right, it's all my fault. Got it."

I sat in the car, shell-shocked. Saskia glanced over at me and at my once-white shirt, which was covered in scrawls, graffiti tags and signatures: all part of the "fun" of our last day at school.

"What does that say on your arm?"

I looked down at my sleeve where one of the livelier boys from my class had written something in big red letters.

"*Suckit.*"

"Lovely."

"Can we stop here a minute?" I said.

"Which house?"

"The one with the three palm trees."

She pulled over outside my house and I jumped out.

"Be quick. *No* hair-straightening."

I looked at her and managed not to give her the finger.

I was so shaky that at first I couldn't even get my front-door key in the lock. Then I kicked off my shoes and tore up the stairs and into Lily's room. I stripped off my school uniform for the last time ever, and put on a long turquoise hippie skirt and a brown sleeveless top from Lily's wardrobe. She had some nice beaded thong sandals and a chunky seashell necklace, so I borrowed those too. I was not going to visit Zeke in the hospital wearing my skanky, graffitied school uniform or any of my faded old beach stuff.

I swigged some mouthwash, spat it out in the bathroom sink and then ran down the stairs, brushing my hair. I stopped for a second to look in the hallway mirror and put on some light pink lipstick and mascara. My face looked tense; it reminded me of my mom.

I got back into the car and sat in the passenger seat next to Saskia.

"Six minutes," she said, looking at her watch. "Not bad."

"What name is Zeke under at the hospital?"

"Jack Johnson. Anders's idea of funny."

Before Jack Johnson became a multimillionaire musician, he was a pro-surfer. Then he wiped out at Pipeline on the North Shore of Oahu, hit the reef and cracked his head open. Right after the one hundred and fifty stitches were taken out of his forehead, he decided to ditch pro-surfing and become a song-writer instead. I wasn't sure I got Anders's sense of humor there.

When we got to the hospital and Saskia went off to pay for parking, I slipped out of the car and went straight to reception, where I asked for Jack Johnson's ward.

I didn't want Saskia to be there when I saw Zeke. I took the elevator up, surrounded by old people dragging oxygen canisters, and I thought about how he would look. I couldn't imagine seeing him all wired up to medical equipment.

The ward was quiet. A nurse sat behind a desk reading a magazine and ignored me as I walked in.

Zeke was at the far end, asleep.

I walked over quietly and stood at the end of his bed. He was very pale, and a cut on his lip was beginning to heal, a mess of purple congealed blood.

He opened his eyes and smiled.

"Hey. Howzit, Iris? Wow, you look *hella* fly."

"Thank you. You don't look so bad yourself, all things considered, like."

"Caught any killer waves today?"

"Uh, no. Mom ragged on me for an hour before school this morning, so I didn't exactly get a chance to go surfing, even if I'd wanted to, which I didn't. How are you feeling?" I said, wishing I'd thought to bring him some surf magazines. But maybe that would just make him feel worse. Like rubbing salt into the wound.

He moved a game console from his lap, slid off the bed and walked to the window.

"Guess I'm not going base-jumping in Utah. Bummer. I've always wanted to see the Moab desert. It's not your fault, by the way."

"It so is."

"I was getting harassed by your ex all night. I thought it was funny. I should have just gone and asked him what his problem was. Worked it out like men. None of this knife bull."

"I'm really sorry."

"Forget it. Wasn't kidding when I said I've gotten better beatings."

I must have looked a bit skeptical, because Zeke said, "This is nothin' compared to getting my knees dislocated, my eye socket shattered and my head split open when I wiped out in the wrong spot and got slammed all over a Tahitian coral reef. Anyways, I'm getting out of here tomorrow."

"Yeah? Awesome."

"But they say I won't be able to surf for a while. Maybe two or three weeks. Not until my rib's all healed up again. It's gonna take a while for my leg to feel OK again too."

"You should press charges. Daniel deserves it. He needs to know he can't go around attempting to murder people."

"Anders and Saskia have been telling me the same thing. I'm not pressing charges. He's just a pissed local, mad at me for coming here and taking a crack at his waves. And his girl. Besides, Garrett beat the crap out of him. Broke his face."

"I'm not his girl, and press charges anyway."

"The kid's nuts about you. He made a mistake. We've all done it."

"You ever beat up someone over a girl?"

"Sure."

"Don't believe you."

"It happened. I was eight."

Not exactly the same thing. I shook my head and smiled.

Saskia walked over and gave Zeke a kiss on the head. "Don't worry about a thing," she said. "I've made all the necessary telephone calls and your schedule is wide open for the next month, so all you have to concentrate on is getting better. We'll get you back to London in the next few days and have you seen by the best physical therapists this country has to offer."

"I'm going no place but Newquay."

"What? Why?"

"Because my planner is blank for like the first time in two years? And I'm not going to waste my time in some city."

"You can't surf, darling. The doctor was very clear about that."

"So I'll eat ice creams and catch some rays."

"Oh yes, on the two days of the summer that Cornwall actually gets sunshine."

"Who cares about the weather?"

"Let me get you a cup of coffee," Saskia said, talking to him like he was a toddler, before swishing out of the ward.

As soon as she was gone, Zeke turned to me and said, "I can still stand-up paddle surf. I have a great new SUP board my sponsor wants me to try out. I'll go explore hidden coves, see if I can spot a new break, one not accessible by land. Maybe name it too."

I couldn't help laughing. Stabbed, bottled and battered, but not broken. "I know I shouldn't say this, but I'm so glad you're staying."

Zeke grinned and said, "Yeah, Iris, it's gonna be real interesting."

Chapter Eleven

On the first day that Zeke was released from hospital, he came around to my house.

I spotted him from the window. He walked up the path smoking a cigarette, which I watched him crush underfoot. Then he picked up the dog-end and put it in what looked like a little black film canister that he fished out of his pocket. I seemed to remember the Surfers Against Sewage gang handing out those film canisters as part of an anti-beach-litter "Get Your Butts Off Our Beach" campaign, because billions of cigarette butts end up in the ocean each year and some of them hang around for a decade, leaching toxic chemicals into the ocean and killing marine life.

Though he seemed to be a tidy smoker, I was still surprised that Zeke smoked. As a vegetarian, yoga-expert surf champ, smoking seemed weirdly out of character. I hoped it was something that he only did when he was stressed, though that would mean he was stressed by seeing me, which wasn't a great thought.

I opened the door just as his hand was raised to knock and caught my hand around his fist, unfurled his fingers and led him into the hallway. Before he could say anything, I reached up and put my arms around him, lightly so I wouldn't do any extra damage to his cracked rib. I just wanted to hug him. It was all I'd wanted to do for days, and now he was here I wasn't going to wimp out. He put one hand on the back of my head and quietly said, "Thanks for worrying about me, but I'm OK now."

My mom's voice called out in the hallway: "Put him down, Iris. The poor boy is walking wounded."

I released Zeke and spun around.

My mom was smiling, and looking curiously at Zeke.

We went into the kitchen and my mom puttered around, making us eggs Benedict, with veggie bacon and wilted spinach for Zeke. I noticed her eyes widen slightly as Zeke carried our plates out of the kitchen and into the breakfast room. Then she gave me a little smile, which clearly said, "Good taste, daughter."

"So what do you do, Zeke?"

"I'm a pro-surfer."

"Oh yes, I think Iris did mention that. And what do you do apart from surfing?"

"I play a little golf, I guess? But pro-surfing pretty much takes up most of my time."

"What about job-wise? I don't suppose that surf contests pay all that well, do they, even if you can win them?"

"They pay pretty good, but it's the sponsorship and endorsements that really bring in the bucks."

"And how much do they pay? Roughly?"

"You really wanna know?"

"Is it a secret?"

"No, ma'am."

"Oh, go on. Ten thousand dollars? Twenty?"

"A little more than that."

I looked over at Zeke and I could see he was mortified.

"Leave him alone, Mom."

"Boys today are so easily embarrassed. You'd never see that sort of coyness in my day."

When we'd finished eating, my aunt Zoe knocked at the door, bringing Cara, my two-year-old niece, who my mom was supposed to be looking after for the day. Cara was holding a small cake tin full of plastic animal figures, which she offered up to Zeke.

"Hey there, little lady," he said to her, pulling out the animals one by one and asking what they were. I was terrible at keeping Cara interested, but Zeke seemed to be finding it totally easy. My aunt went into the kitchen to talk to my mom, where I could hear enough of their conversation and raucous laughing that I went out to ask them to keep it down.

When I got back to Zeke, he was standing, legs apart, arms outstretched, on the coffee table. Cara was watching him open-mouthed and shouting, "More surfing, Zeke," every two seconds.

"Does your aunt have a surfboard for her?" Zeke said.

"She's got two."

"Let's rent a foamie and take her surfing today."

"You're not allowed to go surfing. And neither is she, probably."

"Ask her momma. Go on. We'll only take her in the baby waves."

"I don't know . . ."

"What's this?" my mom said, marching into the room with a tea tray.

"Zeke was thinking we could take Cara to the beach today, if it's OK with Auntie Zoe."

"She's a lot of work," Zoe said. "She needs constant watching. Can you handle that?"

"I have a three-year-old cousin, and I sit for my aunt whenever I'm home," Zeke said.

"I didn't know that," I said, surprised he hadn't mentioned it.

"Yeah—Colton. I'm used to taking care of him, and he has some severe ADD, so looking after Cara will be a piece of cake."

"Well, OK then, but just for an hour," Zoe said. "And don't you take your eyes off her for a second, Iris."

"Can we take her in the water?" I said. And Zeke added, "On a surfboard? Just up to our knees?"

"She's a bit young," Aunt Zoe said.

Zeke's face fell, and I saw my aunt's expression soften.

"Well, OK, but only because you're a young man with years of good seamanship under your belt, and I trust you to be sensible in the water."

"Cool," Zeke said. "Also: do you have any duct tape?"

"Yes, there's a roll in the kitchen drawer," my mom said, looking confused. "Why?"

"The nurse made me promise I'd tape my dressing if I went in the water any time soon. It probably won't get wet if we stay in the shallows, but I should maybe cover it anyways. Guess I don't need an infection."

Mom got the tape and then Zeke went into the kitchen to put it on, while me, my aunt and my mom talked about whether it was, in fact, possible to be a surf addict.

So that was it. Zeke and I were off to the beach, looking after a little kid. People were looking at us, scandalized, as if Cara was our little girl. I felt like writing on my back, "She's my aunt's kid, not ours, and mind your own business."

I went to rent the foamie, as Zeke and I only had fiberglass boards and we needed something really big, stable and soft to take Cara safely out. A foamie could support a twenty-stone kook, so it'd be fine for a wriggly two-year-old.

As I walked away from Denny at the surf-rental shack, I saw a familiar head of wavy yellow hair in front of me. I just knew it was her from her awful bobbing walk and tanorexic arms.

Cass's best and only friend, Rae. Rae was the sort of girl whose greatest hope in life was to be a hippie, doss around some remote islands in the South Pacific and have her name officially changed to Dolphina. What she had in common with Cass I couldn't figure out. She seemed all right, but I didn't want to be reminded of Cass or Daniel.

"Oh hiya, petal!"

This was the way she talked. We were all petal or rosebud or Delilah or some other word that popped into her brain. She couldn't just call a person by their actual name. Some people at school thought she was on drugs, but really she was just incredibly weird.

"Hiya," I said. "How's it going?"

"Not so bad. Had a magic surf this morning and I'm off now for a toasting on the sunbed at Cass's place."

"Fun."

"Sorry. I shouldn't have mentioned Cass, should I?"

"I'm not stopping you."

"You've gone all moody now, see. I honestly didn't mean to mention her. I only did because she's on my mind, I guess, because of the argument."

"You two had an argument?"

"No, her and Daniel had a massive blow-up. Maaasive. I could hear it from my house and I live six doors down. It was mega."

"Yeah?" My ears had definitely pricked up. We were walking down the beach and Zeke and Cara were getting bigger. A minute or two and we'd have reached them. Whatever Rae had to tell me, it had to be then.

"Cass couldn't take it anymore."

"The drinking?"

"Well, yeah, that wasn't helping, but all the rest of it was getting to her even more than him being constantly tanked."

I nodded, as if I knew what she was going on about.

Cass and Daniel were having arguments? It was news to me. Just a few weeks previously, they'd been love's young dream. Even Kelly had to admit that, and she was always waiting for the cracks to appear, as she knew that was the only thing that could cheer me up. Maybe it hadn't all been skinny-dipping and heart-shaped bars of surf wax.

At that moment Cara ran up to me, shouting, "Cara surfing now, please!"

"Hello. And how are you today, duckie?" Rae again.

Holding Cara's hand, Zeke walked up slowly and looked at Rae as if to say, "She cool?" I nodded slightly.

Rae was freaking out.

"Oh my God, oh my God. You are a lej! Zeke Francis. Born 1996 in Oahu. Current holder of the Hawaiian Junior Men's title, and June centerfold of *Surf Girl Magazine*. Earns a quarter of a million dollars every year just from endorsements. I am your biggest fan!"

All Zeke said was "Oh boy."

"You're in *SGM*?" I said, turning to Zeke, surprise probably written all over my face, but also noting that Zeke was apparently pulling in the mega-bucks.

He nodded.

"'Sexiest Athletes 2014.' There's a different guy every month, but June was the best," Rae said, grinning. "You should get a copy, Iris."

"It's probably not on newsstands anymore," Zeke said. "At least, I hope not. They took the pictures last fall but the magazine came out in, I think, May? It's so lame, right?"

"Not necessarily."

"Nanna had her podiatrist buy her a copy of the magazine and she keeps making the nurses in the retirement home look at the picture. It's kind of mortifying."

"I'll have to go into Smith's and order a back copy," I said.

"And look out for *Cosmo Girl* too. I read in their forum that you're nakey in their August issue, Zeke? The feature has Oli Adams, Sebastian Zietz and the Geiselman brothers too, so you should definitely check it out, Iris. It'll probably be out any day now."

Zeke gave Rae a really pained look, which she didn't seem to notice at all.

"Seriously, Zeke? Naked?"

"Um, kind of? But you know, obviously I'm not showing my junk."

"So are you in every girls' magazine in this country?" I said.

"Far as I know it's just those two. And that's all on Anders."

Zeke turned to play with Cara, who was covering the foam surfboard with sand and saying, "Surfboard gone! Zeke find!"

"So are you actually dating Zeke Francis?" Rae whispered.

I wanted to say yes, but that wasn't strictly true so I shook my head.

"Cool. Do you think he might go out for coffee with me?"

"No idea. You'd have to ask him. Be my guest."

At first, I wasn't sure if Zeke heard that, but he suddenly picked up Cara and walked her over to some rock pools, which seemed like pretty clear body language to me.

"Maybe another time," Rae murmured.

"So I guess you're itching to go check on Cass?" I said.

"Oh God, I totally forgot! I better dash. Have a lush weekend, Iris. Say bye to Zeke Francis for me," she said, grinning.

I tried not to suffocate as she gave me a crazy bear hug, and then she went on her way.

I walked over to Zeke, who was knee-deep in a rock pool with Cara clinging on to his back. He was flushed and not in a good way; Rae had really rattled him.

"Can we take her surfing now?" he said.

"Sure."

We waded out into the shallows and started what Zeke was calling "Cara's first step on the journey to pro-surfer."

He was so gentle with Cara, sitting on the back of the board, with his feet touching the seabed and letting her stand in front of him, as if she was riding the wave herself. She kept saying, "Me love Zeke!" and then looking at me, waiting for me to say it too. For obvious reasons I just smiled and said nothing.

"Should we let her try on her own? Just bodyboarding? For like two feet?"

"Probably shouldn't. Board might turtle-roll," Zeke said.

"Just one try." A ripple rolled toward us and I steadied the board and let go.

The board rose up and got swept along with the wave's momentum. The ripple had looked super-weak but the board was so buoyant that the water ran away with it. The board suddenly tilted and Cara was plunged face down into the water.

I rushed toward her, the water slowing my legs so much that it seemed like I was hardly moving at all, even though I couldn't have been more than a second or so behind her. Zeke came out of nowhere and scooped her up in his arms, his face white with panic.

She came up coughing and spitting water. Then she started laughing and saying, "Love, *love* my surfing!"

"Jesus," I said to Zeke. "Remind me never to try that again."

I took Cara out of his arms and went to sit on the beach and dry her off, holding her tight against my body. Zeke fetched the surfboard and carried it over to us. All Cara could say was "Again!" but I shook my head, feeling like I'd aged about ten years in ten seconds.

"We've got to get you back to your mommy now," Zeke said, and then whispered to me, "She's psyched. That wave had some legs on it, huh?"

I turned to look at him, and suddenly our faces were close. My heart stopped as Zeke moved in even closer, this really intense expression in his eyes. In those slow-motion moments, I couldn't blink or breathe.

Cara, who had been watching some herring gulls fighting over a stolen ice cream, turned and started up chanting, "*Zeke kiss Iris!*" and wouldn't stop. Eventually Zeke had to kiss me on the cheek, just to get her to quiet down. "Lips!" she started shouting. I picked her up and she started yelling her head off. I didn't care. There was no way that my first kiss with Zeke was going to be in front of a shrieking two-year-old.

We walked back to the house and Cara and I said goodbye to Zeke on my doorstep. I watched as he crouched down to kiss her on the head. He looked at me for a few seconds, then once again he touched his temple in a salute. He walked slowly out of my garden and over to his van, where he sat for a while before pulling away. I spied on him from my bedroom window, standing back from the glass so he couldn't see my silhouette. Anders had bought him a new iPhone and it looked like he was talking to someone on hands-free. Probably Saskia, I thought darkly.

Chapter Twelve

People aren't the best surfers. Dolphins surf way better than people. Some birds surf better than people. But even if people aren't the best surfers, we keep going back because the sea lures us back. Sometimes, when the surf is good and it's all coming off perfectly, it feels as if the saltwater of your body is responding to the sea; is part of it, even.

I had a text from Zeke asking me to bring my favorite short-board to Fistral. I got suited up and left the house with my six-foot-two-inch board, as the surf report said the waves were a little blown-out and messy.

The first person I saw was Anders.

"Hey there, blue flower," he said, in a sing-songy way, as if I wasn't the girl who was responsible for putting Zeke in the hospital.

"Hiya, what's happening? Everything OK?" I said, looking around for Zeke.

"Everything's dandy. So, are you ready?"

"Huh?" I said, still not quite awake even after two breakfast espressos.

"Didn't Zeke tell you? Today's the day."

"What day? Zeke hasn't said anything."

"Billabong surf trial! Wonder Boy probably didn't want you to be nervous. Anyway, you're only up against three others, so it won't take too long. What we're looking for is raw natural talent."

I looked down to the waterline, where three girls were doing stretches. One of them had red hair, and as she turned to look at one of the lifeguards—who was nagging the bodyboarders yet again to get the hell out of the surfing area and back in between the red-and-yellow flags—I saw that the girl was Saskia.

"What's she doing here?" I said to Anders.

"Saskia?"

"I thought she was Zeke's PA?"

"Oh, she's my PA, although she helps out Zeke too. But she only took the job to get a foot in the pro-surf scene. She's a total shredhead. Her parents took her on international surfing trips from day one. Spent every vacation at some big surf break or other. She wants to be a pro-surfer and she's learning everything she can from Zeke. She worships the ground Sonny Boy walks on."

"Have they ever gone out?" I asked casually.

"I don't know. You'd have to ask them. Doubt it though."

"Why?"

"She isn't his type."

And what is his type exactly? I wanted to ask, but didn't.

Anders walked me down to the other girls. Saskia didn't look at me and I knew she could tell I was annoyed. Neither she nor

Zeke had said a word about her being a surfer. To look at her you'd think she'd never got past her big toe in the sea, what with all the make-up and glam hair.

I caught the eye of the girl next to me, who had a strong build and wavy brown hair.

"How's it going?" I said.

"A bit edgy. What about you?" She had a local accent.

"Not too bad. Where's your home break?"

"Hayle, St. Ives Bay. Fistral's way busier."

"Just keep your head up and your eyes open and you'll be fine."

"I'm Jenny, by the way."

"Iris."

Anders interrupted. "Now, girlies, I'm going to be generous and give you twenty minutes to get some decent rides. The two girls to score the highest will keep our interest. The remaining two we won't be pursuing. Is that clear?"

The girls nodded. We all knew what it meant. The next twenty minutes would be brutal competition.

Two young male surfers joined the group.

"My eyes and spies," Anders said, in a mock-villain voice.

Anders had a pair of binoculars hanging around his neck, but that wasn't good enough apparently. His two assistants would paddle out with us, with tiny head cameras to record us. "In case there's any doubt or argument later," Anders explained.

This was worse than any job interview. We hadn't even stepped in the water, but my heart was already racing.

Before I'd met Zeke I'd never thought of trying to be a serious surfer, making a career out of it, and suddenly I was facing the most important twenty minutes of my life.

A whistle materialized in Anders's hand and we were racing to the water's edge. One of the girls, the blond one, turned her ankle in a dip and lagged behind. Saskia was ahead, faster and stronger than I'd expected.

The waves were total zippers, coming in fast, too close together for my liking, but I didn't have any choice about when I could show off my moves, so this was it. In the impact zone we all duck-dived, pushing our boards down with straight arms and then sinking down over them to avoid the massive waves breaking on our heads.

When we came up after a particularly gnarly wave, I saw the blond girl had taken on water and was in trouble. I shouted to ask if she needed help but she shook her head and continued to paddle out. Saskia had made it through the impact zone and was approaching the line-up.

The sea had settled a little so I paddled over toward Saskia, positioning myself behind one of the best sandbars. The brunette girl, Jenny, had made up the distance and was just off my ankle. The blond girl was miles behind, having lost her nerve and her concentration apparently.

Something changed in the water and I could sense that another set was close. I don't know how. It's just one of the things you pick up with enough time in the water. Where it would hit first was anybody's guess. Saskia turned to paddle north and I turned south. She was right and caught the wave, managing a ten-second ride in which she showed off some serious muscle. I kicked myself for having chosen the wrong spot, but vowed to take the next wave. I had to do well. I wouldn't get a second chance.

Another wave came in and the chase was on. Saskia and I saw it at the exact same moment. It was a paddle battle. Whichever one of us got there first would catch the wave, and once they had it and popped up, the other one couldn't drop in. Surf etiquette said whoever was nearest the crest of the breaking wave owned it, and everyone else had to back off. So if she got there first, she'd win again.

We were shoulder to shoulder, paddling hard, when I felt my board shift to the right. Saskia's leg had caught it and nudged it away. Accident or deliberate? I couldn't tell. She was now a good foot ahead of me and at the speed she was paddling, there was no catching her. Paddling is an art and one she had mastered. Her board skimmed perfectly over the water, her weight precisely centered.

She caught the wave and stayed on it for ages. So in five minutes Saskia had caught two rides, whereas me and the other two girls had caught none.

Saskia was so long on the wave that she had to paddle out through the whole of the impact zone again. She'd made a mistake. I'd have a good few minutes to catch the best wave I could before she elbowed her way into the line-up again. This was my chance.

Jenny and I paddled for the same wave but I got there first, and as soon as I was up I could feel that it had power. The wave was a little short and the ride bumpy and fast, so I didn't have long to show Anders and his spies what I could do. I bottom-turned, traveled up the face a little way, pulled a super-sharp cutback and then leaned my weight backward in the whitewater for a layback snap, only just managing to right myself to vertical. A few more seconds and I was done.

I hadn't gone too far toward shore and Saskia was still getting slammed in the zone, although thirty seconds more and she'd be clear of it. I was out of breath and my arms were feeling the strain of such full-on paddling, but I had to get out back before she did. Jenny was up on a wave and showing quality, and I went for the next one. This ride was even better. It was more controlled and I was able to show some of the sixties-style soul-surfer moves that I'd seen in the old films. It was good to do tricks, but people also liked to see smoothness in a ride, not just shredding a wave, but respecting and flowing with it. I hoped I'd shown some range.

The clumsy girl caught two very short rides where she didn't show anything much, and Jenny caught a right, and went frontside, cutting into the wave confidently. Saskia was trying out every move in the trick book and, apart from one wave, where she wiped out spectacularly, she was amazing, it had to be said, and I hated her for it: the girl could surf. If I was a 5, she was a 7.5, easy.

I'd just have to train harder. Go running. Do more yoga. Build up my strength and my stamina. It was worth it. If I got through this phase, and there was no guarantee that I would, I would have to cross-train to become the fittest possible version of me.

Jenny and I were about evenly matched, so I had no idea if I'd made it through.

Anders was waving his hands on the beach to tell us the time was up and we caught our last waves to shore, just for the fun of it, as anything we did now, even a perfect ride, wouldn't count. We'd done what we could, and the rest was out of our hands.

The young boys were ahead of us, already on the beach and conferring with Anders, who looked particularly indecisive.

Saskia was a given. But me or Jenny? That had to be what he was thinking about. I looked at Saskia and wondered how many hours she trained each day. Whatever she had done had worked, as Anders called her name first.

"The other surfer we'd like to pursue is . . ."

At that moment his phone rang.

"Sorry, girls, I have to take this. I won't be long. Promise!"

Saskia was the creamy-whiskered cat, beaming like she'd won Wavemasters.

Me and Jenny looked at each other nervously. The other girl was getting out of her wetsuit and straightening her bikini, beaten before she'd even heard the verdict. She overturned her board, so the fins were up, then stretched back on the sand next to it to catch some rays, looking totally relaxed now that the stress of the trial was over.

Anders was frowning on the phone. None of us could hear what he was saying, but he didn't look happy. He hung up and walked back to us. With no preamble, he said, "The second girl is Iris."

Chapter Thirteen

"Sorry," I said, turning to Jenny. "You were really good."

Jenny looked absolutely gutted and there were tears in her eyes, but she mumbled, "No worries. Only been surfing a year. I'll keep at it."

"Yeah, do that, and if you're ever in Newquay, Facebook me and we'll go shredding together. I'm the Iris Fox with a profile picture of a pimped-out camper van, so send me a friend request?"

"Thank you. I will."

I was buzzing, but a bit confused. Who had been on the phone? Was it Zeke? Was he watching from somewhere?

Don't look a gift horse in the mouth is what people say, but I couldn't help but think that it wasn't supposed to be me. Had I got in because of Zeke? Was he pulling strings behind the scenes?

Did Jenny or the other girl ever really have a chance? And if not, why go through the charade of including them?

Both of Zeke's friends were in the final two. Saskia deserved to be. I didn't much like the girl, but I couldn't say she was in first place because of nepotism. She was pure class. In Saskia I'd found another surfer I could learn from. In a different universe, obviously. In this one we were competition and I couldn't stand the sight of her, let alone her grating voice and general bossiness.

Anders was filling in a form on a clipboard and he didn't look up when I approached. I cleared my throat.

"Is Zeke here?"

He looked around. "Doesn't look like it, darlin'."

"Where is he?"

Anders brought up a schedule on his phone and pointed to the screen.

"There you are. Zeke has some film-fest thing today. Managed to get him in on it at the last minute. He actually has a small part in one of the festival films. Some eco-documentary about a surf crew trying to stop the dolphin slaughter in Taiji, Japan. The event is at the, er, Lighthouse Cinema—know it?"

I nodded.

I walked across the beach, looking out for Kelly, who was supposed to be covering Fistral and Little Fistral that day. During school vacations she worked as an ice-cream seller, which was cash in the hand and good money, but in the pickle of ten thousand tourists, I couldn't make her out.

I cut through town and made a beeline for the cinema, which was a swanky building, all white walls and steel. I stashed my board in a bike rack, crossing my fingers that it would still be there when I got out. Walking down the steps into the foyer, I could hear music.

There were hordes of people inside the cinema, all dressed in their finest. Even the mayor was swanning around with her ridiculous chain around her neck. The organizers had gone berserk decorating the room. There were posters and boards plastered everywhere for various surf films. It was apparently the first British Surf Film Festival, so they were pulling out all the stops. A long table was set with canapés and I grabbed a handful and wolfed them down while checking out a display of weird five-fin surfboards called bonzers.

I pushed my way through the foyer to the back of the building and saw Zeke signing autographs for the crowd. To the left of him, three women who looked like they'd just finished a shift at a strip club were demonstrating the Tahitian hula. Zeke looked up and smiled at the nearest one, who was edging closer and closer to him, her hips flying around like she was Shakira.

"Excuse me," a deep voice said.

I turned to see a short, bald man glaring up at me.

"Yep?"

"You can't wear a wetsuit in here. Don't you know this is a VIP charity event? Do you even have a ticket?"

"I'm just here to see my, um, boyfriend," I said.

There. It was out of my mouth. *Boyfriend.*

"And does he have a ticket?"

"Doubt he needs one. He's over there, signing autographs."

A ripple of shock passed over his face, and then he looked at Zeke, looked back at me, and smirked.

"On your way, darlin'," he said. "Come back when you've got some proper clothes and twenty-three dollars for a ticket."

A few people were starting to stare, and I really didn't want Zeke to spot me in an argument with the manager of the cinema.

Outside, I took a deep breath and tried to remember the calming yoga breathing I'd learned at Hotel Serenity. I'd have to do more yoga. Seemed like it was the only thing that could counteract the craziness of Zeke's world.

I grabbed my board and walked past the gift shops and arcades, stepping into the road a few times because the streets were so busy with tourists.

Just before the North Shore surf shop, I turned left and swung up the hill to Sainsbury's. I went straight to the newsstand.

The August issue of *Cosmo Girl* was out.

I rested my board against the newspaper stand and flicked through the copy and there was Zeke, totally naked except for a two-foot long skimboard. The photo was in black and white, but you could still see how light his eyes were, and how his hair was bleached on the ends from the sun.

Rae would go nuts for it. It was a beautiful picture that captured his chilled-out vibe, as well as his six-pack. The magazine was five dollars, but I always kept emergency change in the Velcro pocket of my board's leash, so I dug it out and then got in line at the kiosk to pay.

As the woman took my money and put the magazine in a bag, I tried to work out just how sad it would be to Blu-Tack the picture to my bedroom wall. It would be nice to see Zeke last thing at night and first thing in the morning, but then I thought about my mom's reaction and figured she'd never stop laughing.

I walked slowly back to my house, since I had nowhere else to go.

Sitting on my doorstep in the blazing sun and midday heat was Daniel.

I stopped short of him and stared. He was sitting with his arms around his knees and his head turned to one side, like he was napping. His face still had faded bruises from the fight at the Headland Hotel and his nose had a new kink in the middle— from Garrett punching and breaking it, I guessed. He hadn't put wax in his hair and it was fluffy, like a little kid's.

When he looked up at me, I could see he was upset.

"Iris," he said, his voice cracking, my name coming out of his mouth like a plea.

"Get lost."

"I need you. You're the only one who gets me."

"I don't 'get you.' I don't know you at all. The boy I knew would never have carried a knife, let alone stabbed someone with it."

He put his face in his hands, and when he finally looked up, his face was wet with tears.

"What's wrong?" I said, knowing I should just ignore him and go inside.

"Dunno what I'm doing anymore," he said. "Everything I do is messed up. No wonder everyone hates me. I hate me. You'd all be better off if I stuck a rope around my neck like my old man."

He looked and sounded so sad, and I heard myself say, "Damn it, Daniel. All right, come in. Five minutes, that's all."

Kelly and my mom would be upset, and yeah, I'd promised myself I'd never speak to Daniel again, but something was going on, and whatever had happened, whatever mistakes he'd made, we'd once loved each other.

I got up and led him into the living room, which was messy with scattered magazines and newspapers. He sat down on the sofa and looked at the floor.

"I'm really sorry about the Hawaiian dude. Zach, is it?"

"Zeke. And you put him in the hospital. You know that, right?"

"I was so wasted, Iris. I didn't know what I was doing, did I?"

"Course you didn't."

"OK, OK. So I was jealous."

"That's no excuse."

"I know. And now everything is just . . . shit."

"Is it Cass? Has something happened?" I already knew that they'd been arguing. What was I fishing for? Details? Complimentary comparisons?

"No. Yeah. It's her *and* you."

"Me? What've I done wrong?"

"Nothing."

My mom walked into the room then, her face bright red, and she said one word: "*Out.*"

"Chill, woman," I said.

She gave me a withering look. "You are on thin ice, Iris Fox. Wafer thin."

"Don't worry. I'm gone," Daniel said.

"Mom, just let him stay a bit longer."

"After what he did to you? After very nearly killing poor Zeke?"

"He messed up. He knows that."

Daniel had pushed past me and was in the hall making for the front door.

"People make mistakes," I said.

"Yes, and he made one when he decided to show his face in this house. I don't want to see that lunatic here ever again, and that's final."

Daniel didn't shut the door behind him and I saw him walking up the hill toward Pentire, collar up, head down, as if the whole world was against him.

The thing about Daniel was that he was damaged. I'd always known it. It was to do with his dad. Something had happened that was so bad that Daniel just couldn't get over it.

My dad was an artist, so obviously he had his quirks. My mom said all artists were useless and covered their desire to be lazy with pretty paints and fancy words. My dad quoted Vonnegut and said that artists were necessary to society as they were so sensitive. That they were like canaries in the mines—they would keel over before tougher types had sensed anything was wrong. My dad didn't keel over but he did walk out. He told my mom that she stifled his imagination. He kissed me on the forehead for a long time, and told me that he loved me unconditionally.

He didn't love me enough though, because he left, even when I begged him to stay. When I called for him, he carried on walking to his car and he drove away.

My mom spent the next day watching *South Pacific* and singing her own tuneless versions of "Bali Ha'i," "Happy Talk" and "I'm Gonna Wash that Man Right Outa My Hair." It was more disturbing than if she'd sat crying.

Daniel's dad was a different thing altogether. He was a drunk but he was also a character. When his local pub lifted the dog ban and his friends started bringing in their mongrels, he double-checked with the landlord that pets were welcome, then came back later and rode in on a beach donkey. My aunt was working the bar and said it was legendary.

But one day he left the pub in his car and drove so fast through two eleven-year-old boys on a crosswalk that they both died. He went to prison for five years, and when he got out the families of the dead boys made his life a misery. And rightly so, everyone said. Various uncles and nephews took turns knocking seven shades of shit out of him whenever they could, and one day Daniel's dad sat in his local boozer and told everyone he was going home to kill himself. He couldn't take it anymore. Living was too hard. His friends laughed it off, thinking it was just the talk of a man who'd had one drink too many. Nobody tried to stop him. Nobody called Daniel's mom to warn her.

Daniel was with his mom when she found him. Daniel was three steps behind her so she couldn't stop him from seeing his dad's motionless legs. He hanged himself from the landing light. Daniel was only twelve. You can't erase that kind of sadness. It stays. It didn't make Daniel a bad person. It just made him a person who needed second, third and fourth chances.

Nobody else could see that about Daniel, but I knew it. I wondered how Cass was dealing with Daniel's sadness. It was a burden, and it was one I'd taken seriously. I'd thought that with enough time and love I could heal him.

Daniel sensed that, which was why he'd always kept such a tight grip on my hand. I was his everything. Part of him hated me for it too.

The wind slammed the front door and made me jump. My mom sighed and went to make us a pot of tea. Tea solved everything in her world.

I stashed the *Cosmo Girl* in a stack of surf magazines and then locked myself in the bathroom and submerged myself in a hot bath. My head was throbbing with the emotion of the day and for twenty minutes I opted out of it all. Out of Daniel, Zeke, Cass, Saskia and out of the competition.

For twenty minutes it was just me in stillness.

Chapter Fourteen

My home phone rang at 7:45 a.m. I heard my mom pick up and then her thudding footsteps on the stairs. She burst into my room, her face a question mark.

"Some guy called Anders is on the phone. He sounds old, Iris. When you finish speaking to him, we need to have a talk."

"Chill out, mom. He's just an agent."

"What kind of damn agent?"

I just knew she was thinking something dodgy. Strip-club agent, escort agent. Sometimes it was like she would totally forget that A) I wasn't an idiot, and B) I was only sixteen.

"Surf agent."

"A '*surf agent*'?"

"Surfing's a sport. Sports have agents."

"Surfing is not a sport—it's a bad habit. And what in the name of Rice Krispies would a surf agent want with you?"

The phone was in her hand, so Anders was probably hearing every word of this.

"I'll tell you in a minute, all right?" I put the phone to my ear.

"Mornin', darlin'. And how are we today?"

"Er, half asleep."

"Well, we're here waiting, but Flower is a no-show."

"Huh?"

"You were supposed to be here fifteen minutes ago."

"Where? Nobody told me."

"Excuses, excuses. Just get your skinny butt down here pronto."

"I'm there in fifteen minutes."

"Make it ten."

A dark thought crossed my brain.

"Who was supposed to have told me about this?"

"Me. I texted you."

"What number do you have?"

He read it out and the four and the five were switched.

"Who did you get my number off anyway?"

"Saskia."

"Uh-huh."

"Sorry, love. I must have inverted the numbers when I typed it into my phone."

Yeah, right, I thought. Total accident . . .

"Anyway, hon, less chat, more getting dressed, please."

"OK, OK."

"Shorts and T-shirt is fine, and don't bring your board."

"Don't bring it?"

"No. This is something else. We'll be waiting for you in the Little Fistral car park."

I had a quick shower and changed into shorts and a vest.

I had an idea what this might be, and if I was right, it was not going to be a fun morning.

When I arrived at the car park, I saw Anders and Saskia deep in talk. I was walking over to them when Zeke came running up the metal steps from Little Fistral. He was wearing gray sweat pants, a blue T-shirt with the words "It's not the destination, it's the glory of the ride" printed on the front, and he was drenched from head to toe.

"Welcome to boot camp," he said.

"Is that allowed?"

"Hey, I'm not surfing, am I? Anyways, Kelly Slater surfed Teahupo'o and Bells Beach with a broken foot, got through eight rounds and *won* those entire events. He landed *aerials* at Bells. So I can sure manage this."

"Doesn't it hurt to run?"

"Naw, my rib feels OK now; even my leg is way better."

"Wow, just how strong are your painkillers?"

Zeke grinned, and said, "Yeah, the doc gave me the good stuff." He fiddled with some tracks on his iPod.

"How many times have you run up those steps?"

"Not many. Say twenty. Just down to the water and back."

"Oh, just twenty."

He was still messing around with his iPod, trying to find a certain song.

"Got anything good on there?" I said, looking over his shoulder.

I don't know what I was expecting. Maybe Alice in Chains, or Megadeth, which Daniel had all over his iPod. But actually Zeke just had a load of mellow surf music on there. Benjamin

Francis Leftwich, Ben Howard, the Neighborhood, Bon Iver, Newton Faulkner. All pretty chilled-out tunes. The sort of stuff you'd listen to before bed, not in the middle of a workout. Then it occurred to me that maybe he had so much of this mellow stuff on his iPod because it set the mood when he was entertaining girls.

"You and Saskia got through yesterday. You didn't hit up my phone to tell me," he said, giving me hurt eyes.

"I thought you knew." Truth was, my head had been spinning all day, and after the madness of the surf trial, the embarrassment of the Lighthouse Cinema and the weirdness of seeing Daniel, all I'd wanted to do was sleep.

"How would I know?" he asked, sounding surprised.

"Anders is your agent."

"Anders? Anders never tells me anything. You know what he's like. Always busy with some master plan. I thought you'd tell me though. I was thinking of you all morning."

He was? Even when he was at his swanky surf film festival, surrounded by the adoring masses? I felt a warmth come into my chest. A boy I really liked had been thinking of me. Though God only knew what he was thinking about. I hated to imagine how I looked through other people's eyes. There was so much that you didn't see or notice about yourself. It was like hearing your voice on an answering machine. You were always surprised by your own thickly accented mumbling, which sounded so clear in your own ear.

"Sorry. It's been kind of a hectic few days."

"I thought you'd be stoked. You did so good. This could be the moment that the rest of your life hangs on."

"No pressure, then," I said.

He laughed and said, "Your turn now."

He handed me a stopwatch, which I guessed was the boot-camp baton.

I pressed Start, ran down the steps, across fifty yards of beach to the water, turned and headed back. I was feeling OK. I made it back up the metal steps. When I pressed Stop I saw it had taken me a mortifying two minutes.

I looked over to Anders and Saskia but they were busy with press-ups. Great.

Zeke took a look at the stopwatch and pursed his lips to hide a grin.

"This time I'm really gonna cane it," I said.

I managed one minute and forty-eight seconds. It was torture. By the time I had done ten circuits I was ready to drop.

Anders waved us over. Saskia was hard at work on stomach crunches. She was wearing an Adidas peach training top that stopped just above her navel, and white leggings. I mean, who in their right mind wore *white* leggings? You could see everything, or rather the fact that she wasn't wearing anything underneath them. In contrast, I was wearing a black tank top that I'd bought for six dollars in the Ann's Cottage summer sale and camouflage Reebok shorts. If she was *Sports Illustrated*, I was the *Army Times*.

"All warmed up?" Anders asked me.

"Warmed up? Er, I'm done."

"Guess again. Race time."

"Whoop whoop!" Saskia said, as only she could.

"Right, so it's up the hill to the coastguard lookout, back down again, then across the cliff path to Fistral Beach, and the finish line will be the door to Bodhi's. Coffees are on me."

The coastguard lookout was an old whitewashed building at the top of a very steep hill. Once there, the view was panoramic. It was one of my favorite places. Unfortunately, that wouldn't be the end of the race though; we had to get to Fistral Beach and run its entire length before we were through, and given that running on sand was about ten times harder than running on grass, I was pretty sure I'd come in last. Still, finishing—even last—would be some kind of achievement. Definitely more than sleeping in.

I slipped my iPod out of my pocket and the first song that came on the shuffle was Christina Aguilera's "Fighter." Some days it was like my iPod answered to my guardian angel, who knew all the right songs to play.

Just as the first bars of the song were getting going, Anders threw his water in a trash can and shouted, "*Go.*"

Zeke took the lead, racing ahead of me and Saskia, but he stumbled a little when he looked over his shoulder at me. I was slightly ahead of Saskia but she was gaining. In any case, I was running way too fast and I knew it was only a matter of time before my knees buckled and I ended up crashing out.

Zeke reached the coastguard lookout, ran around it for extra measure, and then started belting down the hill toward me and Saskia. Spurred on by the sight of him, I made myself run faster. It was all or nothing. Go hard or go home—and I wasn't going home. I reached the lookout hut first, swung around it and bumped into the back of Saskia. She hadn't bothered to go around. Anders hadn't said we had to, but it was just good form, since Zeke had. Wasn't it? But then maybe she hadn't seen him. I didn't know. All I knew was that she was now in second place and I was trailing in last. I pushed on down the steep hill, feeling like I was flying, legs working too fast again, like Cara's when she was about to nose-crunch into the floor. My iPod was working its way through the complete back catalog of Christina Aguilera and was now on "Dirrty." I used to loathe her music, but got into it for about two weeks after I watched the American version of *The Voice* on YouTube.

I was gaining on Saskia; three more steps and we'd be shoulder to shoulder.

I was there, when suddenly she lurched to the right and her elbow hit me in the ribs. OK, I'd given her the benefit of the doubt in the surf trial, but this was a pattern. I shoved my whole body weight back into her and sent her flying.

"What the hell?" she shouted so loudly that I could hear it over my iPod. Luckily Zeke was so far ahead that he didn't hear Saskia's complaining.

I turned up my iPod volume a few notches, blasting "Dirrty" into my ears, and put even more distance between me and Saskia.

By the time she got to her feet, she was hopelessly behind. There was no way she could catch up to me now. This race was mine.

I cruised up the steps to Bodhi's, dripping with sweat but victorious. Saskia had obviously lost her fighting spirit as she was miles behind, or perhaps she'd just done too many stomach crunches with Anders.

Anders and Zeke were sitting at a table by the window. Lazy idiot that he was, Anders had driven around in his BMW. He had a steaming cup of coffee in front of him and Zeke was downing an entire bottle of water. When Zeke saw me, he got up and held up his knuckles for a fist bump.

"We have a winner," Anders said. "What are you drinking, kiddo?"

I turned off my iPod, where Christina was wailing through the last verse of "Genie in a Bottle."

"Gin and tonic, no ice."

"Try again."

"Pint of Coke."

Zeke stood up and looked out of the window. Checking on Saskia, I guessed. She was just below us, walking up the concrete steps as if they were the most depressing thing in the world.

I had a horrible knot in my stomach. What would she say? Would she tell them I'd shoved her? But how could she, when she'd tried to sabotage me first?

She limped in.

"Lordy, could those steps be any steeper?"

Zeke was at her side in a flash. "What's wrong? Is it your chest?"

I wasn't a fan of Zeke asking about Saskia's chest. If she was worried about that, she should have worn a proper sports bra, instead of that stupid peach crop-top number. I felt incredibly guilty about this thought two seconds afterward, when Anders handed Saskia a blue inhaler.

I hadn't known she was asthmatic.

"Don't worry, my darlings," she said. "I just landed awkwardly and snagged my ankle back at the lookout. If I rest, I'll be right as rain in a couple of days."

I was waiting for her to point an accusing finger in my direction, but . . . nothing.

That was it for the day. Anders was leaving to go and talk on a local radio show. About Zeke, his one-and-only surf megastar, I guessed.

Zeke gave me and Saskia big sweaty hugs and then left with Anders.

Saskia was barely denting a boiling hot latte and I was getting beaten by a Coke that was way more gas than liquid.

The silence was horrendous. I was sure she could hear me swallow.

"You know, Iris, I didn't mean to catch you with my elbow."

"Whatever," I replied, meaning it to sound laid-back. It came across as totally hostile.

She sighed. "Do we have to be enemies, just because we're competing?"

"I don't know. You tell me. Because you've seemed pretty aggressive with me, right from the start. And while we're at it, just what are we competing for? A surf sponsorship? Or something else?"

What exactly was her relationship with Zeke? I wanted to know, and he obviously wasn't going to tell me.

"Just the sponsorship. And of course I'm aggressive. I want to win. But that doesn't mean I don't like you. I think you're great, Iris."

OK, she was psyching me out. She had to be. She had no reason to think I was great. Nobody thought I was great, with the sometimes exception of Kelly and my mother.

I heard myself saying, "Look, I'm sorry about earlier. I just got caught up in the moment. And I was listening to Christina Aguilera."

She frowned. "Which song?"

"'Dirrty.'"

"Oh, then I totally blame Christina too."

And so we spent twenty minutes talking about Christina Aguilera songs and then another half-hour debating the merits of the British *Voice* compared to the American and Australian versions.

As I walked home, I wondered if in another universe, me and Saskia could be friends. Nah, I thought. I could never get used to that accent. It'd be like hanging out with Kate Middleton.

Chapter Fifteen

"Come over," Zeke had said. "It's gonna be fun."

I'd dressed in my nicest Fornarina jeans and a black strapless handkerchief top, which was pretty skimpy as it knotted beneath my shoulder blades and was otherwise open at the back. I'd even borrowed my mom's blue Kurt Geiger pumps, which I could barely walk in as they had a four-inch heel. Kelly had a late shift at Hendra so she said she'd meet me there.

My idea of a fiftieth birthday do was obviously different from Zeke's dad's, whose party was like something out of *The Great Gatsby*. The streets around South Fistral were totally blocked with cars, and when I got to the house the front lawn was covered in a marquee. I couldn't see anyone I recognized in there so I turned into the house and caught a glimpse of Garrett, who handed me a bottle of Budweiser. He was holding a plate of cheese and pineapple cubes stuck together with cocktail sticks.

"Pa made these but no one's eating them. They're all fighting over the caterer's fancy canapés."

"Really? I love these things," I said, stuffing a cocktail stick in my mouth and skimming off the cheese and pineapple with my teeth.

Garrett handed me the plate and said: "You gotta eat at least ten."

"No problem. Cool party," I said, putting the plate down for a second to take a sip of beer, which tasted really strong.

"This? Nah. Basement is where you'll find the real party."

"Yeah?"

"Hell yeah."

"Zeke down there?"

"Where else?"

An older man with a deep tan and a ponytail came up to us. He had a big smile on his face and a "Fifty Shades of Awesome" badge pinned to his chest.

"This lovely young lady your girlfriend, Gar?"

"Not mine. Zeke's, I guess. Bachelor life for me, Pa."

"Well, well, so you're Iris?" he said. But why did he sound so surprised, and what had Zeke been telling him about me?

"That's me. It's nice to meet you, Mr. Francis."

"Call me Dave. So how did you meet my youngest son?"

"Yoga class."

"Christ, his mother will love that."

A couple of girls about my age came up and hugged Dave, before loading brightly wrapped presents into his hands. "There you go, Uncle Dave. Don't say we never get you anything decent. And the bottle of Laphroaig on the kitchen table is from us."

"Too much, girls, but thank you very much, my sweethearts."

One of the girls, who had long ginger hair down to her butt, looked up at me and said, "One of the long-lost cousins from Penzance, are you?"

"Um, no. Zeke invited me."

She smirked at the other girl in an obvious way. "You better get downstairs, then. My favorite cousin is getting stressy waiting for you. No offense, Gar."

"None taken. Can't compete with Superboy, can I?" he said, sighing.

The basement had obviously once been a game room, but someone had tricked it out as a nightclub. There was a proper bar with a dance floor and squashy sofas around the edge of the room. It even had its own cloakroom and bathrooms. For all intents and purposes, it was the nicest club in Newquay.

"Not bad," I said to Garrett, which was something of an understatement.

There were about forty people down there already, mostly teenagers, but a few older hangers-on too.

I sat down on an empty chair, finished my beer and felt hands over my eyes.

I squirmed in his light grip and turned to face Zeke, who was literally glowing with happiness.

He kissed me lightly on the forehead and then grabbed my hand.

"I met your stepdad," I said. "Didn't get to meet his girlfriend though."

"Yeah, about that—better not mention Daisy. She left him yesterday."

"One day before his fiftieth birthday? Harsh."

"I guess his birthday had something to do with it. She was only twenty-four."

Nice going, Dave . . .

"Well, I thought your stepdad was super-nice."

"Yeah, he's the greatest."

A group of younger teenagers were waving us over and Zeke said, "Come meet my Irish cousins."

How many cousins did he have?

After being introduced to all eleven of Zeke's step-cousins, I realized I hadn't remembered any of their names, which was going to be embarrassing if I bumped into them later. Then somebody produced an empty beer bottle and began spinning it in the middle of the dance floor.

Zeke laughed and shook his head, but people were gravitating toward the bottle, like it was the most hilarious idea ever.

In two minutes, me and Zeke were the only ones not in the circle.

"Come on, brah! And bring your girl too. Need all the babes we can get for this."

"Seriously? Aren't we a bit old for this?"

"No way. Who's too old for Spin the Bottle?"

I was pretty sure that I'd never been young enough to enjoy spin the bottle, but still, if Zeke was up for it, then I wasn't going to be the only wet blanket in the basement.

Wes was looking uncomfortable and he said, "Remind me of the rules?"

"There are no rules, bro," Garrett replied. And then added, "Haven't you ever played this before?"

"Yeah, like in kindergarten."

"Well, what's there to know? The bottle points to a chick and then points at you, you kiss her. Easy."

"What if it points to two girls?"

"Winner. Game on."

"Two dudes then?"

"You pass on a dude, obviously."

"And what about if it points at someone you've already kissed?"

"Kiss 'em again."

"OK, got it."

Wes was even worse at this than I was.

The first spin landed on a dark-haired girl who seemed painfully shy and then on a young blond boy who was much shorter than her. They kissed for maybe three seconds before pulling away, embarrassed. Next up was Garrett and a young woman in her early twenties and both of them were dead game and had the sort of comedy kisses that brides and grooms go in for after saying "I do." On the third spin, the bottle pointed squarely at Zeke.

I could see the panic cross his eyes and he looked at me apologetically, because there was no way that the bottle would point to me next. It didn't. It pointed to Garrett again.

"Dude!" Garrett said. "That is wrong on so many levels. Spin again, bro."

I wondered if in his brain Zeke was trying to make some calculation as to how fast to spin the bottle so that it would land on me. It was hopeless though. Like trying to influence the outcome of a roulette wheel. The bottle stopped and pointed between two people to right where Kelly had just walked into the room.

"You gotta kiss that chick, bro," Wes said, laughing.

"That's Iris's best friend," Zeke said, looking scandalized.

"Kiss her!" one of the girls shouted.

"Uh, no, you're all right," Kelly said, grimacing at me.

"KISS, KISS, KISS . . ." There was no stopping it. Horrendous. My best friend was going to make out with the guy I was seeing before I did.

Kelly rolled her eyes but was still digging her heels in. The chanting was getting louder and I could see Zeke was on the point of bailing.

"It's OK," I mouthed to her.

Shrugging, she went over to Zeke and leaned forward.

Garrett shouted, "It has to be a mouth kiss," when Kelly angled for the cheek.

She sighed and pecked Zeke on the mouth. It was over in a fraction of a second but my stomach was burning.

If Cass's betrayal had been hard to take, I realized that I would never, ever, get over it if Kelly did something like that to me.

But she wouldn't, would she? No. And Zeke wasn't Daniel. He was so far from Daniel that he was practically a different species. Still, I didn't want to see Kelly and Zeke kiss ever again. Not even a peck.

I was still shuddering when I realized that the neck of the bottle was touching my knee.

I hadn't seen who had spun it as I'd been in a silent conversation with Kelly, where she was mouthing things like, "Sorry about that," and, "Our lips barely touched."

"Er . . . who am I kissing?" I asked, as casually as I could, to hide the fact that I was freaking out.

Zeke's eyes darted to his brother Wes.

Seriously, what kind of masochist would enjoy Spin the Bottle? The only thing worse than seeing Kelly kiss Zeke would be having to kiss one of Zeke's brothers. It was horrific. And once again my brain was reminding me at one hundred decibels that Zeke and I hadn't even properly kissed yet.

Wes was hesitating and even Garrett was saying something like, "Awkward, bro, real awkward."

And then Wes did the most ludicrous thing. He said, "What the hell?" grabbed my shoulders and kissed my face off.

It was a weird kiss. There was literally no chemistry whatsoever, but Christ almighty he was making a meal of it.

I pulled away and turned my palms upward, in a peace-out way, but Zeke jumped to his feet and said, "Screw this," and stormed across the room to the steps that led out of the basement.

Wes followed him and put his hand on Zeke's shoulder, but Zeke turned and pushed him off, sending Wes halfway across the dance floor. Zeke left and Wes walked sheepishly back.

Garrett smiled at me and said, "Yo, I think Zeke likes you."

"Wes! What was that?" I said.

"What? It's Spin the Bottle. I thought that's what you're supposed to do."

"Yeah, well, you did it," I said. "I better go after him."

"Nope." Garrett put a hand on my shoulder. "Leave him be. He like almost never loses his temper these days, but when he does, he needs space to chill out. Seriously uncool, little brother," he said to Wes.

"What? She's not even his girlfriend!"

"You know he likes her. He's been seeing her almost every day."

It was so strange. Wes had done that deliberately, for some reason. He clearly didn't like me, as there was no spark at all between us. But why would he do that to his brother? There was obviously way more going on than I understood.

Spin the Bottle carried on and I just sat there, waiting for Zeke to come back. The only other person I kissed was Kelly, and that was just a granny peck. Kelly, on the other hand, seemed to kiss about ten guys, and unlike her kiss with Zeke, she really went for it. On the last round she got Garrett, and the moment they touched, I could feel the air in the room change. It wasn't a stupid game kiss: they both came out of it looking dazzled, like they'd just come up from being held in dark water. Kelly actually blushed. I had never in my entire life seen Kelly blush.

Then, as quickly as it had started, the game was over.

Zeke was not in any of the main party rooms or in the marquee. Eventually I found him in the garage, furiously planing a foam blank that would one day be a surfboard—well, if he didn't mess it up, and he wasn't exactly doing a stellar job on it. He looked up at me but didn't smile.

"Fucking Wes. Can't believe he did that."

"He's probably just rendered," I said.

"Huh?"

"Drunk."

"He's totally sober."

"I didn't kiss him back," I said, which should have made it better, but somehow didn't.

"See," Zeke said, "this is the crappy thing about having brothers. It's all swell until they hit on the girl you like."

"You like me?"

"Sure I like you. I really like you. You're different. You're your own person. I knew that from the first moment I met you."

"In yoga class? When I was wearing those horrible old shorts?"

"I wasn't looking at the shorts." He put down the plane and I slowly walked over to him.

"I'm sorry about earlier," I said. "It just seemed to spiral out of control and I didn't really know what was going on. But I didn't want to kiss Wes."

"So kiss me," he said.

Walking backward, Zeke led me deeper into the garage, where there was a blue-and-green striped hammock. I couldn't quite see how we were going to both get in though, as it didn't look wide enough for us to lie side by side.

Zeke stretched back on to it and pulled me on top. Our bodies fell together, and for the briefest of moments, our lips touched.

And that was the moment that a seriously beautiful older woman in a headscarf and a tie-dyed floaty dress walked in with a huge smile on her face.

"Zeke, honey!" she said. "Who's the saltwater betty and why are you squeezing her to death on that hammock?"

Saltwater betty? That was new, and how did she even know I was a surfer?

But all Zeke had to say was, "Mom!"

Chapter Sixteen

Zeke was stoked to see his mother. There was no doubt about that. And who could blame him? Zeke's mom was the coolest mom in the history of moms. At least that was the opinion I came to within about one minute of talking to her.

Zeke had jumped out of the hammock the second he spotted his mother and they hugged each other for ages.

"Iris, this is my mom, Sephy July."

Well, I had finally met someone with a weirder name than me.

"Sethy?"

"With a *ph*, surfer girl. Short for Seraphina, but who wants that label?"

She gazed up at Zeke once more, and said, "You done real good, baby," and then she came over and hugged me, which I was not expecting. As she pulled away from me, very quietly she murmured what sounded like, "Be gentle with him, Iris. He's not as tough as he looks."

"What are you doing here, Mom?" Zeke said, missing what she had just said to me.

"Your pa invited me. Jacob needs to spread his wings, so we had one last day together and set each other free. You know how it goes."

"Mom, I'm so sorry. He was a cool guy. Sure you can't fix it?"

"Pretty sure. A blind woman could have seen the love was fading out of him. Out of me too. Don't you worry about me, honey."

Then she hooked her arms through mine on one side, and Zeke's on the other side, and connected like that we walked into the house.

Even in her late forties she was a head-turner. People were rushing up to her and asking how she'd been, and I caught at least five guys checking out her figure.

Zeke and his family spilled out into the garden, having a great time catching up with Sephy. Even Zeke's dad seemed pleased to see his ex-wife.

The stories she had to tell. She had traveled on her own to rough it in Oahu, living on pineapples stolen from the farms on the North Shore, on the fish she could catch with a spear each night and on coconuts that she climbed for herself. She was still climbing for coconuts when she was eight months pregnant with Zeke.

She was one of the original North Shore soul surfers, but the only girl up there, by the sounds of it. Shunned by the guys, she would go hunt for food and return to find they had buried her surfboard somewhere on the beach, or defaced it with badly graffitied cocks. Once, she had the tires of her woody surf wagon slashed and her board smashed by an Australian dude who couldn't catch a single wave at Pipeline. But still she didn't let it get to her. She kept on trucking and surfed eight hours every single day. Then she married Zeke's biological father, had three kids, divorced him, and crossed paths with a certain clueless but charming dude from England called Dave. Garrett was to blame, apparently. He saw Dave checking out his mom and lobbed a clump of rotten seaweed at Dave's head. Zeke's mom went to apologize for her eldest son and the rest was history.

Zeke's uncle Chris arrived with Zeke's Nanna, who he'd just picked up from the nursing home. Nanna was four-feet-ten-inches of sparkly-eyed loveliness.

"Nanna," Zeke said, going over to her wheelchair and holding her hand. "How are you feeling?"

"Better now. You're a sight for sore eyes, my darlin'. Is this the girl you're courting? Introduce us, dearie."

"Iris, this is Nanna. Nanna, this is Iris."

"Iris, are you a California girl?"

"Nice to meet you, Mrs. Francis. No, I'm from here."

"Do you know, I once visited Malibu. Such a vibrant, busy place."

"Iris is from Newquay, Nanna."

"Is she?" she said, disappointed. "Well, never mind. Where's my Garrett?"

"I'm here, Nanna."

"And what about Wes?"

"He's keeping his head down," Garrett said. "Fallen out with Zeke."

"Fighting? Oh, boys will be boys. You should all go and surf it out. An evening like this, you shouldn't be indoors. Get as much of the stoke as you can, because it doesn't last forever. I only wish I could be out there with you, instead of in this damn chair."

"Did you ever surf?" I said, surprised to hear an old lady use the word "stoke."

"No, no, dear. We couldn't in our day. They wouldn't allow it."

"Who?"

"Our fathers. Our brothers. Our sweethearts."

"No? That sucks."

"Oh, we wouldn't have dreamed of going out and competing with the men."

Garrett butted in. "Nanna, tell Iris about the tandem."

"We didn't surf, but we girls used to ride on the men's shoulders."

"How the heck did you get up there?" I asked.

"They pulled us up, dear. The best girls would do handstands up there. But I used to stand up straight, with my arms out to either side. It was so much fun. We all did it then. Because of Marilyn, you know. She started it."

Zeke looked at Garrett and shrugged. "Was she one of your friends, Nanna?"

Nanna laughed so hard that she had to wipe a tear away from her eye with a hanky.

"Monroe, of course! When she was Norma Jeane Baker she used to compete at tandem-surfing in California with a handsome surfer called Tommy Zahn. She was supposed to be very good in the water. Very athletic and robust. Never complained about the cold. And it did get cold, you know. Because you're in the water and out of it so much, you get cold in a flash. But once we knew Marilyn did it, we had to try it too. If it was good enough for Marilyn, it was good enough for us."

"What was it like?" I asked.

"Wonderful. Water all around. And you really had to concentrate, else you'd fall off. But of course, Newquay was so different then."

"Quieter, I guess?" I said.

"Oh no, dear. It was wild. All of these young men who had dropped out of society and were flipping the bird to the squares. None of your designer labels—no, the boards were like tree trunks, and the wetsuits were so awful back then that they wore woolly sweaters underneath them. None of the money either, just lots of young men living their lives the best way they knew how."

Nanna smiled at some far-off memory. Then she said, "It's been so wonderful to have you here this last week, Zeke, my beauty. I was so worried I wouldn't see you before this old heart did me in. And to see you in love too. Well, it's all I've ever wanted for you."

I squirmed, and Zeke went very rigid in his seat.

"You know, I fell in love with a surfer once," she went on. "He had the widest shoulders I have ever seen." She sat there smiling, and then said, "What I'd give to go tandem-surfing again. Just one last time."

Sephy looked at Zeke. "Will you take Nanna out surfing on your shoulders?"

Nanna squealed with delight and said, "Goodness me, that would be wonderful!"

Zeke looked totally shocked. "You're kidding me, right?"

"What about you, Garrett?"

"Um, that is kind of crazy. Are you high, Mom?"

"So," Sephy said, "I'll take her. I work out."

"Mom! No." Zeke looked horrified at this idea.

Dave said, "Come on, Sephy, you can't be serious. Mom is seventy-five years old."

"And?"

"If anyone's taking her, it's me."

"With your sciatica?" Sephy said. "I don't think so. No, I'll do it."

"What if you wipe out? Can Nanna even swim?" I said.

Nanna, who'd been wide-eyed and giggling, suddenly said, "Of course I can swim."

Dave leaned over and asked me to see if I could round up Wes.

"No problem," I replied. It had been great to sit there, listening to the mix of their lovely accents and laughter, but it felt like they deserved some time together, as a family. So I went for a wander through the rest of the house, dodging the milling crowds of partygoers, and tried to find Wes. It was silly for him and Zeke to fall out over a stupid game of Spin the Bottle. After a few laps of the downstairs rooms, I made my way upstairs.

It was partly nosiness. I thought I would just take a look at Zeke's bedroom. Not to snoop exactly, but just to see what it looked like. I didn't even know if he shared a room with his brothers. All the doors were open, though admittedly the last of them was only slightly ajar. The first room was incredibly tidy, painted lilac and turquoise and had all sorts of incense sticks, candles and tarot cards around. This had to be where Dave slept, and it had probably been decorated by his ex, Daisy. The second room had a double bed, which judging by the porno mags and huge supply of condoms in a massive jar on the nightstand, had to belong to Garrett. At least I hoped so. When I looked in the third bedroom, I saw it was lit only by a single tea light. Two tall figures were standing by the window, the moonlight streaming through and making them a single silhouette. They were tangled together, hands in hair and jeans, kissing. I inhaled so loudly that I thought they would hear. They didn't. Wrapped up in their own world, they didn't know they were watched. One of them had fluffy pale hair loose around his face. The other one was . . . Wes.

Wes was kissing a GUY?

I closed the door and bumped into Zeke, who was racing up the stairs.

"You didn't tell me Wes was . . ." I said, and then I came to my senses and shut my mouth.

Zeke shot me this intense stare. "Wes was what?"

He stood there waiting for me to answer, not moving, hardly breathing; a rabbit in the headlights.

"Nothing."

"What were you gonna say?"

"Forget it."

"He came on to you again?"

"*No.*"

If Zeke had known Wes was into guys, he wouldn't have been so annoyed with him for kissing me during Spin the Bottle. But, in this family that seemed so close, how was it possible that Zeke didn't know his own brother was gay? Or maybe Wes was just experimenting or something? Maybe that's why he'd kissed me?

To figure something out? Or, in that awkward Spin-the-Bottle moment, had I been his cover?

"You're really pale, Iris. What happened? Just tell me already."

What could I say? I couldn't tell the truth. If I told him what I saw, it would leave no room for Wes to deny it if he wanted to.

"Oh, is that Kelly?" I said, "I'm just gonna go get my lipgloss back from her."

I intercepted her at the buffet table and grabbed her by the wrist. "Kelly, we've gotta get out of here."

"No way! This is the best party ever! There's so much talent in here. Zeke's brother is a total hottie, by the way. He's been giving me flirty eyes all night. I'm so in there."

"Which brother?"

"Garrett, obviously."

"Why obviously? What's wrong with Wes?"

"Nothing. There's nothing *wrong* with him."

"You don't sound very sure about that."

"Well, you know, I obviously wouldn't want to be going out with a gay guy, would I?"

"*You know he's gay?*"

"Yeah, course."

"Why didn't you tell me?"

"It's none of my business really."

"*How* do you know?"

"His boyfriend's in our yoga class. Elijah. He was the blond guy I was chatting to, the night you met Zeke. I'm getting quite friendly with him now. Course, I didn't connect Elijah with Wes until I saw the two of them together tonight."

"Zeke doesn't know."

"Well, whatever you do, don't tell him. It's up to Wes to tell his family whenever he's ready. And, you know, he might never be ready to step out of that closet."

"I literally almost just told Zeke. I am the worst."

"Iris Fox, what are you like?"

"I know, I know. I made a right mess of covering. Zeke knows something's up. Come on—we have to leave before this gets any worse."

I looked across the room and locked eyes with Zeke. His face was really tense. Out of the corner of my eye I could see Wes approaching, with a couple of giggly girls behind him. Garrett also picked that moment for a stop and chat with his brothers.

"Seriously, Kelly, let's go."

I gave Zeke a hurried wave and made for the door, which was when Zeke's mother cornered me.

"Iris, I just want to tell you how happy I am that Zeke has you. He's always been such a quiet boy, such a raw soul."

Yeah, right. I was starting to wonder how well any of this family actually knew each other.

She had some orange cocktail clutched in her hand, and as she was talking, she was spilling it on to the cream carpet. I didn't like to say anything so I just watched the falling droplets.

"Sex on the Beach," she said suddenly.

"Sorry?"

"My drink. Haven't you tried it? It is fiiiiine. I *highly* recommend it."

"I'm underage."

"I wasn't talking about the alcohol, honey."

There wasn't much I could say to that, because I was definitely not going to talk about anything sex-related with my sort-of-boyfriend's mother. With a drink or two inside her, Sephy had turned into Ben Stiller's mom from *Meet the Fockers*. Horrifying.

She dragged me back inside the house, where I saw Kelly had slipped by me and found Garrett again. They were dancing like lunatics on the huge kitchen table with about five other people. It was only a matter of time before one of them lost their balance and fell into the fridge.

Still, most of them were surfers, which meant they had to have decent balance. And Kelly had at least taken off her stilettos. Headbanging away to Stevie Nicks's "Edge of Seventeen," which was her all-time favorite vintage song, I could see how happy she was. I watched as Garrett smiled at her. Maybe in some alternate universe Kelly would marry Garrett, I'd marry Zeke and we'd be sisters for real.

Crap. I really was hammered if I was thinking corny stuff like that.

Zeke's mom staggered off to the bathroom and I took the chance to leave before Zeke saw me and started cross-examining me again. I ditched the chaos of the party and cleared my head by walking across the dark beach back to my house.

My mom took one look at me, scowled, but said nothing. She took off my shoes, helped me up the stairs and into a nightshirt and then brought me a glass of water and some aspirin.

"Thanks, Mom. You're the best," I murmured, before swallowing the tablets and passing out.

Chapter Seventeen

The next day I had a shift at Billabong, but thankfully I didn't have to start until eleven, and even then I managed to be five minutes late as I just couldn't face running to work when my head was throbbing and my mouth was parched. Late nights, I was starting to think, were just not worth the hassle. But, every half-hour or so, I let myself think about the party: the one second of Zeke's lips on mine; the shock of seeing Wes kiss Elijah; the sight of Kelly dancing with Garrett; Sephy telling me to be gentle with Zeke; Nanna wowing everyone with her total coolness. And Zeke, again; always back to Zeke. How much did he like me? Did he want me to be his actual girlfriend? Was that possible, or was I just being pathetically optimistic? It seemed crazy on paper, but when we hung out together, Zeke made me feel like he was into me.

Luckily work was crazy, which helped limit my obsessing. The "King of the Groms" contest for surfers under ten years old was being held at the north end of the beach, so there were a lot of people around and tons of families coming into the shop, dropping big bucks on the new line of T-shirts and sneakers for their wonder kids.

I had just bagged up some clothes for one family and charged the dad's Visa to the tune of $480, which seemed ridiculous to me, when I saw that the next person waiting in line was Wes.

He had a nice blue-and-yellow beaded necklace in his hand that I'd been eyeing up for weeks.

"Hi, Iris," he said.

"Hi."

"I didn't think you'd be so busy."

"Neither did I. Forgot about the grom contest. That always gets a bit crazy."

I scanned the necklace and said, "That's twenty-seven dollars, please."

He stuck his card into the reader, entered his pin and I said, "I bet Sephy will love that."

"It's not for my mom."

"Oh," I said, handing him the bag.

He handed it back to me. "It's for you. I'm super-sorry about what happened last night. I don't know what I was thinking. Peace offering?"

"Don't be silly. You don't have to get me a present. No peace offering required. It was just a stupid game."

"I've paid for it now, so you gotta take it."

"You sure? I can refund it for you."

"It's yours."

"That's really sweet. Thanks."

"No problem."

"Have you seen Zeke today?"

"Yeah, he was pissy with me over breakfast, but Pa took us all for a round of golf and after Zeke broke the course junior record, and I'd come in last, he seemed to buck up."

I laughed and then caught the eye of my boss. Billy was gesturing to the line of restless people behind Wes. Wes turned and saw Billy's stressfest.

"I should bounce before I get you in trouble. See ya later, Iris."

"Thanks again, and have a nice day."

I told Billy that one of the customers had bought me a gift, and although he raised his eyebrows as if there was something deeply sketchy about that, he let me take off the tags and wear the necklace over my Billabong T-shirt.

I didn't get home until eight, as my mom had texted me a long shopping list of groceries to pick up from Sainsbury's. By the time I had lugged it all home and packed everything into the kitchen cupboards, I could barely keep my eyes open.

I stretched out on my bed and replied to a few "Hope ur OK"-type texts from Kelly, and a really apologetic one from Zeke saying Anders had sprung some last-minute Ireland trip on him, but that he'd be back in a day or two.

Zeke being out of town for a little while maybe wouldn't be such a bad thing, as it would give me a chance to work out how I was going to deal with the Wes situation.

Yawning every three seconds, I put down my phone and watched a bit of the local news. A blond chick was reporting from Fistral on the contest, which was apparently won by a five-year-old boy from Perranporth. A future Zeke there.

I pulled my dressing gown over my cold legs and figured I'd just close my eyes for five minutes before having a shower, brushing my teeth and changing into my pajamas.

I woke up, ten hours later, to Kelly tickling my nose with a gull feather.

Chapter Eighteen

"Take me surfing," she said.

"Aaargh."

"Do you have plans with Zeke or something?"

"Nah, he's away for a couple of days at some big wave spot in Ireland for a Billabong party."

"Come on then! I wanna stand up on a real surfboard."

Kelly liked to kayak and bodyboard, but I'd been dying to get her on to a real surfboard for years.

I sat up and looked at my alarm clock: six thirty.

"Right this second?"

She gave me a big hopeful grin.

"Well, I s'pose you do have the same first name as the greatest surfer ever."

"Do I? Who's she then?"

"You *are* joking? *He* is eleven-time World Surfing Champion, Mr. Kelly Slater."

"Oh yeah, I forgot him. To be fair, that is a girls' name."

"No, it's not, and anyway that's his middle name. His actual first name is Robert, but Kelly's cooler."

"Wow, I totally have a classic surfer name. Come on, let's go get wet."

"Is this so you can go surfing with Garrett?"

"Yep. So you have to teach me," she said, grinning and pulling me out of bed.

"All right, all right. So, what have you two been up to anyway?"

"We've hung out, and that's all I'm saying," she said, zipping her lips. I knew she'd tell me more when she was ready, but she was superstitious about new relationships and wouldn't say much until she was sure.

The beach was busy, and one of the lifeguards was bombing around on a jet ski, really close to shore and causing huge wakes. Seemed like he was playing more than lifeguarding, bouncing the jet ski over the breakers and only just missing kids, dogs and tourists by the skin of his teeth.

A swell was due in, but the surf was still pretty small. Nice waist-high crumbling waves that were perfect to learn on. I got Kelly a foam swell board, which she couldn't hurt herself on, and I tried to explain to her about good paddling, the importance of arching your back and keeping your shoulders still while relaxing the muscles. Getting a nice plane through the water was the main thing. Paddling was a skill that took years to master properly, but I figured I could give her a decent head start by pointing out her errors.

"You need to move back a bit," I said. "You're too far up on the board and the nose is going to dig into the sea and send you ass over tit." She shuffled down the board and the tail began to drag, slowing her down. "Up a notch," I said.

Eventually she centered her weight so that the board was floating nicely.

"OK, you need to make your hands into cups, dig deep and pull back to your waist. You want the board to maintain a nice steady speed as it glides over the water."

Since she was a total beginner, there was no way I was taking her out into the line-up. That was the sort of crazy that I'd leave for clueless kooks.

"I wanna go out with the hot surfer dudes!" she moaned.

"First off, if you're not good at moving your board around in the blink of an eye, which you're not as you're just starting out, you'll get in somebody's way. A surfer who is up and riding *always* has the right of way, and if a beginner can't, or won't, get out of the way, and the surfer riding the wave isn't able to bail quickly enough, then that beginner could be dead. Surfboards are a major hazard. Even experienced surfers get hurt. And those fins on the bottom of the board are razor sharp. I've cut my hands and feet more times than I can remember. You will only be riding the whitewater."

"OK, the whitewater is my friend, got it."

"When a nice little wave that you like the look of is coming, you turn your board onshore, and then when the wave is ten yards away you start paddling."

"How will I know when to jump up?"

"You might not be able to pop up properly yet, so when your board's caught the momentum of the wave, you'll feel the bite, and then you'll straighten your arms in the push-up position, scoot your knees forward, get on one knee, and stand. You want both feet in line, back foot near the tail of the board, front foot halfway up. You'll ride that wave straight to shore, and repeat. OK?"

I could hear the stress in my voice. It was one thing me taking risks for myself, but it suddenly felt like a massive responsibility to be looking after someone else in the ocean. If Kelly died, I would die. She was my girl. My rock. The only person in my life that I knew would still be there in fifty years.

"Iris, you have got to chill out, bird. I'm not going to do anything crazy," she said, turning to face me.

"Right, well, you never turn your back to the ocean unless you're about to catch the whitewater, OK?"

Just as I said that, I could see a medium set of waves building and coming in fast.

"All right, position your board, now get on it and paddle, paddle, paddle. Faster, or else you'll miss it. Keep the nose up or you're gonna do a headstand and go over the top."

Kelly caught the wave but she bodysurfed it in to shore. I grabbed the next one so I could catch her up.

"How come you didn't stand up?"

"I don't know. It just felt like I was going really fast and it was over in a flash."

"You *were* going really fast. That's surfing. As soon as you're on the next wave, get to your feet, OK?"

Kelly gave me the Zeke Francis signature sloppy salute and started wading out again, pushing her board in front of her.

"WHOA! Never put your board between you and a wave, not unless you want your face smashed in. Push it to the side of you."

My heart was racing. It was like I was looking after Cara or some other little kid. I had turned into Kelly's mother. Luckily she didn't take offense and just hopped the board to one side of her.

"You don't have to worry about this stuff when you're body-boarding," she said.

"Yeah, well, bodyboards are made of foam and don't have fins that will slice your ear off. Right, catch this one."

It wasn't the most elegant pop-up I had ever seen, but she did manage to scramble to her feet. However, she then stood so high that she immediately wiped out backward. I'd forgotten to tell her to keep low with her arms out for balance.

I'd been so busy stressing about her safety that I'd neglected to tell her some of the most important technical things.

She bobbed up with her hair plastering her face and seawater bursting out of her nose.

"I was up! I was surfing!"

"You were up," I said grumpily. "Next time stay low."

"Iris," she said, waving away my instruction with one hand, "you have got me surfing on my second wave. Give me a high five!"

It was impossible to be stressed when Kelly was like this. It made me remember how excited I'd been when I caught my first long ride, managing to stay up as other surfers in the water whooped and hollered in congratulation.

Kelly had a long way to go, but she was my friend and she was laughing her head off, and so I just smiled and said, "You're a surfer now, so let's get you another wave."

We surfed for about an hour and Kelly caught some mellow rides and was buzzing from it, just totally pumped up, like it was the best thing she'd ever done. But after her tenth wipeout she was starting to look tired and I caught her rubbing her forearms. All the paddling and pushing up on her board had probably wrenched her tendons.

"Let's go get a drink," I said.

"Not before I sit on the beach, strip off this wetsuit and wax my board," she said, getting a disk of Sex Wax out of her bag.

"People normally wax their boards before a session," I said dubiously, "and yours is a foamie which doesn't even really need to be waxed."

"I have letched at surfers on this beach my whole life and dreamed of being one of those cool surfer girls with a board under her arm. I am milking this moment, Iris Fox, and there's not a thing you can do to stop me."

I laughed. She was a real kook all right. Funny though.

When she finished her wax job, she took the board back to Denny and I sat cross-legged in the lapping waves at the edge of the sea, just watching the pack. I still loved watching surfers wipeout from the shore, even though I knew how it felt. It looked so comical though, as these little rubber stick figures plunged sideways off their boards.

I felt someone tap me on the shoulder and turned to see Daniel. He sat down next to me on the wet sand. The bruises on his face had finally faded and he looked like his old self.

"How's it going?"

"Can't talk. Kelly'll be back in a minute."

"Ah, Kelly loves me."

"She *really* doesn't."

He smiled and said, "Well, I wanted to tell you I'm not gonna kill myself. In case you was worried."

"Glad to hear it." I was relieved he'd come to his senses. For one thing, there'd already been far too much tragedy in his lovely mom's life, without Daniel piling on more.

"Things are looking good for me."

"Sounds good. Like how?"

"I'm training to be an RNLI lifeguard. I'm gonna join Fistral Lifesaving."

"Seriously? Congratulations."

"That's not even all of it. There's something even better, but it's a surprise."

At that moment, I saw Saskia walking up the beach with a fancy, ten-foot Alaia board under her arm. Alaia boards are wooden, finless and were ridden for centuries in ancient Hawaii. I had never even seen one, except in magazines. It was another thing that emphasized to me just how superior Saskia was in every single way.

She was giving me a hard stare and then my brain engaged. Saskia had found me chatting away to the person who stabbed Zeke.

Daniel chose that second to grab my hand and tell me he had to get back to work since his boss probably had binoculars on him at that very moment.

"Yeah, go," I said. "Please."

Saskia was approaching me from one direction and Kelly was coming from the other. Both of them were giving me confused looks, as if to say, "What were you doing with that loser?" I closed my eyes and tried to clear my head.

Saskia reached me first.

"Hanging out with the guy that assaulted Zeke? Really?"

I opened my eyes and stood up to face her. "It's not what it looks like."

"It never is with you. I'm starting to think you're trouble with a capital T."

"Thanks."

"Honestly, is it so very hard to treat Zeke with a bit of respect, and not flirt with the person that stabbed him? You're drifting terribly close to 'beach skank' territory."

Kelly arrived then and said, "Whoa there. Don't you dare speak to Iris like that. You don't know her, all right? So butt the hell out."

Kelly's eyes were blazing, and Saskia put up her hands in a gesture of apology.

"Fine. Point taken."

"Sorry," Kelly said, rubbing her forearms. "I didn't mean to get all aggressive there. Long morning of surfing, and my arms are frigging killing me."

"It's probably tendonitis from poor paddle technique," Saskia said. "Get some ice on it and the pain should ease off in a day or two."

"Will do. Thank you," Kelly said. That was classic Kelly. Furious one minute, and completely over it the next. She put her arm around my waist and dragged me off toward Ben & Jerry's for celebratory ice creams.

As we walked away I looked over my shoulder at Saskia and saw that she was still staring at us. It occurred to me that for all of Saskia's confidence and gorgeousness, I had never seen her with a female friend. Maybe, just maybe, she was lonely.

Chapter Nineteen

Kelly wanted me to call her asap. She had news. Big news.

"You were just on the radio."

"Um, no I wasn't."

"Not *you* you. But your name. They played an interview with Anders."

"Tell me everything."

Part of Anders's interview had been to drum up publicity for the new British female surfer that Billabong was going to sponsor. He was on Pirate FM talking about how the final show-down would be in September at North Fistral for Wavemasters. Ed Sheeran was going to be gigging the festival and he would be the one to present the Billabong contest winner with a $7,500 check.

"Ed Sheeran, Iris! *Seven grand!*"

I took a deep breath.

"Can you come over?" I said, collapsing back on to my bed.

"Dead right I'm coming over," she said. "And I'm bringing strawberry cupcakes from the Little Cake Shop."

"I don't know if I can eat that," I said. "I already had ice cream and I'm supposed to be in training."

"Yeah, and you've been burning like ten million calories a day. You're eating some cupcakes."

By the time she arrived, I was starving. Or "ravenous," as Saskia would say. I smiled as I thought about Saskia, and then wondered why on earth I was smiling at the thought of the girl who was standing between me and Ed Sheeran.

Kelly arrived with the cupcakes, but I was in the en-suite shower, thinking about Zeke and singing Carly Rae Jepsen's insanely catchy "Call Me Maybe" at the top of my lungs, and I didn't hear her come in. I stepped out of the shower, looking for a new bottle of conditioner, which my mom had annoyingly left in the bathroom cabinet.

Kelly popped her head around the door and said, "Damn, Iris, you've lost weight."

"Stop checking me out, perv," I said, laughing and quickly stepping back behind the frosted glass of the shower stall.

She sat down on the towel hamper and tucked into her cupcake, demolishing it in record time. "You need to eat at least three," she said.

"I haven't lost much weight. Least, I don't think so."

"Have you been on the bathroom scales?"

"No. But I guess I have been doing a lot of exercise lately."

"And have you been eating?"

I thought about it. When was the last time I'd had a real meal? I'd gone from scoffing everything in sight, morose about

Daniel, to hardly eating a thing. Every time I thought about
Zeke, my stomach clenched, a feeling like butterflies but worse,
and I lost my appetite.

Was this more than crazy infatuation? Love was supposed to
make you feel like this. New love, anyway. The long-term love
I'd had with Daniel was a different thing altogether. We were
part of each other. Two sides of the same person. At least until
he'd gone postal. But Zeke was totally new and totally exciting.
What would it be like to spend the night with him? Cry in front
of him? Listen to him talk about his past, his previous relationships, the girls from his phone?

I couldn't imagine it. Not really. It was too much to start
again with someone new. But how could I feel that way already?
I was sixteen, not sixty.

Kelly was giving me a sharp look. "Tell me exactly what
you're thinking. Right now."

"Um . . ."

"Tell me."

"Er, just wondering if I'm tough enough to start a real relationship with someone new."

She properly rolled her eyes and handed me a cupcake, which
I devoured.

"Get dressed."

"Wasn't planning on knocking around naked."

"So hurry up already."

"Where are we going?"

"You'll see. Just wear something skimpy."

I put on a denim miniskirt and a white strappy cami, and
then a fleecy Sea Shepherd sweater over the whole thing, as if

an advertisement for saving the whales could save my trashy outfit.

Kelly changed into a yellow sundress of mine that I hadn't worn since I was thirteen. It was short on me then. It was positively obscene on all five-foot-seven of Kelly.

She shoveled on as much make-up as our faces could take, which included bronzer, liquid eyeliner, lip liner and gloss, and then she handed me a fake ID from her reliable vendor.

"We are going out drinking," she said.

"Now?"

"Yes."

"We'll never get in anywhere. We're blatantly underage."

"Let the doormen be the judge of that."

"It's 12:45."

"Well then, the sun is over the yardarm, as my mom says."

"Are you sure about this?"

We hadn't taken our fake IDs on the town during broad daylight before. Normally we tried to slip into clubs behind groups of older people, so we wouldn't be noticed.

This seemed unnecessarily risky.

"Where are we going? Sailors? Belushi's?"

"The Central."

I groaned. The Central was the most touristy pub in town. During the summer months in Newquay, guys outnumbered girls twenty to one, so the Central would be heaving with out-of-towners looking to impress the local girls with their flashy watches and fat wallets. With my brain foggy from too much sleep, I didn't think I had the stamina to listen to a load of crap from boys I wasn't interested in.

Kelly gave me the once-over and then said, "You need this. Trust me. You need to remember."

"Remember what?"

"How to walk in high heels, for one thing."

She ushered me down the stairs, and I looked for my house keys as she opened the door. To Daniel. Who, for some reason, was wearing multicolored Hyperfreak board shorts which he'd teamed with a T-shirt with a smoking-fox on it.

I was standing right behind Kelly, and I saw her body stiffen. Flying across Daniel's face was a slightly panicky look and then his jaw dropped as he took in my miniskirt and platform shoes.

"Hello, Stabby," Kelly said, without a hint of a smile.

"What do you want, Daniel?" I said.

"You to kick this Zeke dude to the curb."

"Good for you."

"I'm sorry I hurt him. Really sorry. But I still don't like him."

"Yeah, you've made that plenty clear. Just as well you're not going out with him, huh?"

Kelly grabbed my wrist and pushed past Daniel, giving him a hard stare.

"We're going out," she said. "So get lost."

We walked the side streets down into town and I could hear Daniel's footsteps behind us, at a distance, following. Kelly never turned around, so I couldn't either. Finally we crossed into the Central beer garden, and when I looked over my shoulder, Daniel was gone.

We were in the beer garden for all of thirty seconds before the first group of boys approached us: fifteen men in their early twenties dressed as superheroes. A man in a padded Superman costume came right up to me and said, "Would you like a drink, darlin'?"

"I dunno. No."

"Come on, why not?"

"OK, well, just a Diet Coke."

"Nothing in it?"

I shook my head. "Nah, we're detoxing," I said. "A whole month without booze."

"Suit yourself."

"What about my friend?" I said, nodding over to Kelly, who was standing awkwardly and looking through the open double doors toward the bar.

Before he could answer, one of his friends, a boy with blond hair and a Robin outfit, stepped up and said, "I'll get her one."

My Diet Coke arrived and surprisingly it didn't have a sneaky shot of vodka in it.

"What's your name?" Superman asked me.

"Elena."

"That's pretty. But, hey, that's to be expected."

This was something that Kelly and I always did when we were out. We'd fabricate new names, new hobbies and sometimes new accents. Kelly would sometimes go totally crazy and tell boys that she was actually twenty-three with two small children at home and a husband in the navy. I never really got this, but she found it hysterical. I was mostly content with a new name and a few new hobbies. Not bungee-jumping or shark-diving. More snail-collecting and trainspotting. I guess it was a test. To weed out the shallow ones.

These guys weren't creepy or desperate, which couldn't be said for all of the tourists hitting Newquay. They were just out to have fun and were happy to chat with some girls, with no strings attached. They had no idea we were sixteen. They'd have been mortified. But that was the thing about make-up and tarty clothes: they could totally fool half-drunk men.

We finished our drinks and then moved to another area of the pub, where we got talking to some boys from Manchester who were spending the summer in Newquay. One of them was training to be an airline pilot, another had scored a job as a barman at Walkabout and the third was just bumming around with his indie band and learning to surf. His name was Matt and he had fair spiky hair and an eyebrow ring. There was something about him, this crazy enthusiasm, that I liked. He nodded his head at everything I said, and really listened. He reminded me of Zeke.

That was when it dawned on me. I hadn't thought about Zeke, or Daniel, in a whole hour. That was definitely a record. Maybe Kelly had been right to bring me out. Cheesy as it sounded, it had given me a bit of space from the constant worrying.

Matt and his friends walked with us to the next pub, just ten steps away from the Central, a place that had been aptly named Help.

Matt was telling me all about his band, which was called "White Side of the Moon" and he was stoked because they'd been booked for a couple of small gigs around town. He played bass guitar.

"I can teach you, if you like," he said, handing me a glass of Malibu and Coke. Malibu reeked so strongly of coconut that even if my mom smelled it, I could blame it on my shampoo or sunscreen.

"To play the guitar?"

"Why not? It's easy."

"Sure it is."

"And maybe you could give me a surf lesson? Quid pro quo, Clarice."

I laughed. Quoting Hannibal Lecter was a debatable strategy thirty minutes after meeting a girl, but with the huge grin on his face, I wasn't too worried.

I hesitated.

"What, do you have a boyfriend or something?" he said, still smiling.

"Ummm . . ."

"Uh-oh."

He looked really crestfallen. Had I been flirting with him? I hadn't meant to. I was just having fun and trying to be nice.

"Well," I said, "there is someone I really like."

Kelly butted in, dropping the conversation she'd been having about her future career visiting Neptune as an astronaut for NASA.

"She has a thing for a guy, but he hasn't even kissed her properly yet."

"Brutal, friend," I said, giving her the stink eye.

"What's he waiting for?" Matt asked casually.

"Don't ask me," I said, flustered.

And that was when Matt swept in and gave me the most full-on first kiss from a boy that I'd ever experienced. It was as if the pub went silent in response to that mega-watt kiss. I opened my eyes and Kelly was looking really surprised. Matt was grinning like all his Christmases had come at once, which was crazy. It was the second time in a week that a boy had kissed me and I hadn't been able to kiss him back. It seemed like I'd never get the chance to kiss the person I actually wanted to be with.

"I have to go to the ladies' room," I said.

Kelly was hot on my heels. "Iris! Oh my God. What are you like? That boy is totally crazy for you."

"It's this new pheromone perfume," I said, wafting my wrist around, like it had special powers.

"Seriously though. I mean, he's hot, don't get me wrong, but what about the current Junior Men's Surf Champ of Hawaii?"

"It was a one-way kiss, Kel."

"Nice lips. I noticed that right away about Mr. White Moony, or whatever his band is called."

Talking of lips reminded me to take care of my severely sun-chapped mouth. I got out my lipgloss and had a quick dab. Screw being stressed. I'd be young, dumb and full of fun, and for one afternoon I'd forget all the boys that were messing with my head.

Kelly and I teetered back to the bar.

Matt and his friends were gone, which spared us the awkwardness of having to ditch them.

"Let's take a walk," Kelly said. Help had really emptied out, with a mass exodus to the next pub, which was starting a dollar-fifty-a-shot afternoon happy hour.

"Bangarang" by Skrillex slammed through the massive speakers and Kelly wouldn't let me leave the dance floor.

"One song," she said, and then, "Just one more."

I danced with her, and for an hour I felt totally light and free.

Help was our last bar. We took the cliff path home, slinging our shoes in our handbags and walking barefoot. About halfway, Kelly sat down on the dewy grass and stretched out, arms waving above her head like she was making a snow angel.

"What are you doing?" I asked her, laughing.

"It's my being-drunk policy. Conservation of energy. *Never stand up when you can sit down. Never sit down when you can lie down.* Winston Churchill."

"Winston Churchill did not say that."

"He did actually, but I don't think he'd been doing Jägerbombs."

It was good to be spending real time with Kelly. She was so much fun and I knew I would always be able to rely on her. In the fresh sea air, I lay down beside her and closed my eyes.

Chapter Twenty

I was woken at midnight by my phone vibrating on my bedside table. I picked up.

"Hey, sweets."

Zeke.

"You're back!"

"Yep. Party was OK, but the whole time I just felt like I had somewhere to be, y'know? Caught an earlier flight. What ya doin'?"

"Err, sleeping."

"Oh man, is it late? Sorry, I thought it was like ten."

"Are you wasted?" I said, instantly regretting it. Who was I to ask about Zeke's blood alcohol level after I'd been out drinking with Kelly?

"A little. Got home and found my family celebrating."

"Celebrating what?" I said, wondering if Wes had made a certain announcement. Sephy was definitely the type to throw her son a Coming Out party.

"Garrett's been investing his trust-fund money. I'll tell you later." He went silent for a moment and then he said, "Can I come over?"

"Now?"

"I really wanna see you. I've missed you a lot."

"It's the middle of the night. I'm dressed for bed."

"OK, definitely coming over now."

"I don't think my mom will be happy if I have a boy in my room overnight. I mean, she likes you and all, but even she has her limits. She'd think we were up to . . . all sorts."

"So meet me in your backyard."

I turned on my bedside lamp and caught a glimpse of myself in the silver reflective surface of my iPod dock. *Grim.*

"In the morning, yeah?"

"Now."

"Seriously?"

"How about in, say, twenty minutes?"

"Can't it wait?"

"Nope."

I caved. He was determined. I'd never heard him like that before. Perhaps this was what he was like when he competed. I hadn't been brave enough to check out the videos of him on YouTube. I'd tried to, but when I saw that the first video to pop up had over half a million views, and was called "*Zeke Francis Smoking the Competition!*" I'd slammed my laptop lid shut. I didn't want to see Zeke the Brand. I didn't want to read the comments by the haters, or the ones written by the groupie girls who'd give everything they had just to grab a five-minute coffee with him.

"All right, see you in a bit," I said, slipping out of bed and padding across the carpet to the door.

I put on some tinted lip balm, crunched a couple of Extra Strong Mints from a packet on my dresser and tidied my hair as best as I could without putting my main bedroom light on, and then moved really quietly along the landing, avoiding all the creaks of the old floorboards. The front door was the hardest thing. The frame was swollen with the damp sea air and it always made a popping sound when the door was opened. I did it a millimeter at a time, and my mom's voice didn't break the silence.

It was creepy outside, so gray and still. A huge moon—a supermoon apparently—lit the garden and cast weird shadows of the still-full washing line. The seagulls were soaring through the sky and I wondered if they ever quit their mysterious quests. They were restless spirits. Like Zeke and Daniel, I thought. Like me.

There was no wind and I wasn't cold, with my parka wrapped around my pajamas, and my fleecy socks beneath my UGGs.

I didn't hear him coming—he walked so quietly—not until he was standing at the garden gate. He was silhouetted in the moonlight, his hair lost under a cap I hadn't seen him wear before. He looked different.

As he came through the gate, he staggered a little and it made me feel weird to see him like that. He normally had perfect posture.

Without saying anything, he came and stretched out on the sunlounger next to me and we looked up at the stars.

He sighed loudly and I smelled booze on his breath.

"My bad," he said. "Sorry for getting you outta bed." Then he added with a little smile, "So what do you wear in bed?" and then he added another "Sorry," and laughed.

"Nothing nice," I said.

"You'd look sexy in anything . . . or nothing."

What was this? It was embarrassing. You'd have thought a top surfer dude would be better at the come-on. Unless he was just out-of-his-skull drunk, or stoned, both of which were possible.

"What are we doing out here?" I said quietly, so as not to wake my mom. She'd always been able to tune into my voice at a hundred paces—one of her mom witchy powers.

Looking at Zeke there, he seemed so ordinary. You'd never know that in the water he was a superstar, one of the most hard-core surfers on the planet, tackling even the most dangerous waves. My stalkerpants YouTube research had thrown up a list of videos of him surfing Mavericks, Nazaré, Bells Beach, Ours, Cyclops, Teahupo'o, Killers, Jaws and Waimea Bay in Hawaii. Maybe one day I'd watch them, but for now just knowing he'd ridden those breaks was enough. Those were the places that people usually only surfed after decades of experience. Zeke was eighteen and he'd survived them all.

Without looking at me, Zeke said, "I was watching this space show in my motel room last night. The scientists were saying that asteroids brought the Earth its water."

"Asteroids are rocks."

"Yeah, but it's like when the Earth was formed it was this doughball that had been baked for too long in the oven. Just totally dry and barren with no water at all."

"OK. The Earth was a doughball."

"But they've just found out that a ton of asteroids carry water and it was these asteroids striking the Earth over millions, or like billions, of years that gave the Earth its water. People are so afraid of asteroids wiping us out, but if it wasn't for asteroid strikes, there'd be no people, no oceans, no surf."

"That's quite cool."

I really liked the way that Zeke would talk about stuff that nobody else knew about. Daniel could talk for hours about the Manchester City squad but I don't think I had ever heard him say the word asteroid. Even on the moonless summer nights when the stars were bright in the sky, he would never notice them. He was rooted in his everyday life.

Zeke seemed to have the planet at his fingertips.

"Life came from the ocean," he went on. "I think that's why people are drawn back to it. It's like our mother, or something."

In that moment, in the silence there with Zeke, I tried to feel the planet spinning at a thousand miles an hour. Spinning us, spinning the ocean, spinning everything.

"Is that what you came to tell me in the middle of the night?"

"No."

He took a deep breath and for a few seconds he started muttering what sounded like "Ramaramaramarama" under his breath. I had no idea what it was supposed to mean. Then he looked at me, and said, with that beautiful twang of an accent, "I came to ask how old you are."

"What? I'm sixteen. You could have texted to ask me that."

He exhaled through gritted teeth. "Dang. I thought you were my age."

"Right, so you've had two extra laps around the sun. So what?"

"OK, calm down, lady. There was something else too. I wanted to know what you're doing tomorrow."

He scratched the back of his neck and shifted in the sun-lounger. Was he nervous?

My schedule was wide open except for maybe a bit of yoga and a run, but I didn't want to look too desperate.

"Not much. What do you have in mind?"

"Something amazing."

"I'm always up for something amazing."

"You free first thing?"

I wasn't sure I liked the sound of a morning date. "What kind of time are you thinking?"

"Five thirty."

I sighed. One of the least fun aspects of surfing is that you have to get up early if you want to catch the best, least crowded waves. "Dawn patrol," they call it. It's not unknown for surfers to get up at 4 a.m. to catch the best summer waves, but it still sucks. Squeezing yourself into a damp, ice-cold wetsuit at dawn is one of the most miserable things to do five minutes after pulling yourself out of a warm bed.

"Six, then. I promise it'll be worth it."

"It better be. By the way, what does 'Rama' mean?"

"Huh? You heard that?"

"Yeah."

"OK, it means *'the source of all joy.'* Hindu yoga mantra. I guess it's dumb, but it makes me feel better. Like I'm tapping into something."

"Cool. I want a mantra too."

"You'll find yours. Or you can use mine."

I smiled, and said, "Goodnight, Zeke."

"*Aloha*," he said, then reached over and grabbed my hand and kissed my wrist.

In my coat and boots I was warm, but Zeke's hand was freezing. He had such perfect long fingers, pianist's fingers, my mom would have said. And yet these were the hands that had mastered a surfboard when he was a grom of four and the hands that had held trophies for photographs that appeared in the back pages of newspapers the world over. Without thinking, I took his hand in both of mine and blew on his cold fingers. He shot me a bright, hopeful look.

That look in his eyes was something else. I knew then that if I just got up and walked into my house, up the stairs and into my bedroom, he would follow. He couldn't help it. It was like all of these invisible sticky threads were reaching out from each of us and once they touched we'd be tangled together until something violent and painful pulled us apart.

And I had given him that look, that hunger. Me. It was awesome and terrible at the same time to think I could do that to a boy. Daniel had constantly been trying to get into my pants, but always cool and aloof, not really admitting that it was for him. He'd always spun it as something that'd benefit me, but here was Zeke, aching with longing.

It gave me a glimpse of the power I could have over Zeke's heart, the power I could have without even trying. Call it physical attraction, chemicals, lust, whatever, but it was there in Zeke's face and I wanted to see where it would lead, as much as I was totally terrified of it.

I shook my head, like that could clear away my thoughts. "Zeke," I said, "can I ask you a question?"

"Shoot."

"How many girlfriends have you had?"

"Where'd that come from? What happened to talking about asteroids?"

Instantly cagey. He was being defensive. Could he actually be as inexperienced as me? Was that even possible for one of the dream-crew surfer dudes? Just because he had a lot of numbers in his iPhone, that didn't mean he'd slept with all of those girls. He could have just met them in bars and taken their numbers, or gone on a few dates or whatever. They could even be female competitors on the QS who he hung with as friends.

"It's OK, you can tell me."

"Depends what you mean by girlfriend."

Definitely evasive. If he'd had a lot of girlfriends he'd say, because guys were always proud of that. So maybe, just maybe, it was possible that he was also a virgin.

What the hell.

"Are you a virgin?" I said. "Because I am and it's totally OK if you are too. It's all good. In fact, it's cool to wait and be, you know, sure."

I had messed up. He was embarrassed.

Then it dawned on me. He wasn't embarrassed because the number was zero. He was embarrassed because the number was high.

"I wanna make you happy here and tell you that I've never slept with anyone either, but I'd be lying. I'm really sorry, Iris. But I'm eighteen, and nearly two years of surf touring is pretty lonely."

Not that lonely, obviously.

"Girls chase the guys on tour, tell them what they wanna hear, offer a bit of human warmth, right?" I said. "Because gee, it's all so stressful."

"Give me a chance here, OK? Yeah, it's true, hooking up with girls is one of the ways to relax and get your mind off the tour, but it's more than that. Sheesh, this is coming out all wrong."

I let that sink in. He wasn't even talking about girlfriends. These girls were hook-ups. One-nighters and nothing else.

"So how many girls have you slept with?"

"Can't we just leave history in the past? Start from scratch with each other?"

"I think I'd rather know," I said. "It's only a number, so just tell me. How many girls are on the list?"

"Nowhere near as many as there could have been. OK, so that sounded bad."

I had literally no idea what to say to that.

"You don't understand," he said. "It's crazy hard on tour. Not just having to win every damn time, but being around other dudes who want to win as much as I do. It makes them, and me, real aggressive, and I'm already aggressive enough."

"You're not aggressive."

"Wanna bet? Surfing attracts arrogant, competitive guys. You think I do yoga and meditation for the sake of it? I need it. Competitive surfing brings out the worst in me as well as the best, and I have to work real hard to not let the anger get the better of me. Nothing is worse to a pro-surfer than the frustration of missing the perfect A-frame wave and seeing some douche-baggy opponent ace it. It does something to your brain. Eats you up. Being with chicks is one way I can get away from that. Puts a little nectar in life, you know? Does that make sense?"

It did, but I was angry and I only said, "I guess."

"Come on. Don't be mad at me. You don't get it yet. But you will. So no judgment, right?"

The moment passed and suddenly Zeke was up on his feet, telling me that he'd meet me outside my house at six sharp and to wear my warmest stuff. Then he was gone and it was just me and the galaxy stretching out over my head, on and on to infinity.

Before I left the garden for my bed, I thought about how I would probably never understand boys, because the ones who seemed like nice guys turned out to be serial womanizers, and the ones who seemed like bad boys could surprise you by telling you that they wanted to settle down with you forever.

And . . . I had to stop obsessing; had to think of something else. Surfing.

I wondered if I would ever discover how it felt to stand on a podium and be handed a surf trophy in front of screaming crowds, or to pose for photographs that surfers the world over would see.

I had to forget boys for a minute and admit that I had ambitions of my own. Competing professionally at surfing would be really hard and majorly head-bending, but it would be incredible too. Whatever happened with Zeke, I had my dream.

Chapter Twenty-one

That night I dreamed about the time I was besties with Cass. We used to play this game down on the beach during the busiest days of the summer when Fistral was packed with a hundred thousand tourists. Cass created the game and it was called "Find My Figure." We'd play it for literally hours, sizing up all the girls on the beach to see which of them looked the most like us in a bikini. Not that we ever wore bikinis. Both of us were heavier then. Cass hadn't started up with the bulimia and I was what some of the boys in my year liked to call a heifer. Of course they changed their minds when I took up surfing, lost a ton of weight and the sun streaked my hair blond, but back in the old days, me and Cass were sisters in loneliness. Kelly was abroad visiting her dad, who had a placement in a Thai school teaching English, which brought me and Cass even closer together.

Cass's betrayal was worse than Daniel's. Cass had known me forever. I had told her things that I would have never told a boy. Yet she was still ready to stab me in the back when she saw the opportunity. That always surprised me. How a girl could totally change her personality like that.

Cass changed. It took me a while to come to terms with it, to believe it. But that's what it came down to. I looked different, but on the inside I was still the same person. Cass wasn't. Either that or she'd never been who I'd thought she was in the first place. Both ideas were depressing.

In the dream we went from playing the figure-twin game to swimming in a sea full of dark fins. I woke up in a horrible sweat and saw that it was five fifty. I'd forgotten to set the alarm on my phone and had overslept. Zeke would be at my front door any minute.

I brushed my teeth and stepped into the shower. Late or not, I wasn't going on a date with Zeke with greasy hair, so I lathered up quickly, rinsed and then stepped into my clothes, still damp. I didn't have time to blow-dry my hair so I toweled it, scrunched it a bit and left it to air-dry while I put on some waterproof mascara and waited.

Six o'clock passed. He was definitely coming. He was just late. Six thirty came around with no knock at the door, and then seven. At seven o'clock he was still coming. Something had delayed him but there was no way he was standing me up. Not Zeke.

Every dead palm frond that blew across the pavement outside my window was him walking up the garden path, every swish of the cherry tree was the rustle of his board shorts, and every creaking branch was the swinging of the garden gate. It was always him, but still he didn't appear.

It surprised me how my brain fought his no-show. My mind just couldn't seem to accept that he wasn't coming. Not for an hour and a half.

Then it sunk in deep.

Zeke had invited me out for our first ever real date and had failed to show up. My phone was blank, no new calls or messages. No emails, except one from ASOS giving me twenty percent off city shorts for one day only. Big whoop.

Facebook was dead, with hardly any of my friends online, and the only interesting thing I could see on Twitter was a conversation between Kelly Slater and Koby Abberton about a surfer who had broken his back at Cyclops.

I would drive myself crazy, I knew, if I waited around the house. I could surf better than most people twice my age, and in the last week I had got off my butt and really pushed my fitness limits. I was not going to wait around for some sex-addict surfrat to give me validation.

In other words, I was raging.

And how many girls had Zeke slept with anyway? In two years of touring, even if it was just one a month, the list would have over twenty names on it. And it was bound to be more than one a month. It could be one a day, for all I knew. Two a day even. It could be like a thousand girls. No, that was just silly. Realistically, it was probably like thirty. But no way was I being number thirty-one.

At seven forty, I put on my running shoes and took off along the cliffs. I ran the entire Pentire Headland, turned back and ran through sleepy suburban streets down to the mansions overlooking the Gannel River, which was in full flood. I followed the curve of the river from the path running next to the sky-high garden walls of millionaire second-homers.

Hitting the steep steps carefully, I ran down to the sands. The tide was in and with the turquoise water and the reflected mansions, it could have been the French Riviera. My face turned toward the sea, which glistened a half-mile away between the riverbanks. Then I walked to the river's edge, knelt and splashed my face and wrists with its ice-cold water. What was Zeke playing at? Was it fair to get a girl's hopes up like this, only to dash them? What was the point of it? What could he get out of it? An ego boost, yeah, but as a top surfer, wouldn't he be able to get that anywhere with a hundred different girls on any given day? Why me?

I walked for a few minutes, breathing hard and trying to clear my mind. I turned away from the plate-glass river and crossed the road, sweat dripping from my head. Not ready to throw in the towel, I ran a couple of laps of the boating lake and then up Trenance Hill to town. A few cars were around now, just locals on the way to work. The flashy cars of tourists were still tucked outside fancy hotels, their owners enjoying luxurious lie-ins on hundred-fifty-dollar sheets.

At the crest of the hill I turned left toward Towan Beach and ran down through the side streets until I was standing outside the Blue Reef Aquarium, which was just opening up. I popped in to grab a swig from the drinking fountain and then ran on down to the sea. There was no surf at all. It was the flattest I'd ever seen it. Something to do with the supermoon and a super-high tide. The sun was getting higher in the sky and I could already feel its strength. The beach was still empty so I walked in up to my knees, thinking I'd stop when the water reached my shorts. I didn't. I kept going until the water was lapping at my belly button and then I struck out and swam.

After about five minutes, what looked like a gigantic dog stuck its head out of the water just in front of me.

It was just one of the harbor seals giving me the once-over. They were friendly enough, but it was disconcerting to see one so close. I hadn't even sensed another animal around me.

I swam back to shore and collapsed on the beach, the exertion of the run and swim finally catching up with me. I lay flat on my back and stretched out, arms over my head, toes pointed, and just let myself settle there, sand caked in my hair and fingers of saltwater creeping around the edges of my body.

This was where I'd stay. This was where I could relax.

Even with my eyes closed, I felt the shadow cross my face.

How was it that he seemed to find me everywhere?

Chapter Twenty-two

I squinted to see him and noticed that the zip pull of his Adidas jacket was flashing like a lighthouse, spinning on its metal ring in the bright morning sunshine.

"Mermaid alert," he said, smiling down at me.

"Daniel," I said, scrambling up and brushing sand grains away from the sides of my face, which only succeeded in wiping on more sand, as my hands were covered.

"Spotted you from the harbor wall. Been helping with the catch. What you up to?"

"Not a lot."

"Your boyfriend's on Fistral dragging a tree across the sand."

"What?"

"Saw him earlier when I was walking the dog. Rope across his chest. Strength training, I suppose. He has about fifty cheerleaders, including that ginger chick with the weird name and the big boobs."

So he'd ditched me to hang out with Saskia and his Fistral fan club?

"Great."

"Walk with me."

"What if someone sees? Kelly would be pissed. I promised her I was over you."

"And you're not?"

"I didn't say that."

"Come on. Just a walk."

I sighed. "Where are we going?"

"You'll see."

We walked along the beach and up the steps to the harbor. Daniel pointed at one of the small boats, called *Bite Me*.

"My uncle upgraded his fishing boat, and guess who's got the keys?"

"He's letting you take it out?"

"Why wouldn't he? I'm responsible," he said, adding, "sometimes."

He went to pick me up so I wouldn't have to walk through the oily harbor water, but I didn't let him. I could wade through a few feet of dirty water. I clambered up the boarding ladder and stood on the small deck.

"Have you ever driven a boat before?"

"Yeah, lots of times. I'm thinking of getting my own fishing boat in a few years. It's an all-right living. Yeah, I'll never be rich, but my family will never go hungry. So, you up for this?"

I thought about it. Zeke had stood me up. I had no plans for the whole of the day. Stuff it.

"Looks like it."

Daniel steered the boat out of the harbor, almost grazing a wall, and then followed the buoys until, after an hour or so, the land was just a snake on the horizon. It was so peaceful out there. Bliss.

"What now?"

"Let's see what food we've got," Daniel said, and went down into the galley to raid the cupboards.

I stretched out on deck and soaked up the sunshine. I was still angry with Zeke, but the longer I spent with Daniel the easier it was to forget Zeke. Who was he anyway? Just someone I hardly even knew. Someone who was used to turning the heads of girls and who probably had a different one, a different dozen of them, every place he went.

Stick with what you know—that's what people from Cornwall say. Why dream of traveling the world with Zeke when I already had the awesomeness that was Newquay? We had stunning coastline, pumping surf and dozens of surf contests. Zeke would be gone in a week or two and then I'd have to face up to what was going on with Daniel, so why delay it? Why not just fix it now?

Daniel laid out some cookies, chips and cans of beer and we spent the next hour chatting, stuffing our faces and getting pleasantly tanked.

Then Daniel picked up the acoustic guitar that his uncle kept on the boat and started strumming. He was amazing on the guitar and he used to take it with him to the tribe's beach fires. It was something that had once worried me a bit because it made me go weak at the knees and I knew it would be having the same effect on other girls.

It was always the tourist girls I worried about. I thought they'd eye up Daniel when he was out in the waves teaching them to surf, and try to pull him afterward.

But I didn't need to worry about them at all. I should have been worrying about Cass and the lines she was spinning him behind my back. The lies and the promises she was whispering in his ear.

Daniel started singing. An old song that sounded vaguely familiar but I didn't know its name. He had it memorized by heart, not faltering or losing his way, and when he opened his eyes after the chorus, he looked straight into mine. His music was a spell he could cast over me.

When he finished the song, the atmosphere was embarrassingly heavy. I looked at my watch and saw that it was past four.

"We should get back," I said. "Cass will be wondering where you are."

Daniel leaned forward and kissed me very slowly on the mouth.

It was so tempting to just throw caution to the wind. So tempting to kiss him again like we had done so many times before. So tempting to forget Zeke and all the hassle that went with him. So tempting to get my own back on Cass.

But I knew how that felt. To be betrayed.

"Don't," I said, pulling away. "We can't."

He kissed me again, and this time I didn't stop him.

Even though I knew it was Daniel because I had kissed him hundreds of times, the person I could feel against my body was Zeke. I imagined it was Zeke touching me beneath my T-shirt and shorts, and Zeke's soft hair beneath my hands.

I felt a vibration coming from Daniel's back pocket. Somehow, way out here, his phone had got a signal and someone was calling him.

His hand snaked around to turn it off, but that was it, I'd come to my senses and it was over.

"What the hell am I doing?" I said, getting up and walking to the railing. I was suddenly faint and nauseous, and I nearly puked over the side of the boat.

I had just been kissing the moron who had put a good person in the hospital, almost killed him, and all because Zeke had committed the crime of having a life before meeting me.

I really, truly loathed myself.

Daniel came to ask if I was OK or if I needed a glass of water, but he could see by my face that I was a wreck. He went to the bridge, did something to the GPS and turned the boat.

He stayed there and I stayed where I was. I couldn't even bear to look at him. Not that I'd have been looking in any mirrors either.

Eventually we made it back to the harbor, Daniel steering past another cluster of seals.

I clambered out of the boat before he could have a last attempt at talking to me. I didn't want to see his face or hear him try to make it all better. I just wanted to be gone.

I looked across to the harbor beach, and flinched. Sitting on her yoga mat in the lotus position and looking directly at the boat was Saskia.

I'd have to walk right past her to reach the road leading out of the harbor. I nodded to her as I passed and she said, "Really, Iris? Again?"

"What?"

"Hanging out with the lowlife who stabbed Zeke."

"It's not like that," I said.

"You haven't just spent the day on a fishing boat with your ex-boyfriend?"

"Yes, but . . ."

"Is that a love bite on your shoulder?"

I looked down, horrified. "No."

It was only an insect bite that I'd been absentmindedly scratching. The idea of Daniel leaving a love bite on me was too awful, but it was only dumb luck that he hadn't. "It's a mosquito bite," I said.

"Zeke is my friend. What are you playing at? Are you trying to make him jealous?"

"No, of course not."

"So what *are* you doing?"

"Things are complicated."

"Uncomplicate them."

"It's not that easy. I've known Daniel a long time. I can't never see him again."

"Perhaps you could start by not going on dates with him?"

Ouch.

I wanted to beg her not to tell Zeke what she'd seen, to tell her that I regretted it more than anything. I wanted to explain about Daniel; tell her why he was so screwed-up; make her understand that I would always care about Daniel because we had so much history, but that I wanted to be with Zeke. But instead I said, "You just don't get it."

"You're right," she said. "I absolutely don't."

Chapter Twenty-three

Once again I woke up to the sound of my phone beeping. I didn't move; I couldn't bring myself to read the message.

Zeke had tried to call me at 9 p.m., and then again at 9:30 and 9:55, but I'd screened his calls. I couldn't talk to him. Saskia would have told him what she'd seen. He was calling to tell me he never wanted to see me again.

I lay on my back in the morning light of my bedroom and tried not to cry. I'd been awake for most of the night, full of hot shame about what I'd done with Daniel, and then when I finally got to sleep in the early hours of the morning, it was one bad dream after another.

Eventually I worked up enough courage to feel for my phone under my pillow. It wasn't a goodbye text from Zeke. Instead I had a text from a number I didn't recognize. It said: "Saskia told me bout yr ex. Cum 2 Sth Fistral @ 10. Wes."

Saskia had told Wes that she saw me with Daniel and had given him my cell phone number? Why would she do that? Was this some weird way of stirring? Why didn't she just tell Zeke, if she was going to tell anyone? Or maybe she'd told *everyone*.

I checked the time on my phone. It was half past nine and I was still in my nightshirt. I had the world's quickest shower, tied up my hair in a messy bun on the top of my head and got dressed. The sky was clear and the sun already hot so I opted for my uniform of sleeveless top and shorts and ran straight to the beach. It was five past ten by the time I made it to the south end, and with the tide on the way out I saw right away what was going on.

Sephy, Wes, Garrett and Zeke were climbing down over the rocks from the headland, various kinds of surfboards under their arms. Dave was behind them, and in his arms he carried Nanna.

I ran up the stone steps, past Bodhi's and over to the cliff-edge, where I could watch them up close. The sun was right behind me, so if they looked across all they'd see would be a dark silhouette.

So they were actually going to take Nanna for one last tandem-surf?

The guys hadn't bothered with wetsuits but had stripped down to their baggies. Sephy took off her blue sundress and flip-flops and rocked a black bikini.

Their voices carried in the fresh morning air and I heard Wes say, "Mom, you're no way strong enough for this. Nanna's a dead weight."

"Less of the dead, sonny!"

A few dog walkers stopped beside me to watch too.

"I can do it," Dave was saying, but Garrett interrupted, "It's gotta be Zeke. He has the best balance and he knows how to keep cool. Hate to admit it, but little bro surfs better than me and Wes combined. So, what do you say, champ?"

Zeke rubbed his eyes with both hands, and said, "Super."

"Hurray!" Nanna shouted.

"We'll help get her on your board, but after that it's all you, little brother."

Zeke tossed five boards on to the water and he and Wes got on to theirs. Zeke had brought the red and white, heavily glassed sixties board that had belonged to his Pop. Nanna said something I didn't catch when she saw it, maybe recognizing that it was the same style of board that surfers had ridden when she was part of the surf scene.

Zeke was getting knocked about a bit, trying to hold the board still so that Nanna could be helped on to if she was boarding a boat. But the swell kept bumping Zeke and the longboard against the rocks. Eventually they managed to get Nanna on Zeke's back and she held on for dear life, her arms tight around his neck.

Sephy had Zeke's fish board to ride, which was the smallest and most maneuverable of the boards, so she'd be the lookout, paddling wide and deep to keep an eye out for sleeper sets.

Wes and Dave led the way with Zeke and Nanna behind and Garrett bringing up the rear. Sephy veered a bit further offshore, then looked over her shoulder, where the others were paddling close together in a convoy. Nanna had no wetsuit, and was dressed up in sweaters with her white hair flowing freely in the wind.

After a minute of paddling they made position, stopping beyond the range of the headland currents, where the waves would be smallest.

Pulling this off was going to be seriously difficult. It would have to be a party wave, which is when a group of friends catch the same breaking wave. Garrett, Dave and Wes would need to drop in at the same time, so that they'd be on hand to help Zeke if things went wrong. But there wouldn't be any riding the curl. It would have to be a journey straight back to shore.

Garrett and Wes sidled up so that their boards were neck and neck with Zeke's, while Sephy stayed slightly further out to sea to give the signal when she spotted the right wave.

Sephy's hand was up but all the waves coming through were too messy.

No. No. No. No.

And then it was suddenly coming, a beautiful glassy green wave.

Sephy dropped her hand, caught the wave on the shoulder as it approached her and turned a little so that she could see everything that happened without getting in the way.

Dave caught a smaller wave coming through first, probably so that he'd be in the right position in the shallows to take Nanna from Zeke's arms when they'd finished.

I watched as Zeke moved Nanna to the nose of his board and then popped up to his feet, with Garrett and Wes only half a second behind him. Instead of taking the traditional surfer stance, Zeke put his feet together facing onshore and then picked up Nanna like she weighed nothing at all and put her on his shoulders.

Dave surfed through the impact zone, hopped off his board and turned offshore to face his family.

Zeke was really struggling. The wave was moving fast and Nanna kept wriggling her hands out of his. With his eyes looking forward so he could steer past other surfers, Zeke couldn't get a good grip on her, so her weight had slumped to one side. He was working hard to balance and his spine was flexing backward as he tried to find his new center of gravity.

I knew what Nanna was doing. She was trying to stretch her arms out to either side, which is how she'd told us she'd tandem-surfed back when she was young.

Zeke must have had the same thought, because suddenly his arms swung out wide and he grabbed Nanna's small hands.

Finally stable, Nanna straightened her back a bit and looked at the sea rushing everywhere beneath her. From the cliff it looked like some crazy dad was out there with his little girl on his shoulders.

I could only imagine what Nanna must have felt.

The wave uncurled beautifully behind him, and Zeke was able to pump the longboard with his legs so that he could punch through the sloppy sections and ride right to Dave, who stood waist-deep in the water, his arms wide open.

In the slop, with the wave's power bottoming out, Zeke knelt down on his board and lifted Nanna off his shoulders and passed her to Dave.

Garrett, Wes and Sephy were right behind and I watched them jump off their boards and high-five. On the beach, Sephy hugged her boys one after the other, and as soon as Dave set Nanna down on the sand, Sephy wrapped her arms around him and kissed his face off.

In that moment I was quite certain that they were the coolest family on earth.

And yet tears were in my eyes. For the first time, I was watching them from the *outside*. Being part of their world was something I'd taken for granted. I owed Wes for letting me know what they were doing, because I'd have hated to miss Nanna's moment of glory, but I wished I'd been out there with them.

Saskia must have told Zeke that she'd seen me with Daniel. He wouldn't want me around his family ever again.

I watched Zeke's family mount the steps to Bodhi's, with Nanna being carried by Garrett, but Wes stayed behind on the sand, his knees up to his chest.

Keeping my head down, I walked past the cafe and over to Wes.

"Thanks for texting me. That was amazing," I said.

"You're welcome."

"I didn't realize it was happening today."

"Zeke says he's been trying to call you to apologize about something, but you haven't returned his calls. I guess he doesn't know if you're still interested."

"Oh."

"So what's the deal, Iris?"

"What did Saskia say?" I said, feeling sick.

"She brought me up to speed on a few things. She's concerned. Are you actually going on, what, fishing trips with the psycho creep that stabbed my brother?"

"We weren't fishing."

"Did you sleep with him?"

"*No.*"

"You did something. It's written all over your face."

"I might have let him kiss me. Just once."

"Oh man."

"But then I came to my senses."

"Why are you even hanging out with that guy?"

"We have a lot of history. Daniel's had some seriously awful stuff happen to him."

"So has Zeke. Like being *stabbed*, for instance."

I winced. The thought of Daniel's knife plunging into Zeke's thigh was horrendous. I usually tried to block it out of my mind, because it was just too painful to think about.

"I screwed up. I should never have gone on that boat, not after what Daniel did to Zeke. I'm sorry."

"Don't you care about Zeke?"

"Yes, I care. But I don't really know how he feels. He could have a different girl on every beach on the planet for all I know. Also, he totally stood me up."

Wes sighed. "Zeke's serious about you. I don't know why he stood you up, but he sees a future with you."

"Does he?" It was the first I'd heard of it. Obviously I'd done my fair share of daydreaming about a future in which Zeke and me were properly together, but it never occurred to me that Zeke might be doing the same.

"He talks about places he wants to take you, stuff he wants to show you, breaks he wants to surf with you."

I let that sink in for a gorgeous moment.

"But why hasn't he told me any of this?"

"I guess he doesn't want to freak you out."

"I wouldn't have freaked out. Maybe I would have assumed he was exaggerating, or just being nice . . ."

Wes rolled his eyes, as if I was completely clueless.

"So what's next, Iris? How are you gonna handle this?"

It was a good question.

"Uh, I don't know yet."

"I like you, Iris, but it seems like you still have feelings for your ex, and I don't want my brother to get burned. I'm giving you one day to come clean to Zeke. Let's say, by nightfall tomorrow? Otherwise I think I have to tell him."

"Please don't do that. I'll talk to Zeke, I promise. I just need time to think first."

"Choose Zeke or choose the juicebox ex-boyfriend. You can't have them both. Zeke would not be into that."

I thought briefly about Elijah and wondered how Wes was going to come clean about his own secrets to Zeke and the rest of his family.

"I've gotta catch up with my folks now, but I'll see you tomorrow, right?"

"Right. Thanks, Wes."

"No problem. Go do your thinking."

Chapter Twenty-four

Thirty-two hours later, I walked past the Beached Lamb cafe, past the Red Lion pub and across to Fistral. I'd gone gig-rowing with Kelly, done a circuits class up at the Atlantic Hotel, and swum thirty laps in the pool at Waterworld because I didn't want to risk running into Zeke or his family at the beach until I'd sorted through my feelings and cleared my head. I hadn't eaten anything decent all day and I was starting to feel light-headed, but there was no way I was turning back.

I only had twenty minutes to get there so I had to run. I walked quickly across half a mile of sand, over rocks, up stone steps, across the esplanade, through sliding doors and into the ballroom of Hotel Serenity.

I didn't stop to think what I must have looked like tearing into yoga class with my hair in a big tangled mess from swimming in chlorine and not a scrap of make-up on my face.

A few heads turned but there weren't many people in the class. I grabbed a mat from the box and tried to calm myself down. Zeke would come to this class, I knew he would. I just had to wait.

Five minutes into the class, I was trying hard to think about nothing. There was a different teacher today, a quiet Scandinavian woman called Astrid, who talked a lot about the theories behind yoga. Thinking about nothing was a vital yoga skill. One I definitely needed to learn.

"If thoughts come into your mind, acknowledge them and then let them float away like clouds. *Be the sky.*"

Be the sky. If only it was that easy.

We were halfway through this being-the-sky exercise when the door opened and Saskia walked in, followed by Zeke.

Zeke was wearing a colorful T-shirt and he had his hair swept back in a headband. He gave me a worried look and made the phone sign.

I shrugged, since I couldn't exactly shout out in the middle of a yoga class that yeah, I'd screened all his calls because I'd been busy with some epic soul-searching.

Astrid was telling a story about an elephant who was walking in a parade and kept getting distracted by the food stalls ahead of and behind her, instead of just being happy with where she was, when I stood up and walked over to Zeke. I must have looked schizo, because Saskia's face was all alarmed, as if I was about to punch him or something.

I put out my hand to him, which he took, and I hauled him up. "How about we hit the beach for a private yoga lesson?"

Literally everyone was looking at us, trying to figure out what was happening. For a second I thought he was going to say no.

Then he broke into a grin and said, "Sure, why not?"

Astrid smiled, and Saskia sat on her mat frowning.

This was it. I was going to tell him exactly what had happened and how I felt. Expecting him to be a mind-reader was just stupid.

We left the hotel and as soon as we'd walked down the slate steps Zeke turned and gave me a long hug. "I'm sorry I let you down," he said, his voice warming my hair.

"That's all right, but . . . what happened? Where were you?"

A group of German tourists swarmed out of a bus and headed toward us.

"It's a long story. Can we talk on the beach?"

I nodded and followed him to a battered green Kawasaki motorcycle. "Whose is that?"

"Garrett's. He said I could borrow it for a few days while my van is in the repair shop."

"Cool of him."

"Least he can do, since I'm buying him an apartment."

"For real?"

"I'll own it, but he'll be living in it rent-free."

"You're like the best brother ever."

"Not really. I'll have someone I trust looking after the place. Don't wanna leave it empty. Pa has me putting as much of my money into property as I can. You know, so I won't spend it all on coke and strippers. Kidding."

I winced at the very idea of that.

"Garrett's staying in Newquay for a while, is he?"

"Yeah, he likes it here. Likes Kelly too, I guess."

"I suppose you'll be coming back a lot then, if you have an apartment here."

"Sure hope so."

He gave me a spare helmet and I climbed on to the back of the motorcycle, wrapped my arms around his waist and held on tight as he kick-started the bike and revved the engine.

We burned around to North Fistral, the roar of the bike turning heads, and parked up. He went to feed the meter and I carried on down past the huge lifeguards' building and slumped down in its shadow on to the soft sand. I saw Zeke come down to the beach and look for me, not able to find me in the crowd of tourists.

I was still struck by how much I liked watching him, just the way he moved, his posture, the way his T-shirt hung down from wide shoulders.

I whistled with two fingers and he looked into the shadow and saw me. "Hey there," he said, sitting next to me. I went to say something but he placed his finger over my lips.

"I have to tell you something," he said, before I could say that exact same thing.

"OK," I said, moving his hand from my face.

"Well, first, I wanted to tell you that before I met you, I was sorta in a relationship with another girl. Do you have the word 'umfriend' over here?"

"I never heard it."

"OK, well, it's that thing where you're kind of seeing someone but they're not your girlfriend yet. So like when you introduce that person to your crew, it's all, 'This is my, um, friend.' Does that make sense?"

"You were just seeing a girl, but you weren't going out."

"Right. That's it. And it was pretty much over by the time I met you."

"Who was it? Not Saskia?"

"Maybe . . ." He grimaced a bit.

So I'd been right. Out of all the girls he could have hooked up with, why did it have to be the most irritating one on earth?

"Anders said she wasn't your type."

"I don't have a type."

"Open to all, are you?" I said, smiling despite myself.

"I guess so."

"Gaah," I said. This was the sort of word I'd normally put in a text or email. It had never come out of my mouth before and it sounded ridiculous, like a lazy baby.

"It was only for a few months, and it just kinda fizzled out. Then I met you."

"Amazing. No wonder she hates me."

"She doesn't hate you. She thinks you hate her."

I wanted to say, "And she's right." But instead, I said, "I don't hate anybody," which was a lie on so many counts. It was like I'd suddenly grown incapable of honesty. I had to change that.

The sea wind blew harder and I looked down to see my hands were white with cold and the hairs on my arms bristling. Zeke noticed, got to his feet and went to collect driftwood, which he brought back and set down in front of me. He carried on like that, piling it up, and I helped. When there wasn't a piece of driftwood left to find, Zeke took out a lighter, lit a receipt from his pocket and set it to a twig.

"Thanks," I said, smiling.

"Iris, here's the thing: I wanna explain why I didn't show up. I guess you don't know this—which is totally my bad—but—"

"Hey, guys, OK if we edge in on your fire?"

We both turned to see some surfers, fresh out of the water, looking to get warm and be sociable. Before we could answer, one of them gave us a cheeky grin and said, "Our friend's bringing lotsa beer. Be here any minute. Booze for flames: what say ya?"

Zeke looked at me with a blank expression that I couldn't read at all.

"Yeah, cool. More the merrier," I mumbled, secretly wishing they'd all evaporate.

There was soon a big group of us, maybe twenty, twenty-five. Someone had a guitar. People started talking about their tales of perfect glassy surf in foreign countries. Zeke was quiet. I wanted to talk to him more, but it seemed like he just wanted to think. What didn't I know? What did he want to tell me? What was going on with him?

A half-hour passed, and I was about to crack and ask him anyway, when Garrett, Wes and some of Zeke's cousins showed up. Wes raised his eyebrows at me and I shook my head. He tapped his watch.

I got it: time was running out.

Garrett was joking around with another guy and trying to get the surfers to have an arm-wrestling tournament.

A few of the guys were up for it but Zeke said, "Maybe later, bro. I'm not in the mood. Plus, I promised Iris we'd do some beach yoga."

"Seriously?" Garrett said. "Only girls do yoga in public."

Zeke sighed but didn't say anything.

"Just one minute," Garrett said. "Suck up to your girlfriend later."

"Back off, dude."

"OK, be a homo."

I didn't mean to, but I looked over at Wes and caught his eye. He was bound to be upset by that and I half expected him to storm off. Wes didn't even give Garrett a dirty look though. Instead he gave me one, and then he side-eyed me hard.

I couldn't seem to do anything right: I'd upset Wes, I didn't know what Zeke was thinking, and I *still* hadn't told him what I'd done with Daniel. Maybe, I thought, if I told Zeke some of the history I had with Daniel, then just maybe he'd understand.

Zeke showed me a few new yoga poses I hadn't done before, and he stood in front of me, making himself into a wall so that I could kick up into my first-ever headstand with his chest supporting my feet. It felt nice to be upside down, and the dull headache I'd had all day vanished.

The sun bobbed on the horizon; Zeke had been roped into playing beach baseball with his brothers and cousins, and I found myself alone. I psyched myself up and walked purposefully over the powdery sand at the foot of the dunes to the flats where they were messing around. I stood for a second to watch them. Zeke was batting, Garrett was pitching and I watched as Zeke whacked the ball, sending it sailing all the way down into the water. The ball was being sucked by the backwash and Wes was running after it at a hundred miles an hour. Zeke was running flat out too, zooming past the second baseman, but laughing at the same time, which was making him cough like the twenty-a-day smoker he probably was. Wes had the ball in his hand and I watched as he leaned back and whipped forward, using his whole body weight to throw the ball to his fielding team. It was an immense throw and one of Zeke's cousins, Nils, caught it, got to the plate and Zeke was out.

Wes caught my eye and glared. I walked straight over to him and said, "I'm really sorry if I made it worse for you back there."

"What?"

"You know."

He looked over his shoulder. Nobody was close enough to hear us.

"Just what do you think you know, Iris?"

"I saw you kissing Elijah in your bedroom."

"At my pa's party, right?"

"Right."

"Knew that was a mistake. Did you say something to Zeke?"

"I wasn't thinking and I almost told Zeke what I saw, but I didn't. I started talking about you, then stopped in my tracks, so he was suspicious. But he probably figured it was to do with you kissing me during Spin the Bottle. I don't think anybody knows about you and Elijah, except Kelly, and that's only because she knows Elijah from yoga."

"Elijah told Kelly about me?"

"No, but he talked about his boyfriend and then Kelly noticed you two hanging out and she put it all together. I promise I won't say anything to anyone, OK?"

"OK. Thanks, I guess."

"Do not thank me. I am a total moron."

"No, you're not," he said, breaking into a rare smile. "But maybe I am for trying to keep Elijah a secret. We're gonna get busted someday. I feel like I'm at this crossroads, and I need to pick a direction, especially since Elijah's roommate just moved out, leaving him with a ton of utility bills and rent arrears. He seriously needs someone to move in, like yesterday, or he'll lose the place and have to go live in Truro with his parents."

"Elijah wants you to be his new roommate?" I said, wondering if that would be the thing that made Zeke realize the truth about Elijah and Wes, or if he'd just shrug it off as two bros splitting bills in a bachelor pad.

"Uh-huh, and I said yes."

"What about your folks? Will you tell them the truth?"

"Elijah is really bugging me to. But I just can't even——"

"Zeke can handle it."

"He can? And you've known Zeke how long?"

"OK, not very. But I know he loves you. He talks about you and Garrett loads. Even if it's weird at first, he'll be fine in the end."

"Maybe, maybe not. Garrett is gonna flip out big-style."

"So he'll just have to get over it."

"He'll never speak to me again, and he'll probably kick the shit out of Elijah. That would kill me."

"You love Elijah?"

"Maybe . . . It blows. This would be so much easier if it was just physical."

"And Elijah totally wants you to come out?"

"Yeah. He thinks I'm ashamed of him. Plus, he's majoring in psychology with a minor in gender studies, so he's all amped up on queer theory. He figures I'm betraying the gay community by not coming out. Says that every queer person who stays in the closet is making it harder for the people who are out."

"How's that?"

"Gay visibility. Making gay guys seem like a smaller minority than they actually are. *We* are. Whatever."

"Wow, that's rough."

"He's just so much cooler than I am. He like totally knows who he is, and he's not afraid of anything, or anyone."

"You're pretty cool yourself, you know?"

Wes sighed and said, "I'm so the dorky Francis brother."

"Which is still ten times cooler than most of the other guys in this town."

He grinned. "I mean, so yeah, I do have a hydrofoil surfboard."

"Why, yes you do. Don't worry, you'll figure this out, and you can talk to me whenever. Or I could talk to Elijah for you? Try to get him to take the pressure off? Actually, maybe Kelly could. They get along really well; they keep going out for mocktails and pancakes at Cafe Irie."

"Appreciate it, but I don't wanna drag anyone else into this jam, and it'd suck if I messed up their friendship, especially as Elijah doesn't have so many chick friends."

I nodded.

"Besides," he said, "you have your own problems."

Chapter Twenty-five

I looked into Wes's eyes, which were so similar to Zeke's, and my gut clenched. How could I tell Zeke that I still had feelings for Daniel? That I'd gone out to sea with him and let him kiss me?

A shadow came across Wes's face, as if he was deciding whether or not to say something he was supposed to keep to himself.

"Zeke's been through a lot."

Had he? It seemed to me like Zeke had practically walked on water for the past two years. Win after win, culminating in his epic storming of the Pipe Masters contest in Hawaii, and zillions of girls and sponsors wanting a piece of him. But maybe it was more complicated than that.

Zeke looked up, saw us and jogged over.

Zeke and Wes did their usual forearm-to-forearm handshake and Wes walked back to the others to rejoin the game.

"Wes OK?" he said.

"Yeah, just saying hey."

"Glad it's not awkward for you guys after that whole Spin-the-Bottle thing."

"We're fine now."

"So, you wanna play some ball?" he said.

There were no other girls playing, but any other day I would've given it a shot.

I shook my head. "But when you're finished, can we go for a dip?"

We walked down to the swimmers' section of the beach, which tended to be less busy in the evenings as it wasn't as good for surfing, and Zeke slung his T-shirt on the sand above the tideline and we piled our shoes on top of it. I already had my bikini on under my boardshorts, so once I ditched my flip-flops, I was good to go.

We swam out in the channel between sandbanks, letting the weak rip take us into the deeper, calmer water.

"Part of my training has been underwater work," Zeke said. "Anders has me grab a rock so that I don't cork back up to the surface, and then I walk with it a little way across the ocean floor. Not too deep, just say fifteen or twenty feet down. But it's really helping with the wipeouts. I figure if I can hold my breath for longer, then the risks get smaller."

"Wow, that's hardcore."

"It's working. I'm definitely not freaking out as much when I'm held down."

"Do you think that you should maybe move into surfing normal-sized waves?"

"There's nothing like the endorphin rush of riding the heavies. If you win the contest, you'll get to ride some of the big wave spots and you'll see what I mean."

"Come on, Zeke. Be real."

"That's OK. You don't believe yet. But you will."

Before I could answer, he grinned at me and said, "Race ya." He took off, swimming really fast overarm.

He was quick, but he wasn't quicker than me. I was right on his tail and within a minute, I was able to grab his foot. He swung round, smiling, and I released him. He grabbed me around the waist and kissed me lightly on the mouth. My lips tingled. I knew he was about to go in for another, deeper kiss and I had to stop him. We'd waited this long, and our first real kiss couldn't be messed up by my incredibly crappy judgment.

"I want you to know something," I said.

Bad choice of words. I could see by his embarrassed expression that he thought I was going for the "I love you." Shit. I'd screwed this up on top of all the other screw-ups.

"I'm so sorry. I've really messed up," I said. "When you didn't turn up the other day, and after that horrible conversation we had, I went out on a boat with Daniel and he, aah, kissed me."

He flinched. He'd had no idea. I could tell I'd totally shocked him. He spat some sea snot over his shoulder. When he looked back at me, his eyes had a look I hadn't seen there before. Confusion.

"What do you mean, 'kissed you'? Like a peck on the cheek?"

"More than that." This was torture. I wanted a wave to come and wash me to the moon. "I sort of let him get off with me."

"*Get off* with you? What the hell does that mean?"

"You know, a, um, French kiss."

"This is fucking bullshit," he said. "Why would you do that? Just because I banged some chicks before I even knew you?"

I shrugged, which in hindsight was not the best thing to do.

"I haven't been with *anyone* since I met you, Iris. And there've been tons of girls throwing themselves at me the past few weeks. We haven't even said what we are yet. But OK, I like you, so I've been waiting to figure out what this is. Then you go running back to your scumbag ex?"

Zeke shook his head like he couldn't believe what I was telling him, and then he said, "I'm outta here," and he dived down under the water and disappeared. He swam underwater all the way to shore. I was still bobbing in the calm waters beyond the break when I saw him reappear out of the surf and walk up the beach. I followed him, my face burning with every slow stroke of my arms.

I let a wave carry me through the last of the impact zone, and when I stood up on unsteady legs I saw Zeke sitting cross-legged on the sand, watching for me. When he saw I'd swum back to shore safely, he got to his feet and walked away. I saw him go past his brothers, but his head was down and he didn't answer their calls.

Garrett put down his baseball bat and followed him. Wes and Nils were right behind. The game went on without them. I saw Garrett catch up with Zeke and put his arm across the shoulders of his younger brother. Then Garrett looked back at me with this surprised look on his face. Wes caught up with them, turned to nod at me and together they disappeared into Fistral Blu Beach Bar, a swarm of starstruck girls following.

I'd really, truly blown it.

Chapter Twenty-six

OK, so I'd blown it, but that didn't mean I had to be silent for evermore. There were things I had to say to Zeke. Even if I never saw him again, there was stuff I needed to get off my chest. I texted him.

"I am so, so sorry."

My phone began to ring, belting out the special ringtone I'd picked for Zeke, which was "Fly" by Rihanna and Nicki Minaj. It just seemed right for him. What he did, racing down the curl of a wave, was pretty close to flying. For Daniel I had the chorus of Radiohead's "Creep."

I answered, but the line was silent and at first I thought he'd hung up. I spoke, in case.

"Daniel is damaged. I know that. I know I can't fix him. But I feel bad for him. Something happened with his dad and it messed him up."

"Like what?"

"Daniel's dad was an alcoholic who went on a drinking spree one day and drove home. He ran over two boys. They both died."

"No way. That's horrible."

"Yeah, and that's not even all of it. A few years after that, his dad got drunk again and committed suicide. Daniel was with his mom when she found the body. Daniel blames himself. Thinks he drove his dad to drink because he was such a naughty little kid."

"He really believes that?"

"Yeah. Obviously it isn't his fault, but he thinks it is. His dad's death affected him in all kinds of ways. Plus, it's the reason he won't let anyone call him Dan anymore. That's what his old man used to call him. I don't think Daniel will ever be OK again. But for a long time I thought I could help him, and even though I realize now I was wrong about that, I'll always care about him."

"OK, I get it," he said.

"You do?"

"Yeah, and I'm coming over."

We'd been here before.

"In the morning, yeah?"

"Now."

"All right."

I used the light from my phone to put on some dark-red lipstick and black eyeliner and I picked out the clothes I'd worn to the bars with Kelly and redressed in them. Cold or not, I wasn't going down to see Zeke looking like a slob. Not this time. He'd seen enough of me looking a state. Let him see me in a miniskirt for a change.

I waited in the garden for two minutes in that denim miniskirt before I went in to get my parka and some jeans. It was damn freezing, worse than the rookie mistake I used to make of winter surfing in a summer wetsuit, when it takes your feet forever to feel warm again, and you can't even speak without slurring because your lips are so frozen and numb.

When Zeke appeared, he was carrying a bunch of wilted flowers that looked as if he'd torn them from some hedgerow. It was a nice gesture though.

"My mom says wildflowers are the prettiest," he said, looking up at the window of my mom's bedroom.

He took my hand, and without saying anything more we walked out of the dark garden and toward the esplanade. Even blindfolded, we could have found our way. The pound of the waves was a constant, getting louder and louder as we got closer.

Zeke and I sat down with the wildflowers between us.

"It's not all your fault," he said. "I know I've been giving you mixed signals."

"So where were you the other morning? I know you apologized, but you never actually told me why you stood me up."

"I'm really sorry. I choked."

"So you just left me hanging? Like all day?"

"I got myself all worked up and I choked. It happened to me in the Waikiki Pro. And once at Pipeline too."

"You choked?"

"I know, I know. But it was like a panic attack or something. I let myself really feel it, you know? What was going on between us? I let myself feel what you mean to me. Suddenly I couldn't breathe and I didn't know what to do."

"You could have maybe called. Saved me from waiting for you all morning."

"I couldn't speak to you."

"Text message, Facebook, Twitter?"

"But what would I say? I didn't know how to explain it. I thought it would come to me, but it didn't. I called you that night a bunch of times, but you never picked up."

"Yeah, I wasn't in a great place either." I thought about the long, horrible night of shame after my boat trip with Daniel.

"What were we gonna do that morning, anyway?" I said. "What was the big plan?"

"Garrett's bought stakes in a couple local businesses. One of them is this insane Tough Mudder-style, SAS-designed obstacle course, which is like eight miles long and has electric shocks and fire. It looks awesome, but don't worry, it wasn't that! Not exactly first-date stuff. But he also bought into this other local business and he talked me into booking one of their rides. It cost like six hundred bucks, but when I thought about it, I worried you might think it was corny."

"Er, what kind of ride costs six hundred bucks?" I said.

"Hot-air balloon. They go out at sunrise and sunset, and travel real low along the coast. They've seen whales and dolphins out there, and I thought we could look for some new surf breaks."

"That sounds awesome," I said. "I would have loved that."

"Sorry I messed up," he said.

I sighed.

Then he said something that brought a small smile to my face: "So you want to date me, right?"

This was not exactly the way I'd have put it. For one thing, it would have been a lot nicer if he'd phrased it like it was something he wanted too.

He followed it with, "Because I really want to date you."

I looked at him and he was looking at me really earnestly, but there was a sadness in his eyes.

"Sounds like there's a 'but' coming up."

"There is."

"Don't tell me, you have a girlfriend in every stop on the surf circuit?"

"No." He laughed, as if he found the idea genuinely funny. "No, definitely not that. But I can't stay in Newquay forever."

"You have contests abroad. I know that."

"Yeah, I do. Indo, Hawaii, Chopes, Huntington Beach. And I have training weeks lined up in Dungeons in South Africa, Belharra in France, Puerto Escondido in Mexico, Outer Reef in Australia, El Buey in Chile. More tow-in big-wave training at Peahi in Maui. Anders wants me to settle on one specialism, but I can't seem to do that: I'm on the QS, but I also take off whenever I can to ride the code-red swells with the big-wave surfers. And I wanna keep making surf movies, so their publicity tours will take me pretty much everywhere else in the world. I'm gonna be homeless for the next five years at least."

He pulled out a cigarette but put it away when he saw the look on my face and said, "I'm quitting."

"OK," I said. "So this thing has an expiry date. I can live with that. I knew that it wouldn't last forever the moment I found out who you were."

An expiry date. Gross.

"It doesn't have to."

"You're totally not going to give up your career for me. You're too talented. People would think you were crazy. You're winning pretty much every contest you enter, and you stop? For a girl? You'd be sent to the loony bin. Plus, the last thing I want is a boyfriend who hates me for standing in the way of his dreams."

He nodded and looked me straight in the eyes. "I couldn't give up pro-surfing, even if I wanted to. I'm tied into contracts with my sponsors, and it's the only thing I've ever been any good at. I could never work in an office or something, and I'd be hopeless at college. I'd ditch my exams if the surf was good. So this is it for me. It's not just what I do. It's who I am. There's something else too, and it's bad."

"I promise I won't judge," I said, thinking guiltily about the last time Zeke had confided in me.

"That night at the surfboard launch party? When Anders asked me if I'd taken anything?"

"Yeah."

"He wasn't worried about some marijuana joint."

"OK. So why did he ask you that?"

"Because this time last year I was pumped up on meth."

"Huh?" I said, completely shocked. "You can't surf and do drugs."

"Yeah, you can. There's a reason the contests don't screen for drugs: too many guys would fail. Crystal meth gave me more energy, more stamina and more confidence. And it almost ruined my life."

"Seriously? You were a juice-head?"

He nodded. "At first it was small stuff. I got high and made an ass of myself in a few interviews: bragging about how I was gonna be World Champ by the time I was twenty, bitching about contest judges, throwing shade on the other guys on tour. One time a reporter asked me this super-obnoxious question about Andy Irons on the anniversary of Andy's death, and I pushed the guy into a pool. He had to be rescued by his photographer, 'cause he couldn't swim."

Andy Irons was a really popular pro-surfer from Kauai in Hawaii. He was a contest machine, the star of the Billabong team and he'd won three World Championships. Everyone thought he'd keep winning forever, because as well as being a really nice guy, he was unbelievably talented and massively driven. Andy died in a hotel room from a heart attack. He had drugs in his system.

Even though it happened a few years back, the surfing community was still shocked by his death, and I imagined it would have been especially bad for Zeke. As a Hawaiian surfer, he had probably grown up idolizing Andy Irons.

I gave Zeke a hug and could feel that he was shaking.

"Did the reporter press charges?"

"No, but he ran his mouth. Some other surf journalists had seen I was out of it and word got around quick. I lost a couple sponsors. I was lucky I didn't lose them all. Then things got real bad when I was on this surfari at Macaronis in the Mentawais. You ever been out there?"

"Er, no. I think I saw a picture of it once. Indonesia, right?"

"Yeah. I was with Garrett and Wes and one night they found me passed out in the bathroom of the hotel bar. I'd had the sweats all day and my heart had been beating hard, but I thought I could ride it out."

I absolutely hated to think of Zeke going through that and I wished I'd been there for him.

"I can't believe your brothers didn't notice."

"They noticed my eyes were messed up, but I told them it was arc-eye from the glare on the water."

"Arc-eye?" I said, racking my brains but coming up with nothing.

"You know, like snow blindness, except you can get it if you surf too long in tropical places. The UV light from the sun burns your cornea."

"They believed that?"

"Yeah, Garrett made Wes wash out my eyes with some chick's contact-lens solution and then someone found some local eye drops, which actually turned out to be nasal allergy drops and burned like a *mother*. But that's a whole other story. You gotta remember I was majorly secretive and they were drunk off their asses from too much Bintang Beer most nights. I'd taken some other shit that day as well as smoking meth, and I was ODing bad, but I was in denial. When my bros found me, they said they could barely feel a pulse. Lucky for me, they got to me before it was too late and I was medevaced to a hospital in Padang. Garrett said it was terrible."

I could feel my throat tightening up and the ache starting behind my eyes.

"Oh my God, Zeke. Your poor brothers."

"I know, right? I can't even imagine. I hung around the hospital for a day and then discharged myself. There was a thing, but Anders made it go away."

"A thing?"

"This one surf journalist was gonna run the story. Part of this big 'drugs in surfing' exposé. Anders stopped him."

"How'd he manage that?"

"No idea. Anders said it was best I didn't know."

That sounded like Anders: scheming away behind the scenes.

It was so much to take in. I just couldn't get my head around the idea that Zeke had been a druggie.

"Do you still crave meth?"

"Yes. Every damn day. Yoga and meditation help. I'm not perfect, Iris. You need to know that, because otherwise you're gonna be real disappointed."

"You don't have to be perfect. Why meth though? *Meth?*"

Meth was such a scary drug, and it seemed crazy that Zeke would risk his life by fooling around with something like that.

"Pro-surfing is a life of putting yourself out there to be judged by strangers. It messes up your head."

This from Zeke: the most confident, relaxed person I had ever met.

"I thought you loved being a pro-surfer."

"Sure I do. It's the best job in the world. Surf contests fuel my fire, because I'm super-competitive and, I mean, I love doing the giant-killer thing and beating the older, more experienced guys. The day I beat Kelly Slater in a contest heat was one of the best highs of my life."

"So what's the problem?"

"It's way hard. They don't call the QS 'The Grind' for nothing. It's constant travel and stress, and mostly you have no family or friends with you. You move around the world with the same group of surfers and hang out with them over and over and you start to think they're your friends, but the minute you hit the water for a contest heat, they hate your guts. My last contest in Steamer Lane, Santa Cruz, all the tour surfers were watching from the cliff, which is like thirty feet in the air and twenty yards from the line-up, so you can talk to the people up there if you want, and I could hear the guys on the cliff cheering for the other guy. They're my friends, but he's known them longer so they're cheering for him, hoping he beats me. Stuff like that makes you feel insecure, I guess, which is the last thing you need when your sponsors and team coaches have been hassling you like crazy to win."

I nodded. I knew I'd be psyched out in that situation.

"And sometimes you have a total shocker and get knocked out in the first round, even though you've done all the right training and followed the strategy. It's the pits. You're like, 'I'm surfing smart so why am I losing? Why isn't it coming together?' It's constant pressure. When I started winning, the pressure got even heavier. Every contest I surfed, I was being marked out of ten and people wanted to see eights and nines from me on every single wave. Meth just made it feel easier."

"Didn't it affect your surfing?"

"Sure. Methamphetamine gives your brain this intense high that makes you think you're invincible. I started taking crazy risks. Late drops, ignoring the shark flags at training grounds, trying to surf close-out sets. Slept with too many girls."

"Yeah, I figured out that last part."

"It was a crazy time. Before the thing in the Mentawais, Billabong had paid for a yacht for me and five of the other guys they sponsor. We lived on it for a couple months, sailing along the west coast of Australia. All we had to do was surf as much as we wanted and show up for contests. Obviously we checked out a lot of bars and clubs too. Not just in the cities. We found all kinds of cool little towns."

"So a group of six pro-surfers rock up to some small town bar? Girls must have been all over you."

"It's weird. We felt this pressure to act up, give them a good show, almost? Because like for us it was just a normal day, but for them it was the biggest night in their social calendar. That sounds super-egotistical and sketchy, right? But I'm being honest here and that's how it felt. So we just went for it, I guess."

"I kinda noticed you had a lot of girls' names in your phone."

"You checked out my iPhone?"

"Yeah, I'm so sorry. I didn't exactly mean to, but I picked it up and saw it was open on the Contacts page, so I caught a few names. Then I accidentally dropped it in your hot tub. I'm really sorry."

"Forget it. It's just a cell phone. Some of those girls are friends and some are girls I've dated. I keep their numbers in my phone so I know who's calling me. I've been blindsided a few times. I should just change my number."

"Honestly, don't feel like you have to. I was acting crazy insecure. Stuff with Daniel screwed me up. But I don't wanna be that person anymore. I wanna be here for you. If you ever need to talk, I'll listen. I'm really sorry you had to go through all that stuff."

"You know, I kidded myself that I was having the best time of my life. I was doing well financially. I paddled some monstrous waves. Got the covers of surf magazines. I picked up so many injuries, got more scars than I needed to get, broke bones, but somehow got through it alive. Anders sent me to rehab and got me clean. Wes and Garrett helped. Now I have to pay them all back by winning the QS and getting on to the ASP World Championship Tour. So I couldn't give up surfing, even if I wanted that."

"Right. So why can't we just see how it goes? Have a cool summer together?"

"Because I'm falling in love with you. And it gets worse every day. You're all I can think about. Even when I'm in the ocean, where I've always been able to relax and switch off, I'm thinking of you."

Why? I wanted to ask. Nobody had ever let me get into their head like that before. Daniel had been with me for ages and never even told me he loved me, and here was this amazing boy who was thinking about me when he should have been catching waves, and telling me that he was falling for me. It was nuts.

"If I'm ruining your surfing practice, we definitely shouldn't be going out."

"No, it's not like that. You're good for me. I'm just, I don't know, like, *better* or something around you. I want to work hard, so you can know me at my best. But I'm not stupid. I know you're sixteen. I get that."

"So what's the problem here?"

"I don't think I can do long distance. It's just not for me. I'd be no good at it."

"You'd cheat on me."

"No. I'd really miss you. It'd suck and I'd hate it."

"So what am I supposed to do? Run away with you and travel the world?"

"No . . . Yeah. Maybe."

"Like you said, I'm sixteen."

"If you get sponsorship and parental approval, you can come on tour."

"I'm up against Saskia. There's no way that I'm going to get sponsorship. I only started surfing a few summers ago. I'm not good enough yet."

I didn't want to point out that I'd never in a million years get parental approval.

"You are good enough. Anyways, Lisa Andersen didn't start surfing until she was fifteen."

Lisa Andersen lived rough under a pier, or on a bench or something, after running away from home. I wasn't tough enough for that. I also couldn't make my mom worry about me. She didn't deserve that. True, Lisa Andersen had gone on to win four World Surf Championships, but what were the chances that would happen to me?

"Anders thinks you have what it takes."

"Anders thinks I look nice in a bikini."

"Sure you do, and that does count. Looks are important in this business, and especially the female side of it. It's stupid, and my mom is totally right when she says surfer girls shouldn't have to be 'the patriarchy's cutest dolls' or whatever. But it comes back to money. The surf companies run the major contests, and the whole surf industry exists through selling merchandise, mostly to non-surfers who want to look like surfers. Good-looking chicks sell stuff. Queebs do great in pro-surfing. They've got the looks and the own-it attitude."

Queebs were queen bees who strutted around the beach like they were God's gift. I hated them. There was no way I was going to be one.

He was right about them bringing in money though. So many surfer girls were growing their hair long, getting nose jobs, even boob jobs. In the past it didn't matter so much what you looked like. No surfer was a mainstream celebrity. I guessed people like Kelly Slater and Lisa Andersen had changed that. You had to look good now, especially if you were a girl.

It wasn't easy though. Surfing builds up muscle, which is why so many female surf pros are built like brick shithouses. They're not at all fat, but once you hit twenty, it's hard for all that strength training not to bulk you out. So if you want to be a celeb surfer, a pin-up girl, you really have to break out while you're still a teenager, while you're still at your lightest and leanest. I knew from reading *Surf Girl* magazine that the pressure to be thin and pretty had destroyed careers.

"OK, so just say we *can* run off together, what then?"

"Then life happens. We see a lot of really cool places, catch a lot of sweet waves and have the time of our lives. What's not to like?"

I thought about that. I would miss my family and Kelly. But this would be an incredible opportunity and I'd be stupid not to consider it. But then the sensible side of my brain kicked in again. I imagined myself after a fight with Zeke, stranded somewhere like Morocco. Not knowing the language, and not having any money, or any way of getting home. All my female acquaintances would be my competitors. I'd have no Kelly. No Lily. No Mom. I'd be totally reliant on a boy. This boy I'd only just met. I'd rushed head first into an intense relationship with a boy once before and it had ended in disaster.

"What if we split up?" I said.

"Let's just live for today and see what happens. I wouldn't be suggesting this if I didn't think we had a really good shot of making it work."

I sighed and stretched back on to the cold grass. The crazy thing was that we were discussing things that were months and years ahead and *still* he hadn't properly even kissed me. How much longer could this go on?

And then the stars were darkened by his silhouette leaning down to me.

I can remember the kisses I'd had with other boys quite clearly, and lots of the vanilla kisses with Daniel. But it wasn't the same with Zeke. Something different happened with Zeke.

It was a really deep kiss and I remembering thinking, *Wow, our mouths and noses fit together perfectly.* No awkward readjustment; just totally in sync with each other. But there was more than that. It was the most hardcore intense feeling. I wasn't thinking about what to do with my mouth, or if my breath smelled of coffee, or wondering how many other girls Zeke had kissed and how this kiss compared to them. I was just totally one hundred percent in the moment.

I was still kissing him when I rolled so that I was on top of him. I could feel that things were getting serious when we were interrupted by a drunk old man who'd walked quite close to us and shouted, "Young lovers."

Then he added, "Should get a room."

We laughed and sat up. Zeke's lips had a faint stain of my dark lipstick.

"So, are you my girl, Iris?"

"Damn straight," I said, laughing and reaching to move a strand of hair that had fallen across his face.

It was a killer high. And I realized that the more I was around him, the more comfortable I was becoming with him physically. I was even getting used to that gorgeous face, although I still got butterflies whenever he looked right into my eyes and smiled.

Still, I knew we had to accept the fact that if I didn't succeed at Wavemasters and grab the sponsorship from Saskia, Zeke and I would be over. He would go back to his life as a surf champ, adored by zillions of girls the world over, and I'd go back to my life working in a shop and being completely ordinary.

Something I'd learned from being around someone extraordinary, someone with extraordinary talent, was that it was addictive. I wanted a bit of Zeke's magic to sprinkle down on to me and make me extraordinary too.

I looked at him, at those eyes, which for once weren't full of laughter but were deadly serious. And I felt the pull between us, the air rushing away and sucking us closer together. He fell away beneath me and the ache in me was lost to the feel of his body under mine, and my lips on his throat and down to that stomach, which I'd first caught a glimpse of in a yoga class forever ago.

We rounded second and third bases, but stopped it there, as neither of us was prepared, figuratively or literally.

When the sun came up, I saw him at the edge of the grass staring out to the sea.

He was watching the surf, figuring out how it was working, where the peaks and rips were, how the wind was moving, and how the tide was affecting everything. To plan his next surf was in his blood.

When he turned to me, his look of pure happiness showed me that I had been wrong. He wasn't weighing up the surf after all. His eyes were just drifting as he thought about something else. Us.

Then I knew that, for now at least, I was his and he was mine and it would take a lot to mess that up.

If I could just win sponsorship, the years ahead of us could always be this golden.

But how could I do that?

Chapter Twenty-seven

The Saltwater Pro Junior Men's Contest was in full swing. Me and Kelly were on a stripy beach blanket with a picnic and an umbrella, and about fifty thousand other people had the same idea. The skateboard contest was heating up behind me, with all kinds of lunatic stuff going down in the half-pipe, including a broken leg. To my right, the *Nuts* magazine Wet-T-shirt Competition was being judged, and there were more news cameras at work there than in any other area of the beach. Only five long lenses were on the men's surf event and not many beach-goers seemed to be watching the contest either.

The buzzer had just gone for Zeke's first-round heat. He was in the blue jersey and a Brazilian surfer called Silvio was in the yellow. Word in the pro-tent was that Silvio had a reputation for dangerous charging and a bad attitude. He was currently placed fourth, and Zeke was placed sixth, due to him missing a contest while he was convalescing and hanging around in Newquay with me.

Despite the general lack of interest in the surf contest, Zeke still had a following. At least a dozen girls made a guard of honor for him to walk through on the way to the waterline. They didn't care about surfing. They wouldn't care less about what he did in the water. They just cared that he was relatively famous guy with a hot body and a gorgeous face. As the days went on, Zeke had been getting noticed more and more around Newquay, probably because of the *Cosmo Girl* feature.

I wondered how many girls had that picture on their walls. I hated the way girls would look at Zeke, even when I was right there. A couple of girls had even gone in for the blatant ass-pinch, which I thought was just sad. I totally got why girls were attracted to Zeke, but it was still horrible to see how they threw themselves at him. Garrett told me that this kind of thing happened to Zeke pretty much everywhere they went and that certain girls who followed the surf scene were always desperate to get a one-second grope of a high-ranking pro-surfer. More, if they could. *Pro-hoes*, Garrett called them, which I thought was a bit strong. Zeke shrugged off the attention, but after the ass-gropes I could tell he was embarrassed and fed up of being treated like that. Like some brainless piece of meat.

I looked over to Kelly, who was texting on her phone, saying something flirty to Garrett by the looks of it. Then I turned my eyes back to Zeke and Silvio and watched as the two of them dipped through the impact zone, Zeke reaching the line-up first. He took the first wave, threw a really sharp turn on the steepest, most shreddable part of the wall with a vertical snap off the lip, but whitewash was coming at him from two directions and there was nowhere to go. It was a bad wipeout, with him twisting kind of funny as he hit the water. He came up after a couple of seconds and went straight back out. That wave was scored a 4.79. Silvio took the next wave—the biggest in the set—made the drop and got tubed. The judges awarded him a 7.68.

Zeke had a lot of ground to make up. In the lull I could see him talking to Silvio, laughing about something. So much for the Brazilian's bad attitude.

Silvio went for another wave, gathered speed and found a ramp for the air section, but mistimed it and did a backflip while his board went in the other direction. Wipeout. 3.92 score. Then a beautiful right-hander peeled away and Zeke was in the perfect position on the perfect wave. All of his grace and flexibility came together in a sequence of moves that he'd practiced on our first surf together when we'd paddled out after yoga class.

I couldn't believe that was my boyfriend out there. He was incredible. I knew he had a serious work ethic and said the ocean was his office, but seeing him work those waves, my whole body ached with longing for him and I knew for sure that I was the luckiest girl in the entire world.

I crossed my fingers for a big score but was pretty confident, because that last wave had to be considered a "wave of conse-quence" and Zeke's ride would surely be scored in the excellent range. I was right. 8s and 9s from all five judges, averaging a 9.23. The buzzer sounded again. Zeke had won the heat and would advance to the next round. The Brazilian looked annoyed, but that was to be expected. He shook Zeke's hand and ran off to the competitors' tent, where he was greeted by a couple of big-boobed massage therapists in polka-dot bikinis.

I jumped up to greet Zeke. I went for the fist bump, but he swept me off my feet and kissed me. I could tell he was psyched. He was literally trembling with the high of winning. After two years of pro-surfing, I thought all the contest craziness would be normal to him. Apparently not.

Zeke set me down and said hi to Kelly. Then he looked around and said, "Have you seen my parents? They said they'd swing by for my heats."

"No, sorry."

"I guess they lost track of time. It's OK. They've watched me surf a million contests."

He had a few hours so I bought him a veggie burger, chips and Coke as he was ravenous and needed all the calories he could get for the next round heat. All eyes were on us in the cafe. I wasn't sure if Zeke was recognized, or whether the stares were because he had stripped down to just his boardshorts. I had bought a strappy orange dress from the Quiksilver summer sale and new flip-flops, but even at my most glam I still felt like a total trog next to Zeke. As usual, he was ignoring the stir he was causing, and I wasn't going to flag it up.

"You were great out there," I said. "You really knew how to read those waves."

"I came down to the beach last night with Garrett to watch the water."

"Couldn't sleep?"

"Oh, I was super-sleepy, but I knew I'd be starting my heat at midday, so I thought I'd come take a look at midnight, to see how that tide level worked against the ocean floor."

I smiled. That was just classic Zeke: always trying to learn more and figure out ways to surf better.

I offered to pay for a beer from the downstairs bar for Zeke, but he was absolutely against that. He couldn't even risk one bottle of beer, he said, because even that small amount of alcohol could screw up his balance. We walked back down to the beach and the results board showed that Zeke was up against a wild-card entry, who would be wearing a white jersey. Zeke was getting suited up again and pulling his blue jersey over the top, when I spotted the wild card.

Daniel.

He had been invited to compete in Saltwater? Every year they invited two locals, but the organizers had picked Daniel? Maybe his new lifeguard crew had arranged it for him. Whatever, this was mega. The whole of the professional surf scene was here. All the sponsors, all the agents and promoters. If Daniel caught a perfect wave here, things could change for him overnight. All that stood in his way was Zeke.

Zeke spotted Daniel about two seconds after I did, and I saw the realization pass over his face. Daniel waved, but Zeke only gave him a chilly nod.

"He's just a wild card," I said.

"I know."

"I guess if you'd pressed charges then he wouldn't be here."

"He'd be here."

Daniel came over, put his hand out and Zeke shook it. Daniel could barely make eye contact.

"I didn't know I'd be up against you, man," Daniel said. "I didn't expect to win my first heat."

"No sweat."

"I feel shit about what went down, but I still have to beat you here, OK?"

"Well, you can try, dude."

Daniel shrugged and said, "May the best man win."

"Yeah," Zeke said. "He's gonna."

The buzzer sounded and they ran down to the water. Kelly and Garrett were walking up from South Fistral, where they had been surfing, judging by the beginner foamie under Kelly's arm and the fish board under Garrett's. Kelly's eyes were popping out on stalks as Zeke and Daniel ran into the water.

They came straight over.

"Am I tripping or is that the guy whose nose I broke?"

"Yeah, he's the wild card."

"He's like scabies," Kelly said. "He gets everywhere."

"Gross, but accurate," I said.

Daniel caught the first wave, but a big section closed out and sent him flying. Zeke was on the second and almost took off Daniel's head as Daniel surfaced in the zone. Somehow Zeke missed him and turned toward the lip, floated on the crest and dropped back in. At 7.33, Daniel would find the ride difficult to beat. Daniel punched through and made the line-up, took off too fast and wiped out again. It was embarrassing. He had to calm down, or he was going to score zero. Zeke stayed away from Daniel in the lull and looked toward shore for a moment. I waved but he couldn't find me in the crowd and he didn't wave back. The next set was pristine and breaking in one long beautiful curl. It was slightly outside, so Daniel and Zeke stroked out to position themselves for takeoff. Whoever reached the crest first and got to their feet would have right of way, so it was a full-on race. Zeke had better paddle technique and his board skimmed perfectly through the water, but Daniel had desperation on his side, and they were neck and neck.

Daniel messed up the turn to shore, and Zeke got to his feet first. Zeke had priority, but Daniel went for it anyway and was flagged for interference. Daniel slid down the back of the wave, and watched, just totally humiliated, as Zeke pulled a frontside grab-rail reverse aerial, which was something I'd never seen any surfer manage. It was a highly technical aerial trick, where a surfer grabbed the edge of the board and then did a 360 high in the air, but rotating in the opposite direction from whatever momentum they'd built. It scored Zeke a 9.62.

With only one minute left on the clock, Daniel scratched for the next wave but it was junky slop with no power and he was only riding for five seconds. He managed a 3.90. That was his only scoring wave. It was a total hammering. Daniel had been humiliated by Zeke in front of the entire competitive-surf community. He'd choked and blown it, big time. The buzzer sounded again and Zeke paddled in, but Daniel stayed out there, desperate to catch another wave to redeem himself. He was being warned over the loudspeaker to come in but he just ignored it. An overhead wave reared up and Daniel took off, only to wipe out once more. It was not his day. He should have quit when he was told, because now a lot of people were watching.

Eventually he came in, tore off his white jersey, threw it on the ground and went straight to his car without saying a word. Bad, bad loser. Zeke was trying not to grin, but failing. His fan club surrounded us, the cameras on their phones clicking overtime.

Zeke never got to surf his next round heat.

Running up the beach were Wes and Elijah.

"Come on," Wes urged Zeke and Garrett. "We've gotta get to the hospital."

And then he said it:

"Nanna's had a stroke. It's bad."

Chapter Twenty-eight

Nanna was only in the hospital for two days before they moved her to a hospice.

"Come visit her with me?" Zeke asked.

"Yeah, of course I will," I said, grabbing his hand.

Zeke drove us there in his camper van, but hardly said a word during the whole journey. As he reversed into a space in the hospice car park, I saw Garrett's green motorbike and pointed it out to Zeke.

"Wes is here too," he said, nodding at the hospice entrance, where Wes was talking to someone on his cell phone. I jumped out while Zeke was rooting around in the van for a card and a basket of flowers and I heard Wes say, "That's bull. You know how I feel."

Wes turned around, saw us and flinched.

"I gotta go. I'll hit you up later," he said, and hung up.

"Chick troubles?" Zeke asked.

Wes just shrugged and said, "Tough day. Go sign in and then I'll show you to Nanna's room."

Nanna was lying flat in her bed. The left half of her face had slumped, there was drool at the side of her mouth, and she could hardly talk. But when she saw Zeke, she smiled and started moving her good hand in an undulating motion. Then she grabbed a Get Well Soon card, turned it on its side and skimmed it along the bedcovers, like a surfboard.

"I think she's saying she wants to go to the beach and watch some surfing," I said. "Is that right, Nanna?"

She nodded vigorously.

"Nanna, you wanna go to Fistral?" Garrett asked.

She nodded again, her eyes wide with hope.

"We can't take her," Wes said flatly.

"Why not?" said Garrett. "The doc says she's only got one or two days left, if she's lucky. Her body's, like, filling with fluid or whatever as her heart shuts down."

"Dude. She can hear you," Zeke said.

"She knows. So let's give her one last awesome memory. Take her to go see the surf."

"What if it kills her, bro?" Wes said.

"Then she dies by the ocean instead of in this fugly hospice."

"Feel how cold her hand is, even under all these covers," I said. "She is gonna be freezing in the sea air."

Zeke nodded. "Iris is right. So we're gonna have to keep her as warm as possible. We'll have to take a ton of blankets."

"Can we really do this?" I said.

"No," Wes said. "We can't."

"Just one hour," Zeke said. "And then we'll bring her back."

Garrett exhaled. "OK. We're making this happen. Let's go."

"Right now?" I said.

Zeke raked his hand through his hair and said, "We can't just waltz her through the lobby. How are we supposed to get her out of here?"

"Window," Garrett said.

Nanna was smiling her lopsided smiled and waving her fist around.

"Seriously, bro?" Wes said.

"Do it."

Wes sighed and cracked open the window. Garrett went to Nanna and gently lifted her out of her bed.

I stood next to Wes and looked out of the open window. The hospice was on a hill, so it was going to be a drop of maybe seven feet.

"It's gonna be tricky getting her out," I said.

Very gently, Garrett handed Nanna to Wes.

"I'm not throwing Nanna out a fucking window," Wes said.

"So you wanna catch her then?" said Garrett.

"OK, so I'll pass her down. Man, this is not gonna end well."

Zeke turned to me and said, "Baby, can you go tell the receptionist that Nanna is resting and that we'll be staying with her for a couple hours? Ask her to give us some time to say goodbye?"

I nodded and tried not to blush because Zeke had just called me baby for the very first time.

He carried on: "Then, once you're back, lock the door. We'll get her back before they even know she's gone."

I did it and the receptionist smiled and said that was absolutely fine and that she understood that people needed to say goodbye in their own way and in their own time.

Little did she know.

When I got back to the room, I asked, "Who's catching her?"

"I am," Garrett said. "Zeke's driving."

I watched as Wes passed Nanna down to Garrett and Zeke, then I gathered some of her blankets and scrambled out after them, landing in Zeke's waiting arms. Garrett wrapped Nanna in the blankets and carried her into the back of Zeke's camper van. Wes and I jumped in the back too, holding Nanna still so that she wouldn't get slammed against any of the surfboards as Zeke took the corners. He drove at maybe ten miles an hour, if that, all the way to the esplanade.

Nanna's eyes sparkled with excitement when she clapped eyes on the surfers out in the line-up. Seventy-five years old, but she was buzzing like a grom.

"Water," she whispered.

Garrett took Nanna in his arms and carried her down the old stone steps and past Bodhi's, where Zeke's family had gone to celebrate after they'd taken Nanna for her final tandem-surf.

How quickly things could change.

Nanna kept saying "ocean," so Garrett waded into the sea up to his knees and Nanna tilted her head back so that she could see the surfers, the breakers rolling in and the backwash swirling around Garrett's legs.

We were standing a little way behind Garrett, in the shallower water, but Nanna moved her head and motioned for us to wade deeper so she could see us and the waves. Wes, Zeke and I stood apart, thigh-deep in the sea, and looked back to Nanna. Then Zeke threw his arm over Wes's shoulders and turned to me to take my hand.

Nanna smiled.

Garrett's face was stern and I could see that he was only just holding it together. Then Nanna started wriggling in Garrett's arms, her fingers reaching for the baby waves. Garrett bent his knees to let her splash the water. When he looked up, I couldn't tell if his face was wet from the sea or his tears. Maybe it was both.

The tide was coming in fast and the sand getting even more tightly packed with tourists. Garrett wanted to walk up the beach where it was quieter, but someone was having a fire and Nanna started whimpering when we walked past.

"I think she wants to stay here," I said to Garrett, who looked down at his grandmother and smiled.

"Then this is where we stay."

Some of the surfrats were passing around a bottle of whisky and, as it went past, Nanna reached her hand out for it.

"Is she on meds? Is she even allowed to have some?" Wes asked.

"Yeah. And yeah," Garrett said.

"She wants it, she gets it," Zeke said.

Garrett took a swig, then put the bottle to Nanna's lips. She drank deeply, and then lay back on to the sand and looked up at the sky.

"Tired," she mouthed.

"You can't sleep here, Nanna," Wes said. "We gotta get you home."

She waved her good hand around at the beach. This was her home. The beach was home to all of us.

Then she whispered, "Kiss me," and Garrett, Wes, Zeke and I planted light kisses on her cheeks, lips and forehead.

"She's shivering," I said.

Half a dozen of the surfrats sitting around the fire handed hoodies and sweaters down to me and one kid passed down his beanie hat. Garrett, Zeke and Wes loaded her up with the clothes, covering her head, lap and shoulders. Then they huddled around her: Garrett behind, with his arms wrapped around her waist; Zeke and Wes on either side of her. A triangle of body heat keeping their grandmother warm. Their own little boat.

Nanna closed her eyes and almost immediately strange gasps and gurgles started up in her throat.

Wes turned to Garrett and said, "She's hardly breathing. We need to get help."

"Leave her be," Garrett said.

"Zeke, come on. She's gonna croak out here."

"I think I can live with that," Zeke said.

"We're gonna be in deep shit if the cops find out about this. Zeke, you could get into trouble with your sponsors. And you really don't need any more heat in that department."

"Screw 'em."

Nanna took one huge breath and then stopped breathing altogether. Her face looked calm, ancient and beautiful.

Garrett's eyes were full of pissed-off tears and Wes was white as a sheet. Zeke stroked Nanna's hand, his fingers light on the paper-thin skin.

The surfrats gathered around, quiet and respectful. Garrett gave them back their clothes and then carried Nanna in his arms across the beach to Zeke's camper van, laid her on the spare duvet and pillow that Zeke kept in there, and Wes and I jumped in next to her. Garrett and Zeke walked around to the front of the van.

I closed Nanna's eyes and then Zeke drove back to the hospice.

He swung into the car park, backed up the van so it was near Nanna's window and we got her back in the way we took her out.

Zeke ran at the wall, scrambled through the window and into the room and then leaned back out, hands stretching down. Garrett and Wes held Nanna up and Zeke took her.

Garrett gave me and Wes a leg-up, and then he climbed the wall and shut the window behind him.

The room was so silent.

Zeke brushed the sand off Nanna's cheek and I combed it out of her hair. Then Zeke laid Nanna gently in her bed and Garrett pulled the covers up and over her.

Wes was silent, Garrett was flushed with the effort of holding in tears, but Zeke looked at Nanna and smiled.

Because, even after she had passed, on Nanna's face there was a look of pure stoke.

Chapter Twenty-nine

There was to be a Paddle Out for Nanna, which is how surfers remember their fallen comrades.

Everyone was welcome. Nanna's family and friends were there and plenty of the Fistral tribe had turned up with their boards to paddle out to the calm water beyond the break, where they would sit in a circle and honor Nanna.

Garrett, Wes and Zeke stood together on the beach. Dave was there, supported by Sephy. Elijah was there too, standing next to Kelly, who had a rented swell board under her arm. Anders and Saskia were in Florida, meeting with a few New Smyrna Beach surfers that had started to get attention, but they both sent bouquets of roses, which we stripped for petals.

I went up to Kelly, and Elijah turned to me and said, "How's Zeke doing?"

"Devastated."

"Garrett too," Kelly said. "He's been telling me all these stories about her and then he gets angry when it makes him cry. He couldn't sleep properly so he's smoking this rank damn weed to try and make himself all calm and chill, but I think it's actually making him worse. He's all over the place."

I nodded. Kelly would help him though. She was really good at striking a balance between tough love and sympathy and it seemed to me that Garrett needed both.

"What about Wes?" I asked Elijah.

"I dunno really. Shut down. Not saying much at all. I just wish he'd let me in, you know? But he won't. Says he can handle it. He's so self-contained it drives me crazy. It's like he doesn't trust me enough to let down the walls. He hasn't cried *once*. But he's hardly eating, and I caught him necking vodka on the sly."

"Just be patient," Kelly said. "He'll open up when he's ready."

"Don't think so. If anything, this has made him pull away from me even more."

"He knows you care about him."

"Does he? I don't think he has any damn idea. It's like he finds the whole concept of two guys caring about each other absolutely excruciating. Yesterday, I said, 'Wes, I really love you,' and he just looked at me and said, '*Mahalo*.' Then he went surfing."

"Ouch," I said, remembering the many, many times that Daniel had pulled that sort of thing with me.

"Do you think he's going to tell his folks about you?" Kelly said.

"Probably not. He hates confrontation and is scared to death of any big emotional scene that might involve, you know, feelings being talked about. I don't know how much longer I can go on like this. He acts so weird in public. I have to stay like two feet away from him at all times. I touched his hand in the Central last week and he flinched so hard he almost choked on an ice cube. So now we practically never leave my apartment."

"He wants to move in with you though, and he invited you here today, right?" I said. "That's gotta mean something."

"Dunno what," Elijah said. "All I know is that I can't stand being put in the closet again. I already busted out of it once."

Kelly took Elijah's hand, and I could see the strain in his eyes. She gave him a long hug and then we all turned to look at the three brothers, grouped so closely together—Zeke gesturing and shouting something to Sephy, Garrett sucking on a cigarette and Wes waxing his board—and I thought about how they'd totally changed our lives. It was scary to think how gray my days would have been if Nanna hadn't moved back to Newquay. I'd never have met the Francis family; they'd just be another bunch of strangers living their lives in a foreign country that I'd probably never visit.

A bunch of kids joined our group and looked around, waiting for someone to give the sign to start. There were silver surfers present too, who didn't look much younger than Nanna. Maybe they had even tandem-surfed with her back in the day.

After twenty minutes there were at least a hundred surfers gathered for Nanna. Dave thanked everyone for being there for his amazing mom. Then he gave the nod and we all paddled out together.

It took a while for so many of us to get into the right position, but eventually we'd made a wide circle.

Dave wanted his family to read out a poem that Nanna had loved. We'd all been given a line to recite, even me, Kelly and

Elijah. We'd practiced in the morning, and we had our lines scribbled on the noses of our boards.

The poem was "The Deep" by John G. C. Brainard, and it went like this:

There's beauty in the deep:—
The wave is bluer than the sky.
And though the light shine bright on high,
More softly do the sea-gems glow.
That sparkle in the depths below.
The rainbow's tints are only made
When on the waters they are laid,
And Sun and Moon most sweetly shine
Upon the ocean's level brine.
There's beauty in the deep.

There's music in the deep:—
It is not in the surf's rough roar,
Nor in the whispering, shelly shore—
They are but earthly sounds, that tell
How little of the sea-nymph's shell,
That sends its loud, clear note abroad.
Or winds its softness through the flood,
Echoes through groves with coral gay,
And dies, on spongy banks, away.
There's music in the deep.

There's quiet in the deep:—
Above, let tides and tempests rave,

And earth-born whirlwinds wake the wave.

Above, let care and fear contend,

With sin and sorrow to the end:

Here, far beneath the tainted foam,

That frets above our peaceful home,

We dream in joy, and wake in love,

Nor know the rage that yells above.

There's quiet in the deep.

Sephy sang a Polynesian song about love, her voice sounding out over the water as clear as if she had a microphone, and the rest of us threw handfuls of sunset-colored petals into the sea.

Dave paddled into the middle of our circle and upturned a bag of ashes on to the water, where they glistened in the sunlight, silver and perfect, before melting away.

Then, we surfed.

Chapter Thirty

The Nike Night Surf Amateur Men's Event was gearing up. Locals were invited to compete, and Elijah, Wes and Garrett had entered. Zeke, as a sponsored professional surfer, was excluded. Dave worked as a paramedic and had to do a night shift, but Sephy, Zeke and I had come out to watch and cheer.

Wes had arrived earlier in the evening and had already paddled out by the time we got there. Garrett hadn't suited up yet, but was up to his knees in the sea over by the rocks, watching Wes surf. Garrett was smoking the biggest joint I'd ever seen, which maybe wasn't that clever, since a ton of photographers with long lenses were hard at work in the shallows and he was standing right in the middle of them.

It was almost eleven o'clock, but the whole of North Fistral was lit up with floodlights, chill-out dance music was blaring through the PA system and, in the freakishly windless night, the smoke of countless barbecues was drifting like sea fog. Plenty of kids were out with their parents, and hundreds of surfers were gathered outside Fistral Blu Beach Bar, huddled under the patio heaters, drinking beer. All in all, it seemed like a perfect night to watch some kick-ass surf tricks.

I caught Zeke staring longingly down at the break, and I couldn't blame him. The sea looked fabulous: the surf was heavy and clean, the tide was in and the breakers were glowing neon green and luminous white in the phosphorescent lights.

Zeke had driven us there, and he was probably the only person to actually pay for parking that night, as one of the surfrats was dishing out lines of black electrical tape to cover up number plates, so the Parking Eye cameras couldn't catch out any motorists and slap them with a hundred-and-twenty-dollar fine.

"But parking costs, like, a dollar fifty for the whole night!" Zeke said, laughing, as he slid his money into the parking-meter slot.

So that we wouldn't drift off, Zeke and I took a walk down the beach and watched a flock of oystercatchers bombing over the waves. He kissed me for ages, even though I was quite embarrassed about his mom seeing.

"She knows how we feel," he said, shrugging. "You can probably stay over with me at Pa's place any time you want, by the way."

"Really?"

"Yeah, but I guess you should maybe keep your head clear for your training?"

"I suppose. And we couldn't, you know . . . Not with your folks in the house. It would be too weird. They'd *know*."

"We wouldn't have to do anything and it'd be way cool to wake up with you, but yeah, we probably shouldn't, like, torture each other," he said, laughing, and looking at the bottom of my jeans, which were wet and caked in sand. My feet were so frozen on the icy night sand that they were starting to go numb.

I rolled up my jeans, and Zeke crouched down so I could jump up on to his back. I hooked my arms and legs over him and he gave me a piggyback ride up to our deckchairs, both of us squinting in the lights beaming down at us from eight different directions; I knew it would be super-difficult for the surfers to position themselves in the water with those blinding spotlights in their faces and I hoped the guys could handle it.

The Night Surf wasn't a normal surfing event. There'd be no competitive man-on-man heats, but instead there was going to be one big Expression Session, with everyone out there scratching for waves at the same time. Whoever got snapped doing the best trick, as decided by a team of Nike photographers, would win a vacation to a surf camp in Lacanau in France, plus a grand in cash.

By the time we got back to our spot, Kelly had arrived and she'd brought a bag of old-fashioned sweets with her, which she was sharing with Sephy. Just as we'd finished the sweets and had started on the free energy drinks that various Nike reps were handing out, Elijah turned up and walked over to us.

Kelly jumped up to say hey.

"Wes around?" Elijah said to her.

"Already out there and absolutely ripping. Come on, I'll show you."

Kelly took his arm and they walked down to the waterline. Zeke pulled me up out of my deckchair and we followed them down to the water's edge, while Sephy kept an eye on our stuff.

Garrett waded out of the water to meet us. He nodded at Elijah, stuck the surfboard under his arm and said, "You know how to ride that? Had you figured for a dick-dragger."

"Been surfing a stand-up for ten years, dude."

"Never saw you on Fistral before."

"Mostly surf Watergate Bay and Crantock. Quieter."

"Wes surfs Watergate. That how you know him?" Garrett said, eyeballing Elijah quite blatantly.

"Nope."

Garrett blew out his smoke so hard that it whirled around Elijah's face.

Zeke looked at me, no doubt picking up on the hostile atmosphere. And that was when a group of boys who'd been standing nearby, earwigging, decided to walk our way. As they moved past us, one of them made eye contact with Garrett and then another one bumped Elijah and coughed a word that sounded a lot like: "Faggot."

Kelly spun around and said, "Get lost," and then added her new favorite insult: "microwang."

Zeke looked taken aback and murmured, "Wow, there are some real assholes in this town."

Garrett raised his eyebrows and said, "That why you don't surf Fistral, Elijah?"

"Is *what* why?"

"Y'know."

"Because everyone here hates fags and they know I am one?"

"You tell me."

"Garrett," Kelly said, "don't be such a prick."

"He's asked Wes to move in with him. You know that, Zeke?"

"Yeah, he knows," Elijah said, coolly. "Wes gave Zeke our spare key and he's helping with the boxes."

"So they'll be roommates. What's the big deal?" Zeke said to Garrett, looking uncomfortable.

"Wes is moving in on Monday," Elijah continued, looking Garrett straight in the eye, "if you want to lend a hand."

Garrett and Elijah were getting really close to one another. Each of them had their shoulders back and their chests were sticking out.

"Why don't you leave my brother alone? You're always following him around. Sucking up to him like some ugly-ass leech," Garrett said. "Does he even know what you are?"

Zeke slid in between them and forced them apart. "*Stop*," he said. "Y'all need to chill the hell out."

"He's trying to turn Wes gay."

"You can't *turn* someone gay. They're, like, born that way or whatever. And we'd know if Wes was gay, so cool it."

Sephy, smelling trouble, had come down to the waterline. She plucked the joint out of Garrett's mouth, took a drag, and said, "Garrett, Wes is waiting for you. You too, Elijah. Paddle out together."

"No," Garrett said, through gritted teeth.

"No?"

"Stay out of it, Mom."

Sephy smiled and said, "Out of what, Garrett?"

Garrett looked at his mom, and then looked back at Elijah, and said, "Screw it," and stormed off without even bothering to take his board with him. We watched as he walked between the Nike sails, past the lifeguards' building and on toward town, where he would no doubt hit every pub on the main street.

"You going after him?" I said to Kelly.

"Why should I? If he wants to act like a toddler, that's up to him, but I'm not his babysitter."

"Right on, sister," Sephy said, taking another drag and looking up at the stars.

Kelly squeezed Elijah's shaking hand and whispered so quietly that I could only just hear it, "He doesn't know how great you are yet. But he will. One day he totally will," and Elijah looked down at her with real affection in his eyes.

Then Zeke looked back at the giant digital clock suspended from the beach-complex railings behind us and said, "You'd better get out there, man," and we watched as Elijah struck out into the waves and paddled straight for Wes.

Two hours later, the Nike photographer projected the winning photograph on to the long white wall of the judging marquee and presented Elijah with an envelope of cash and two air tickets. The trick that won him the contest? A perfect board-switch. The photographer caught the split second that Wes and Elijah were in midair, as each of them jumped on to the other's surfboard while riding a crumbling wave. It was the best photo of the night and probably one of the coolest surf pictures I'd ever seen.

Wes let Elijah keep the prize money. "I have a trust fund. You don't," was all he said.

As the fireworks exploded overhead and the Chicane dance mix of Sigur Rós's "Hoppípolla" blasted out of the PA sound system, the cheering crowd surged around us and hauled Elijah and Wes up on to their surfboards and carried them up the beach. I saw Zeke watching closely, and I wondered if he could see what I could see: just how desperately Elijah and Wes wanted to kiss each other.

Chapter Thirty-one

Zeke had given me his key to Wes and Elijah's apartment, which was in the middle of town, overlooking Great Western Beach, and I was under strict orders to pick up Zeke's favorite skateboard. Zeke had accidentally left it at Wes's, but he'd been promising to lend it to me for ages and said if I could be bothered to pick it up, it was mine for the week. I'd never ridden a carveboard before, as they were stupidly expensive, but they rocked to mimic the motion of the ocean, and I was excited to give it a whirl. As I walked up the stairs, all thoughts of sidewalk surfing went out of my head: I could hear loud music and raised voices.

The door to the living room was open and I saw Wes and Elijah in the middle of a blazing row.

"I'm so sorry for interrupting," I said. "I'll go."

"No, stay," Elijah said. "He's giving me a headache. Maybe you can talk some sense into him."

I looked at Wes.

"Elijah is wigging out because I won't do romantic stuff with him in public."

"Eating our lunch outside *one time* is not 'romantic stuff.'"

"Two guys having a beach picnic is probably the gayest thing ever."

"God forbid a total stranger thinking you might possibly be gay. What a disaster."

"I just don't dig unnecessary drama."

"Oh yeah, you're all warm and toasty in your velvet-lined closet. Screw the rest of us who actually have to deal with reality."

"Way harsh," Wes said.

I turned to the door.

"Iris, please stay," Elijah said.

"I really don't think you need me here," I said. "I should probably get to work anyway. Billy goes crazy when I'm late . . ."

Elijah turned back to Wes, and said, "You're living this horrible lie, and, sure, that sucks for you. But you're getting the best of both worlds. You get to date whoever you want in secret, but you also get to enjoy the approval of the straight world."

"And that makes me a bad person?"

"No. I'm not saying that. You know how much I love you. I just can't keep doing this. Today I woke up and realized that you could go on pretending you're straight for like *years*. And if that's the plan, I am out of here."

I heard a cough behind me. Standing in the doorway, with a huge cardboard box in his arms and a blatant look of disgust on his face, was Garrett.

"So, I thought I'd bring over the last of your stuff. Try to patch things up. But I guess you're busy." He dropped the box, and half the contents bounced out, sending old video-game cases across the carpet.

Wes froze, but Elijah walked across the room and pushed past Garrett in the doorway.

"You're not going anywhere," Garrett said to Elijah.

"Wanna try and stop me?"

"OK."

"Jesus. Everyone just calm down," I said, stepping between Garrett and Elijah.

Wes suddenly found his voice and said, "Garrett, this is my bad. Leave Elijah out of it."

"I don't need your help. I'm not scared of your homophobic Neanderthal brother."

"Elijah, seriously, chill out," I said.

"I'm homophobic? You've talked to me like once, ever?"

"Yeah. That was bad enough."

"Kiss my ass. Except you'd probably like that."

"Garrett!" I said. "That *is* homophobic. Saying stuff like that is not gonna help."

"Yep, total gay-hater," Elijah said, nodding at Wes.

"I'm texting Zeke," Garrett said, getting his phone out of his back pocket. "You? Sit there," he said, pointing to Elijah. "Wes, you're coming with me."

Garrett got Wes by the arm and dragged him out on to the balcony. Through the glass doors, I could see that Garrett was giving Wes a hard time. Wes was shaking his head and looking seriously upset.

Elijah turned to me and said, "I should leave."

"Please, just wait another few minutes. Wes is gonna need you."

Zeke came bounding up the stairs, sweaty and sandy from another one of his beach workouts.

He nodded to Elijah and said, "Hey man," and then turned to me. "What's happening? Garrett sent an SOS."

"It's all kicking off," I said, and nodded over to the balcony. "You'd better go ask them."

Zeke strode across the living room and slid open the glass doors. I didn't catch what was said, but after a few seconds the brothers came back into the room and Wes sat down next to Elijah.

"Wes has something to tell you," Garrett said.

"Yeah?"

Zeke looked expectantly at Wes, who exhaled loudly, then turned and kissed Elijah on the mouth.

Zeke blinked.

Elijah gripped Wes's hand and both of them looked at Zeke.

"*That*," Garrett said. Then he turned to Wes and said, "Who *are* you? 'Cause you're sure as shit not my brother."

"What the hell?" Zeke said to Wes.

Garrett took a swig from a can of Heineken he'd helped himself to, and said, "I know, right? Don't even. You don't know him. I don't."

"Yeah, you do," Wes said, his voice faltering.

"You're fucking *gay*," Garrett said, "and how many times did you ask to borrow my porn? What is up with that?"

"I dunno. I wanted . . ." Wes's voice got really tight, and then he looked down and I saw tears roll off the end of his nose.

This just enraged Elijah, who jumped up and said, "So he looked at some tits in a magazine? Who gives a fuck."

"Eat shit and die. No one cares what you think. You're nobody."

Wes looked up and, in this quiet voice, he said, "Don't speak to Elijah that way."

"What?" Garrett said, giving Wes a full-on hate stare.

"You need to apologize to Elijah."

Garrett laughed and looked like he couldn't believe what Wes was saying. "Yeah, that's gonna happen, uhhh, never."

"Elijah's not nobody," Wes said.

"Who is he then, bro? Who's he to you? He your *boyfriend?*"

"I guess so."

"Is this real? Is this actually happening?"

"Can you calm down for like one second, Garrett?" I said.

"I remember you telling Nanna how you only had the hots for biker chicks. You lied to *Nanna*. And you've been lying to us your entire life."

Garrett turned to me and said, "Don't you get how messed-up that is?"

"He lied because he knew you'd act like this."

Zeke sat down on the sofa next to Wes and said, "Can't believe you didn't tell me. You could've told *me*. I tell you like everything."

"Everything?"

"OK, not everything. But the big stuff. The stuff that counts."

"You don't know how it's been for me. Man, how would I even get into it with you?"

"I don't know," Zeke said. "But you could've tried."

"I was scared of losing you guys. I can't lose my brothers."

Garrett said, "Too late. Brothers don't lie to each other for nineteen years. You ain't no brother of mine."

"Garrett, don't say that shit. That's not cool," Zeke said, his face twisted up with pain.

"I'm gonna go," Elijah said, standing up.

"Good idea, and take Wes—sorry, *your boyfriend*—with you."

Garrett was way out of line. I saw Zeke make a fist and for a second I thought he was actually going to punch Garrett. I put my hand on Zeke's fist and felt it relax. Instead of punching Garrett, Zeke said, "This is their home. You go."

"Cool. I'm gone."

And then Wes said something to Elijah that made Garrett flinch so hard that lager splashed out of the can he was gripping.

"I shoulda said it before, but I love you, E. You know that, yeah?"

Elijah nodded and said, "Right back at you."

Garrett slammed down his can on the kitchen table and left.

The next day, Kelly had come around to Dave's house to see Garrett and, when me, Wes and Zeke got back from an awkwardly wordless walk on the beach, they were holed up in the basement with the stereo system blaring. Kelly was ferrying food down there and every time she opened the door, epic clouds of weed smoke drifted out. Luckily, Dave was working, and Sephy had taken her camera on an all-day dolphin-watching boat trip.

"He's coming around," Kelly whispered, giving us a thumbs-up. "In another two, three years he should be totally fine with it."

"What's he been saying?" I asked.

"He's actually really upset. Granted, he's acting like a complete knob—and, don't worry, I've told him that—but he just can't get his head around the idea that his own brother is gay and he didn't know."

Wes looked over at Zeke and said, "You mad at me too?"

"Gimme a break. How am I mad at my own brother? Don't be such a douche."

"Did you never, like, suspect anything?"

"Honestly, no. But this does explain a lot," Zeke said.

"Like what?"

"Er, like the fact that you only ever had one serious girlfriend and she rode a Harley in the Hawaiian 'Dykes on Bikes' parade."

"Yeah, Megan's a cool chick. I guess our bi-curious phases overlapped . . ."

Suddenly the door to the basement swung open and Garrett stood in the doorway. He was unsteady on his feet.

"I hate you for this," he said to Wes.

Wes closed his eyes for a moment, his face pale and drawn. "I know. But I can't help liking dudes. It's just the way I am."

"I don't care who you bang. It's your dick. Do what you want with it. I mean, yeah, maybe I'd prefer it was in a chick for the sake of normal, but I don't really wanna think about my brother having sex with anyone. It'd be gross, whatever. But all the lying and shit, I can't get over that."

"I was gonna tell you. But, like, how? You said it: we watched a ton of porn . . ."

Garrett shook his head and for a moment I thought he was going to cry. Kelly threaded her fingers through his, and Garrett stooped to kiss the top of her head.

Zeke had gone quiet again too.

"What about you, Zeke?" Garrett said. "You OK with this?"

"I'm not crazy about the fact Wes lied for so long, but I'm happy he's finally being real with us. So when are you gonna tell Mom and Pa, Wes?"

"Mom's known since middle school."

"*No way*," Garrett said.

Zeke looked really shocked and said, "Seriously? She never said anything, and she totally sucks at keeping secrets. Did she bust you making out with a dude?"

"Um, I was eleven, so no. She found a picture of a half-naked actor under my pillow one day and she asked me straight out if I was crushing on boys."

"Who was the actor?" I said, curiosity getting the better of me.

"Vin Diesel."

"That tough guy from *The Fast and the Furious*?" Zeke said.

"Yeah. He was rocking the super-oily-Levi's-with-no-shirt look."

Kelly chipped in with, "*Vin Diesel?* He is Elijah's exact opposite!"

"Again, I was eleven. My taste in guys has refined since then."

"Thank God," Garrett said, looking severely grossed out. "Because that dude is like forty and *bald*."

"Hey, so is Kelly Slater," I said, "and he's hot."

Zeke raised an eyebrow at me.

"Well, he is," I said, and Zeke shrugged in a way that seemed to say "OK, maybe."

"Completely hot," Kelly confirmed. "His eyes are just . . . wow."

With the banter beginning to kick in, I really hoped they were going to be OK. I kissed Zeke goodbye, waved to Kelly and legged it across the beach to work.

Chapter Thirty-two

More and more I'd been thinking about Nanna and her relationship with the sea, and how it had lasted until her final breath. My mom once told me that, from the very first days of my life, she and my dad would take me to the beach whenever I was teething or sick, and the noise of the waves would soothe me. And if it was nighttime or too cold to take me outside, they'd make the sound of the sea to calm me down, just ssshhhssshhhssshhh, and I'd stop crying and fall asleep in my dad's arms.

I was making a point of listening to the sound of the sea as Zeke and I were carrying our boards back up the beach. Then he surprised me by saying, "Wanna come to my apartment? I got the keys yesterday, and Garrett doesn't move in until next week."

"I thought you said it was best if we, you know, avoided temptation and all that?"

I turned my back to him so he could unzip my wetsuit. He did this slowly and he helped me pull my arms out, so that I could fold the suit down to my waist and peel it off, as for once I had a rash vest, board shorts and a bikini on underneath.

"I dunno. I guess I was thinking we should forget that."

"Aren't I supposed to be in strict training for the biggest day of my life next month?"

Or maybe the biggest day of my life was today, I thought, feeling a rush of something in the pit of my stomach.

Zeke turned around and I reached up to grab the zip of his suit, moving the wet blades of his hair that had grown longer and were starting to graze the top of his shoulders. The zip stuck a little and it took me a moment to loosen it and thread it down his back, the tanned skin opening up in a triangle beneath the wet rubber.

My board clattered on top of Zeke's and he turned around and held me in his arms. The strong arms that teeny-bopper surf groupies had been so eager to touch, just for a second, just to say they had.

I decided right then. I was going back to his apartment.

I was going to end up there eventually. Why couldn't it be when I was crazy emotional and amped?

"OK," I said to him. "I'll come."

I texted my mom to say that I was staying over at Kelly's.

She was bound to be getting suspicious, but like she'd always said to me, she'd done her fair share of crazy stuff when she was a teenager and she didn't have her mother hovering over her like a helicopter. My grandma had trusted my mom's instincts and, despite all appearances, my mom trusted mine.

Zeke had bought a second-floor apartment in a brand-new development just off North Fistral. There were only seven apartments in the building and the architect had obviously gone for Californian beach-style, with massive windows, fancy cedar boarding and timber-decked terraces. It was the coolest building in the whole of Newquay.

The apartment had its own front door and Zeke led me up a flight of stairs and into a bright and airy living room, empty apart from a mattress in plastic wrapping and three surfboards, which had been delivered the day before and were still zipped up in their soft silver covers.

A huge kitchen was set off to one side, and on the island in the center there was a vase of yellow roses and a bottle of champagne. Zeke walked over and plucked a small card off the granite worktop.

"Don't suppose that's from Garrett," I said.

He looked up and shook his head. "No, just the lady who sold me the apartment. Let's crack this open, huh?"

The cork rocketed out and hit the art deco light fitting, champagne fizzing over pristine floor tiles.

"You have any glasses?"

"Don't think so."

"Swigging time, then."

I took a deep gulp of warm champagne and it fizzed up and out of my nose, leaving my eyes streaming. "Never had that before," I said, rubbing my face on my rash vest. "It's kind of rank actually."

"Gets better the more you drink."

We walked into the living room, which didn't even have a sofa. Zeke docked his iPod in the inbuilt surround-sound system and loaded *An Awesome Wave* by alt-J.

"Love this album," I said. "Especially . . . 'Tessellate' . . . is it called?"

He nodded. "Garrett got me hooked on them. They look like these really goofy skinny guys, but, wow, their music is insane. I've been listening to 'Dissolve Me' all week, like, on repeat."

He put on "Dissolve Me" and the music hit us in small ripples at first, but then the song built in power—the speakers in Zeke's new place so perfectly positioned that it sounded like the band was in the room with us.

I sat down cross-legged in the pool of light by the window. Zeke stretched out on his back, his head resting on my thigh.

"Are you, er, prepared?" I said.

"I swung by Garrett's room earlier, yeah," he said.

I remembered the glass jar on Garrett's nightstand which was overflowing with condoms.

"He won't miss them?"

"I doubt he keeps count."

"Cool."

"Uh, Iris?"

"Yeah?"

He looked over at the new mattress, lying on its side by the front door. "I don't have a bed yet."

"Beds are for wimps," I said.

He grinned, got up, tore the clear plastic off and dragged the mattress over to me, letting it fall to the ground with a thump.

I crawled on to it and flaked out on my back. He was still standing and, as he looked down at me, I cocked my head to try to see him the right way up, though even from that weird angle he still looked totally sexy. Then he knelt and quickly kissed me upside down, which felt surprisingly nice. He walked around and rested on me, his knees on either side of mine. I kept my eyes open, still not quite believing that this surf god was actually putting the moves on me; but there he was, his face bearing down on mine, his eyes sparkling with a hunger I recognized.

This was it.

As he kissed me, my body started to respond to his, my hips moving in a rhythm of their own. He pulled my vest over my head, and fumbled with the knotted draw-cords on my board shorts, which I slithered out of, leaving me in just my black bikini top and bottoms. He took off his T-shirt, so he was just in his boardshorts. Then he kissed me again, the feel of skin against skin upping the intensity.

"Iris," he said, bringing me back to reality. "What are we doing here? Because if we keep at this, in about three seconds I'm gonna, umm, y'know, in your belly button."

"Sorry," I said, a bit embarrassed. "Maybe I was getting carried away there."

"Hell, I don't mind. I just don't want you to do anything you're not ready for."

I thought about that for all of one second.

"I'm ready."

"You sure?"

"Yes."

"You won't be mad at me tomorrow?"

"No."

"Totally sure?"

"For God's sake! Yeah, I'm sure."

"Awesome," he said and gave me the most beautiful smile.

Chapter Thirty-three

I stayed the night at Zeke's. In the end, I didn't even lie about it to my mom. I called her up and told her exactly where I was, and promised I'd keep my phone ringer on at all times.

She wasn't happy, but as she said: "I'm glad you're being straight with me. I'd rather know you were safe with someone you trust, than drunk at a party with some opportunist sleazebag."

I put down the phone and smiled at Zeke.

In a luxury apartment with no furniture except a mattress was not how I'd imagined my first time would be. But then I never imagined I'd meet someone like Zeke.

I thought it would hurt. Or that I'd be sore afterward. But Zeke was really slow and patient and I was relaxed enough that my body didn't tense up. I always thought surfing was the most intense experience a person could have. I was wrong.

Zeke left at 5 a.m. to do circuits with his brothers on Great Western Beach and grab a morning surf. I lay by the window, curled up on the mattress with a silver surfboard cover for a sheet, and I watched the sun arc across the sky.

Normally I would have gone with Zeke for a dawn workout, but I wanted some time alone, some quiet to adjust.

I felt different, knew that if I looked in the mirror my face would be different.

It was.

Something in my eyes was new. Serious.

It had been a trippy experience and I was really happy we'd done it, but I still had a lot buzzing around my head. After a couple of hours of chilling, I was ready to go surf it out.

I was looking through the window at the break when I saw Daniel jogging down Headland Road. He must have sensed he was being watched, because he looked right up at Zeke's window, and I could tell he recognized me.

It wouldn't take long for him to realize what had happened. I was standing in a four-hundred-grand beachside apartment that nobody from Newquay could possibly afford. Daniel would know it was Zeke's and he'd know I'd stayed the night. What else would I be doing there at eight thirty in the morning?

I strung up my bikini, and pulled my shorts and tank top on.

Then I ran down the stairs two at a time, flung open the front door and slammed it behind me.

"Daniel!" I called, but he didn't look round. I only had flip-flops, so I couldn't run properly and I wished I had a skateboard with me.

I jogged behind Daniel all the way to Towan Headland. I knew where he was going. It was obvious from the moment I'd opened Zeke's front door, when I'd heard the deep pounding.

Finally, at the cliff-edge, Daniel turned to me. "You slept with him, didn't you?"

I didn't have to answer that. He had no right to ask.

"Yes," I said, because even if I hadn't spoken the word, my face would have said it.

"Knew you would. Knew it the first time I saw you with that dude." He smiled grimly, shook his head and then said, "Oh well, see you on the other side."

"You can't be serious."

The Cribbar waves were breaking due to a tropical storm that had occurred thousands of miles away. Distant low-pressure weather systems affected oceans like pebbles dropped into a pond. The ripples were swells that traveled for days until they made landfall. In this case, the landfall was the Cribbar reef, and the waves were enormous. Faces that were twice the height of the ones I'd watched at the Headland Hotel with Zeke. They were pushing forty feet, at least.

And Daniel wasn't even wearing a wetsuit, let alone a flotation vest. Just a black rashie and some blue baggies.

"If your poser boyfriend can do it, so can I," Daniel was saying, clutching an electric-green board that looked familiar.

"Uh, he grew up in Hawaii."

"So? I've been surfing all my life. I get the sea. I'm, like, connected to it or something."

"You've been surfing beach breaks. It's not the same as a crazy reef break. Wake up to yourself. This is the Cribbar. You'd be surfing a mountain."

"Yeah, well, who says that's impossible? I can snowboard great."

"On a dry slope. And this is a mountain of water that wants to crush you. A mountain that you have to jump off at the scariest possible moment and somehow survive."

"Your boyfriend does it like twenty times a year."

"Come on, Daniel. You know that's junk. It's not a competition."

"Yeah, it is."

"And what's the prize?"

"You, probably."

"Don't be so psycho. You can't win me."

"I'm doing it anyway."

"Where did you get that board?"

"Found it."

"Where?"

"On your boyfriend's camper van. So what?"

"So first you're now a thief, and second you are actually contemplating riding the Cribbar on an unfamiliar board?"

"I can do it, Iris. I know I can."

"Yeah, like you thought you could beat Zeke Francis in the Saltwater Pro?"

"What? I was just unlucky."

"No, you lost your cool and it all went wrong."

Suddenly, he smiled and said, "Eddie would go."

I thought of the Eddie Aikau tribute tattoo on the top of Daniel's butt, which had those exact words.

"Eddie *did* go. And Eddie damn well died, remember?"

"If I die, I die. But I'm gonna go."

"Go home."

"No way. This is my day. This is it. I'm riding the fucking Crib-bar, and if it kills me, at least I'll have gone out doing something awesome. Something I love."

It wasn't even Kodak courage, because there was no one watching except me. He wasn't trying to get his picture on the news or on the cover of *Surfer* magazine. He was just going.

He picked up the board, a leashless ten-foot gun, and started jogging to the cliff-edge. Just the clamber over those crumbling rocks to the water was dangerous. I ran after him and caught him at the ledge.

I grabbed his arm, digging in my fingernails.

"Don't do this, Daniel."

"I have to. I have to find out."

"What?"

"Who I am. What I'm made of."

"Oh *come on*."

"Don't worry. I got this."

"Please don't waste your life. It's pointless."

"Nah. You'll see," he said.

I looked at him. He was looking out at the set, which was feathering out just beyond the cliff. His whole body vibed with determination. Nothing I could say would get in the way of that.

"You just get as far down the face as quick as you can before it sucks you back up again, OK, and if you wipe out, cover your head near the bottom, because if you don't, your head is smashed in and you're dead. Do you hear me?"

"Gotcha."

Then he went over the cliff and clambered down toward the rocks.

Chapter Thirty-four

"Be careful," I shouted. Either it was lost to the wind and he didn't hear, or he didn't give a shit, because he didn't answer. He was totally committed. He climbed down the rocks and pushed off, stroking powerfully out to the channel that would take him around the reef break and out the back. I saw when the rip took hold, pushing him fast out to sea.

He looked so small and hunched, bobbing out there like a seabird.

The first set came through. Daniel let the first wave pass, and the second, trying to tune in and sense which would be the best wave, I guessed. Then, as the line of the third wave approached, he swung around and stroked hard to take off. It was cresting, and still he was paddling hard to get up enough speed.

Then he started the vertical plunge, carving down the face, this gray wall of water rearing up behind him, getting bigger and bigger. The right rail dug in and he was off, riding down the curl of the wave. It was the wave of his life, no doubt, and it seemed like he was riding faster than was possible. But it was a jerky ride, the wave rising up with weird kinks, drops and lifts, and the board's tail shaking because of the wave gurgles, which were totally unpredictable. All this was happening in the blink of an eye.

Daniel hung on, but suddenly his positioning looked all wrong to me—too much speed, the tail of his board whipping left and right like he was about to lose control. I don't know what he was thinking about out there in that awful moment, but if it was me it would have been my life flashing before my eyes, because those would probably be the last seconds of it.

Then, as he shot the curl, it reduced in size to double-overhead, then overhead and suddenly it was just a normal wave. Daniel was hollering, "COWABUNGA" and "BANZAI!" like some kid in a cheesy beach-blanket movie. And he rode that wave all the way to the channel and then he hopped off the back, bellied down on his board and paddled.

He'd made it. I couldn't believe it. No one would believe it.

For a brief moment he looked toward the cliff where I was standing and did the shaka sign with his hand, and that was when I saw it. Line after black line stacking up much further out to sea.

He was too far away to hear me shout, so I started jabbing my hand toward the horizon. He stared at me. I waved my hands some more, flicking my index fingers to show him what was behind him, but he couldn't hear, and in the dip of the swell he couldn't see.

Daniel broke the first rule of surfing: never turn your back to the ocean.

Finally he saw it, but by then it was too late. The line-up had changed. A sneak set was approaching and Daniel was caught inside, deep in the new impact zone. All he could do was stroke out hard toward it. He was on full RPM, going as fast as if he was trying to take off on a wave, but in the other direction, paddling desperately out to sea, hoping that he could get to the other side. The first wave he made and I watched him bob over it, just. I hoped that the speed and momentum he'd built would take him to the next wave. The next wave was twice the size and it was jacking up, monstrous. Daniel was like a stickman desperately trying to paddle over the top of it. For a second I thought he'd made it, thought he was over it, scratching for the next one. Then I saw him sucked backward. Going over the waterfall.

Holy shit.

I knew he was dead. No one could survive that wipeout.

I screamed because I couldn't help myself. It was just this primal noise that came out of the depths of me. My eyes scanned the sea, but there was so much whitewater that everything between the cliff-face and the break was like frothy cream. Then I saw a board pop up and a head and shoulders appeared not far from the boneyard. The body wasn't floating face down. I saw arms working furiously, heading away from that rocky graveyard and toward the calm waters of the channel. On the waves of the wind I could have sworn I heard laughing. He was alive.

His rash vest had been sucked right off him, and his baggies too, I noticed when he kicked up to swim. It took a scary amount of force to rip the clothes off a surfer. The wave would have been like a tornado in the water. His board, or rather Zeke's board, was somehow still in one piece and swirling in circles about fifty feet from him and I watched open-mouthed as Daniel swam for it, hopped on, and rather than head for shore to go to hospital, he paddled out again in the lull to catch another wave.

He had lost his mind.

Chapter Thirty-five

It took him ages to get position again, and just as he'd figured out the line-up I heard someone calling my name. I turned.

Zeke.

Fresh from his session at Great Western Beach, with his orange longboard under his arm. It was one of his favorite boards, a super-fast gun shaped by his mother.

"Wow, check out the set from Tibet! Totally knew it was breaking," he said. "There were these insane ripples in my Styrofoam coffee cup just now. Boom, would you listen to that!"

And then before I could say a word, his eyes fixed on the small figure out at sea waiting for the next set of waves to come in.

"Damn, someone's riding it?"

"Daniel," I said.

He sighed an awful sigh. Just like his whole chest deflated.

Daniel was just sitting on his board deep outside, resting after the violence of the axing, maybe trying to stop his brain from freaking out. He didn't go for any other waves, and for the time being at least he was safe.

Zeke said, "Is he even wearing a flotation vest?"

"He's not wearing anything. The wave ripped his clothes off."

Garrett and Wes were coming around the headland, carrying shortboards and stuffing their faces with chips.

They could see something was wrong.

"Cribbar bombin', eh? Who's out there?" Garrett asked.

"Some kid trying to be the big kahuna."

"Some kid?" Wes asked, looking at me.

Zeke didn't tell them it was Daniel. Unfortunately it must have been written across my face.

"Not Knife Boy?" Garrett said, looking from me to Zeke.

Zeke just shrugged.

"Iris," Garrett said, "is that the psycho gremmie who tried to kill our little brother?"

I nodded.

Wes exhaled and shook his head. "What the heck is he thinking?"

"He's not thinking," I replied.

Garrett ate another handful of chips. "Bummer for him. The little squid's gonna be sea froth."

"Iris, you have a cell phone?"

I shook my head, mentally kicking myself for not bringing it with me. Zeke and his brothers obviously didn't have one either, as they'd just been surfing and no one in their right mind left expensive belongings on the beach while they went in the water.

"OK, where's the nearest emergency phone?" Zeke said, walking to the edge of the cliff.

"There's two: North Fistral and Little Fistral. Wait a minute . . . one of them's broken," I said, vaguely remembering an "Out of Service" sign. I racked my brains, but couldn't remember where I'd seen it. "I dunno which one. We'll have to try both."

Zeke said, "Wes, you go to Little Fistral. Garrett, you run around to the main beach."

"You're not going in there," Garrett said. "He's made his decision. Let him be."

"In about two minutes he's going to paddle for a wave and wipe out, because these sets coming in right now . . . ? Those waves are not makeable. Too hollow, too ledgy, too choppy, boils bubbling up on the face that will stop his board dead and send his ass sailing to the wind."

"His choice, brah."

"He might make it," I said. "He's survived two."

"No. This set right here is all wrong. But out back, where he's paddling, he won't be able to see how they're jacking up. Teahupo'o is more ridable than this."

"Don't," I said, so choked up I could hardly speak.

"Just get to a phone and call the lifeguard and an ambulance," Zeke said to Garrett and Wes. "Now."

I couldn't take my eyes away from the water. The deep rumble of the breaking waves was so loud that I could feel their vibration through my whole body.

Zeke walked toward the cliff. I grabbed his arm to stop him, and he turned to me and said, "He's gonna need help, and who else is there?"

"Wait for the lifeguard."

I said wait, and yet my heart wanted him to go out there and save Daniel. To make everything all right again. To put it all back to the way it had been.

Zeke just looked at me with those beautiful blue eyes, and it was like he could read my mind. Then he committed.

"Stupid freakin' kook," he said.

At the edge of the cliff, he turned back to me, and I said, "I love you, Zeke."

"Love you too."

Then he was gone.

Chapter Thirty-six

He paddled out, taking nice fluid strokes like he was just going out to any other normal wave.

Garrett was running toward me, steaming back from the emergency phone and I knew that within twenty minutes a lifeboat would be in the water and approaching the headland. With every heartbeat, though, it seemed more and more likely that I was about to lose the only two boys I had ever loved.

I saw the moment when Daniel spotted Zeke coming around the break, and he must have known what he was there for. Daniel had been taking a breather, psyching himself up to overcome that defense mechanism that stopped a person from doing crazy suicidal shit, whatever, but as soon as he saw Zeke, it was like he was electrocuted into action and he started stroking hard, too late, way too late, to catch a wave that had passed a few seconds before.

Zeke was taller than Daniel and he had this graceful paddle style in the water, super-fast and efficient, and he started dropping in further down the wave on the shoulder, away from the peak, so that Daniel would back down. He'd have to. Otherwise he'd risk taking the full weight of Zeke's board. It just wasn't worth the risk.

Daniel kept going, paddling to get enough speed to take off. Zeke, by this time, was a couple of yards to his right, burning through the water like his life depended on it. Daniel popped up at the exact moment that Zeke got to his feet. Both of them were up and riding, but both were too late to drop in on the wave face. Zeke cut back and turned his board slightly toward Daniel, going against every rule of surfing etiquette that he'd lived by so religiously his whole life. Taking control, like the pro that he was, but this time he was also trying to save Daniel's life. Zeke's arm shot out, fist bunched, and caught Daniel in the chest, sending him off the back of the wave, where he'd be safe.

Zeke, though, was nearer to the falling lip of the wave than he'd thought.

Chapter Thirty-seven

I saw Zeke's orange board, pointing the wrong way, get sucked over the falls. Attached at the ankle, Zeke followed his board and was pulled over the wave, nothing he could do to stop it.

I closed my eyes.

Garrett had arrived and was roaring by my side, already running for the cliff-ledge. I grabbed him and he shook me off like I was so much trash.

The wave didn't pick Zeke up like the other wave that had grabbed Daniel and sent him down in the lip. Seconds stretched out like hours and all I could think was: *air*. He needed to swim like hell for the surface and get some air. But I knew that down deep you didn't know where you were, didn't even know which way was up. I remembered Zeke telling me about giant waves he'd ridden, where the wipeout was so fearsome and his back was hyperextended so far that he'd thought he was paralyzed.

"When you panic, you make stupid mistakes," he'd told me. "It's all about staying calm, staying loose and believing you'll get through it."

"It's so dangerous," I said. "Macho bullshit. Why do it? Why risk everything?"

And now, here he was, in the grip of the most hideous wipe-out I had ever seen.

The board didn't surface and neither did Zeke. He wasn't wearing a life vest either. There was nothing to engage and send him like a cork to the surface. There was too much water exploding over him; he couldn't fight his way up.

The wave had passed and another was forming, and still Zeke hadn't come to the surface.

And then Daniel came sailing over the next monster wave, totally oblivious of what had happened to Zeke. This wave was a little smaller than the first, but Daniel was all over the place. Too jerky, his board rearing up, and way too much speed. The bottom fell out of the wave. He was thrown off the front.

I thought of the calmness. The moment of calm when I first met Zeke, lying in the ballroom of Hotel Serenity, looking at twinkling stars.

I thought of the day Daniel had joined my school, riding up on his skateboard like he didn't have a care in the world.

Garrett was in the water now, streaming through the swell, under-gunned in his tiny shortboard that wasn't at all suitable for such crazy conditions. That was when I committed.

I could do it. I'd been practicing my yoga routine every day. I knew how to calm my mind, and my body was stronger than it had ever been.

If Zeke and Daniel were dead because of me, I couldn't go on. I had to fix it. I didn't have a board with me, so I walked away from the cliff-edge, then turned and ran at it and went sailing over the top, just clearing the slashing rocks below.

As soon as I cleared the froth, I saw that half a board was tombstoning not far from me, and much further away again a figure had popped up, a head and shoulders. Gasping, spitting salt-snot.

It was Daniel.

Zeke was still down.

Garrett was ahead of me, not far from Daniel. The half-submerged board had come up only after Garrett had swum over it. He never knew his brother was down there, trapped, fighting to get free of his leash. He had been down too long. There was no way to hold your breath that long. Not even for Zeke, who had practiced free-diving in the Maldives, sitting on the ocean floor alongside the kaleidoscopic fishes as he held his breath for three minutes. Possible if you're calm. Impossible in this kind of beating.

Before Garrett had even turned, I dived down, using every ounce of the new strength in my arms to follow the board's leash, hand over hand like I was climbing a rope, only downward. Then I felt a handful of soft hair.

Chapter Thirty-eight

His body was moving gently, anchored as it was by the urethane leash which had wound tight around an anvil-shaped boulder. It was murky, but up close I could just about see how the leash had snagged. I shook it with everything I had, but there was no way I could loosen it. I didn't know if Zeke's eyes were open because I couldn't bring myself to look at his face.

The sea would not take him. With my lungs on the brink of exploding and the force of a broken wave rushing over us, I worked my hands down his body, only just stopping myself from springing up to the surface, and I took hold of the Velcro strap around his ankle and released the leash.

I gripped Zeke around the waist and let the air in my body take us up.

Garrett was right there to take hold of Zeke; behind him, I watched Wes dive from the rocks into the sea. I turned around and saw Daniel swimming toward us, his face a mask of panic.

Three words looped around and around my brain.

Zeke is dead.

Chapter Thirty-nine

Two days later, his board washed up with the sunrise. Relentless waves had eventually split the board in two and dislodged Zeke's leg-rope from the boulder. The pieces floated ashore with a mass stranding of tiny white jellyfish. My knees buckled. The palms of my hands burned. The swell had died like it was never there and I looked right past the headland, out to where the Cribbar breaks.

It was like an inshore lake. Nothing. No sign of what had happened that terrible morning.

The gannets were diving far out in the bay, sending up plumes of spray, and behind me I could hear London voices say that it was dolphins' breaths, water spray chucked out by the blowholes. But they were wrong. It was just birds pulling out fish after fish after fish.

They talked like nothing was wrong, wrapped up in their own worlds and oblivious to what was happening ten feet from them. Not understanding the significance of this broken surfboard.

A few weeks after I first met him, Zeke had told me, "A leash snagged on underwater rocks is every big-wave rider's nightmare. After a bad wipeout, a leash can be a lifeline or a death sentence. Down in the deep water where it's so dark, you're disorientated and you don't know which way is up, so if push comes to shove you can literally climb your leg-rope, because it's attached to something that is way more buoyant than you are: a board. And odds are that your board is floating on the surface. I've climbed my leash to the surface and it's saved my life, given me that one precious mouthful of air, which is all it takes to survive. But if that leash is snagged on underwater rocks? And you can't pull it free, or get it off your ankle? You're a goner. You're holding your breath as best you can, twenty feet down, or forty feet down if a second wave has broken on top of you. You try pulling off your ankle leash then, with the current pinning your body. It's like doing a stomach crunch with an elephant sitting on your chest."

This conversation came back to me with such clarity that dread rose through my body. I just stood there, looking at the pieces of his board, one at my feet, the other a hundred yards down the beach.

Surfing was rough and Zeke never, ever, went easy on himself. I knew the scars that marked his surfboards as well as I knew the ones on his body. I recognized everything: his board-waxing pattern, the replacement fins, and the small ding that he'd fixed with epoxy resin. I'd been there when he put his mouth to the hole and sucked out the saltwater.

That orange board was like a bright lamp in the gray early-morning water. A little bit of *aloha* in Cornwall.

I couldn't stop crying.

I carried the halves of his board over my head as if they were a coffin. No one helped me, no one stopped me.

I made a quick stop at my place, and then I went to Daniel's house.

Chapter Forty

I placed the two pieces of surfboard on the concrete outside Daniel's front door and then I knocked hard, staring at the flaking blue paint without blinking.

He opened the door and gave me a look of such pain that I almost turned around.

"They just washed up," I said.

He stooped to pick up one of the pieces, and he turned it over in his hands, respectful and somber like he was touching a dead body.

His shoulders sagged and he placed the piece back down on its other half.

"I'm sorry."

I shook my head at him.

On the way back from the beach, I'd stopped back at my place as I knew there was something that could do what my words couldn't. In a bag hooked on my wrist I had an old Nike shoebox that was so full the lid barely stayed on.

I handed Daniel the box and he opened it, looking down into it.

It was everything. I'd kept all of the bits of jewelry that Daniel had bought me for Christmas and birthdays. Even after I met Zeke, I kept that stuff. Beaded bracelets and necklaces that Daniel bought me when we were falling in love with each other. I even had a cardboard case from an old deck of cards where I kept all the ticket stubs from cinema trips, as well as receipts from coasteering and all-you-can-eat Pizza Hut lunches. Daniel had no idea how sentimental I was. None at all. I never let it show, because I didn't want him to realize the power he had over me. Which was a joke. As if he didn't know all about that.

I had been so weak. Back then, I had loved him so much that it caused me physical pain whenever I was away from him for more than five minutes. On one school science trip to Bodmin Moor, where we weren't allowed phones or computers, I wrote Daniel a letter every single day, kissing the envelope before posting it.

Daniel glanced into the shoebox and looked at me. He hadn't kept anything like that. Of course he hadn't. What he meant to me, I had never meant to him. We were two people in one relationship but it wasn't the same one. I'd thought he was parasiting off my strength, but it was the other way around: I'd been addicted to his pain.

And look what I had allowed to happen. Look how reckless he'd become, because I had encouraged him to be that way, with my head in the sand and constant excuse-making.

Daniel had not meant to hurt anyone else. He hadn't meant for Zeke to drown. He couldn't have known Zeke would show up and try to save him. But Daniel was toxic. And I had made him worse.

"I'm so sorry, Iris. For everything I ever done."

Then he added, "I never meant to hurt anyone," like it was the most important thing in the world that I believed that. "I'll always love you, Ris. You know that."

I couldn't answer him. The lump in my throat burned so fiercely that I could barely swallow.

I looked straight into Daniel's eyes, those lovely dark eyes framed with black lashes, and I felt the strength go out of my legs. I put up a hand to support myself, took a deep breath and said, "Have a good life, Daniel. Be happy." And then I turned on my heel and I didn't look back.

Chapter Forty-one

At the apartment, I laid the board fragments against the wall and pressed the buzzer. When Garrett answered, I said, "Come down. It washed up."

"Be right there. Just gotta find some clothes first."

He appeared in the doorway, looking surf-sore and disheveled in crumpled jeans. He was rubbing his eyes and sand was splashed across one side of his face. He'd obviously gone straight from a set of waves into his bed. I watched as he pulled on a bright purple T-shirt.

"Dawn patrol, huh?"

"Best waves always roll in at 6 a.m."

I nodded at the board fragments propped against the apartment block.

Garrett slid past me out into the fresh morning air to stare at Zeke's broken board. A gust of wind caught one of the pieces and sent it flying. I went after it, and when I turned around I saw Garrett kicking the other half, leaving his own dents and scrapes in the fiberglass.

I didn't know what to say, and he must not have either, because we just looked at each other. His blue eyes were full of pain, and I guessed mine were too. I stood waiting for him to tell me what he wanted to do with the board, but he was silent.

I knew why: throwing the board away would be impossible. But the thought of keeping it was equally painful. In that moment I wanted to hug Garrett, or reach out and grab his hand, but I couldn't.

Then he snapped out of the trance, scooped up the orange board pieces and carried them up the stairs.

"Come on," he said, over his shoulder. "There's a pot of coffee on the stove."

Garrett hadn't blamed me for what happened. He could have; should have. Zeke had been trying to help my ex-boyfriend. If Zeke had never met me, he wouldn't have been on that cliff-edge. Garrett should have hated my guts, but since the accident he hadn't even raised his voice to me.

In the living room, the board pieces stuffed under his arm, Garrett paused. Then he made a clicking noise with his tongue, walked across the room and dropped the board on to the kitchen island, where it landed with a clatter.

He turned to the fridge, opened it, rooted inside, and then slammed its door shut.

"Gotta run to the store to get milk. Back in five." He jangled his keys, put his head down and left the apartment.

My gaze drifted through the window to the waves beating against the shore, and then I watched Garrett jog barefoot toward the corner shop and I wondered how long he'd stay in Newquay. Sooner or later he'd return to Hawaii.

The noise of a door opening jolted me back to the present. He came out of the bathroom wearing gray pajama bottoms, a razor in one hand and a strip of bright white shaving foam across the right side of his jaw. Even shaving, he looked gorgeous.

"Hey, Iris."

"Hey, yourself."

"Wow, it finally came loose."

"Yeah."

He reached for the tail of the broken board, his fingers settling where the leash attached.

"*Creepy*," he said.

I looked at Zeke, at the color back in his cheeks and the light in his eyes. "Feeling better?"

"Yeah," he said, smiling. "That whole being-dead thing? I think that's outta the way now. For maybe fifty years, anyways."

Chapter Forty-two

You're not dead until you're warm and dead.

There on the rocks, Garrett had punched his brother's chest. Blown into his brother's lungs and pushed down on his heart, over and over, counting aloud to get the timing right. The sight of Garrett's face is something I will never forget. Puffy blue eyes, ringed red. Nose streaming with snot. I stared at Garrett's face, then at Wes's, because I couldn't bear to look at Zeke's.

Over and over Garrett pushed down on Zeke's chest, and nothing. Just nothing. Until I sobbed with the pain of it all.

But Garrett kept his cool and carried on.

"Let me help," Wes said, the knuckles of his fingers white around my hand.

Garrett said, "It's OK, bro. I got this," and kept going, on and on, beating that heart to keep the oxygen moving, and breathing hard and fast. Two breaths, thirty compressions, again and again. Hundreds of rounds of CPR. He kept on because it was the only thing in the world that mattered. And then came the sound. The best sound we had ever heard. A deep gurgle as Zeke threw up a belly's worth and two lungfuls of seawater.

In the days after the accident, the memory of it was like footage playing over and over in my mind. I remembered it all. Every second of it. It was with me every night and every morning when I woke up drenched in sweat.

In those dreams, I could never set him free. I would pull at that ankle leash and it wouldn't move a millimeter. Or Garrett couldn't bring him back. I would be slumped on the rocks with Wes as Garrett worked and worked on his younger brother, and nothing happened until the terror coursing through my body woke me up.

Standing in the light pool from his huge apartment windows, even while he was still taking in the sight of his broken board and the dazzle of a blue, blue sky, I jumped up, wrapped my arms around his neck, kissed him on the mouth and then rested my cheek against his shoulder and breathed in the smell of his shaving foam. Zeke picked me up, my legs wrapped around his waist, and he carried me into his room.

It seemed bizarre to think that in another universe I might never have got the chance to meet Zeke Francis, but thanks to Kelly dragging me to one little yoga class, somehow it had happened.

I couldn't stop touching him, like my brain kept needing to check in that he was actually there. And I was spending every spare second I had at his apartment, which was cool as Kelly was there visiting Garrett almost as much as I was there with Zeke.

Saskia popped in a couple of times and brought food baskets, embroidered silk cushions and scented candles as housewarming gifts. Zeke always seemed pleased to see her, and she was always polite to me, but we were just so different. Apart from 1) being female, 2) being surfers, and 3) Zeke, we had nothing in common.

Wes was sometimes around at the apartment too, playing video games with his brothers, and they seemed as close as ever. Elijah and Garrett still avoided each other though, and one of them generally left as soon as the other turned up, which was awkward.

So Zeke and I didn't get much privacy as, fair play, various members of Zeke's family kept popping in, including Dave, who insisted on taking Zeke and his brothers out on a long fishing trip, where Zeke threw back into the sea every single fish they caught.

Sephy was a regular feature too. She hadn't gone back to Hawaii and she was getting on great with Zeke's dad. In fact, they were getting on so great that it looked a lot like they were back together.

My sister, Lily, finally came home for a week and, appreciating the irony, she took Zeke to the new Wetherspoon pub that had opened up which had been named "The Cribbar." She sprang for lunch and a few beers, just so she could scope him out, telling me afterward that Zeke was a nice dude, a bit out there, and did I know he was a vegetarian?

I couldn't help laughing. I remembered how odd Zeke had seemed to me when he first showed up, so chilled out and confident. No one could actually be that happy and relaxed, I'd thought. And now I couldn't figure out why everybody wasn't like him. I wanted to be around that positive energy all the time.

I could feel myself changing too. As time passed, I began to sleep through a whole night, and one day I woke up just buzzing with the stoke of being alive.

It was, I thought, the Zeke Effect.

Chapter Forty-three

The rest of August was a blur of shifts at the Billabong shop and evenings spent at Zeke's. On one rainy day, Kelly and I got our GCSE results. Kelly checked hers first and was stoked that she'd done well enough to stay on for A levels. Mine were mainly Bs, with an A* in geography and an A in math. My mom was so pleased that she gave me a congratulations card and a check for three hundred dollars. My dad sent a card too, with one hundred dollars in cash. A day later, I owned a Flash Bomb, which was supposed to be the world's fastest-drying wetsuit as it had an inner lining that dried in twenty minutes. It took all my exam money to buy it, but it worked and was therefore worth every penny because it meant no more putting on a damp, ice-cold suit first thing in the morning.

Then it happened. We were sitting in front of Zeke's huge windows, watching the sun go down in a riot of gold, the windows of the bay-side houses reflecting the sky, cuddling on his massive sofa and drawing warmth from each other. Lightly I touched the red knife line that Daniel had left on Zeke's thigh, and I traced my fingers along the old scars on Zeke's chest and shoulders. So many hidden reefs and rocks; so many near misses.

Zeke was too quiet.

"You thinking?" I said.

"Maybe we should talk about it tomorrow."

I was filled with dread at that moment. I just knew he was going to tell me he was leaving.

"You're off?" I said.

The hesitation before answering was enough to send my heart into overdrive.

"Yeah, tell me tomorrow," I said, suddenly not wanting, or needing, to know.

The next day, when he'd told me, I sat there numb.

After everything we'd been through. All the highs, all the pain, he had to go. No choice. And he was going in less than three weeks.

And, if I didn't win some stupid competition, I couldn't follow.

I didn't want to be one of those blond girls that trailed around the surf scene, just someone's girlfriend, some pro-surfer's groupie. Getting in the way. An embarrassment.

If I didn't earn my place, I'd have to stay in Newquay and do my A levels. It would break my heart and I could hardly bear to think about it, but it had to be that way.

It was all down to me. Compete and win, or stay at home. I'd barely been in the water since Zeke's near-death experience; I didn't even know if I still had an inner waterwoman.

It was like Zeke had told me before: he would never stop surfing. He had to get through the QS and qualify for the World Championship Tour. Not just for himself, but for all the family and friends that had helped him through his meth nightmare.

"I have to prove to them, and to myself, that I can do this without drugs."

So, if I wanted to be with Zeke, I couldn't stop either. I would have to be as brave as he was. I would have to give it everything I had. And I would have to win.

Chapter Forty-four

September arrived, and with it Wavemasters.

Anders had officially entered me and Saskia for the Face of Billabong Showdown Contest, and another top surf agent had found a girl from Saunton Sands in North Devon, who could apparently carve so hard she'd been nicknamed Shank.

Billabong was trying something new and wanted a girl who could dominate on both shortboards *and* longboards, and since the first trial had been shortboards, this time we'd have to ride out on Malibus.

Whereas shortboarding was all about keeping fairly motionless and balanced on the board, longboarding involved much more movement. Longboard riders had more buoyancy to work with and could move back and forth along the board's wooden centerline or "stringer." It was incredibly difficult, but I'd spent my first year of surfing on a nine-foot Watershed longboard, so I could do some cool stuff.

Still, I had so much training to do, and only one week to prepare. I was already running and doing yoga every day, but I knew I'd have to add in beach circuits, gym sessions and sea swimming. I needed to be as fit and strong as possible. Most of all, I needed to stop being frightened of the sea.

The outcome of this final contest would determine whether I'd have a life of thrills, waves and Zeke, or a boring job in a shop and a life of regrets.

Zeke and I had battled life and death, and suddenly our future together depended on me catching some 6.0 or higher-scoring waves. I'd have laughed if it wasn't so painful.

September 7th came and, at eight o'clock I arrived at the beach. I made sure I was there early, before the other girls got there, so that I'd have time to look at the waves, just watching the swell rise and fall. Zeke had wanted to come with me, to feed me snacks and distract me from feeling nervous, but I hadn't let him. I needed two hours of pure concentration on my own, to prepare.

On the doorstep of his apartment he'd kissed me, wished me good luck and told me he'd be waterside for the buzzer at 10 a.m.

As a surfer, the stuff you did on the beach was almost as important as the stuff you did out in the waves, and I needed every bit of advantage I could get. I needed to see the pattern of the sets rolling in. Conditions were always changing but, if you spent sixty or even thirty minutes watching, you could get a feel for the ocean, an idea of how everything was developing.

None of it was totally predictable though. And if, during the few minutes I'd have to prove myself, the surf went totally flat; well, then, too bad. That was just the way it went. You couldn't complain, because it could happen to anyone. And anyway, bad surf was the best teacher. You learned to make the most of what you got. You learned patience.

I made my way past the council litter pickers and the old guys with metal detectors, and walked down to the water's edge.

It was going to be really shifty out there, first because a heavy rip current was sucking through the line-up, and second because the faces on these waves were steep, and with a longboard—which was slower and less responsive than a shortboard—the waves were going to be hard to handle.

I could feel myself losing the little bit of nerve I had left; could feel the brakes kicking in. And I knew I had to deal with that because, as all the surf lore tells you, if you feel uncomfortable, then you should get out of the water immediately, because the battle is as much mental as physical.

What was I doing? How did I think I could do this? I had hardly been in the water since Zeke had drowned and been brought back to life by Garrett. I had thought that was only because I was afraid, but I was beginning to realize that it was also because I was distracted. I couldn't concentrate enough to tune into the ocean and become part of it.

Nine a.m. arrived. I only had one hour left of my prep time in which to warm up. I turned to face the dunes, checking out the already heaving beach bar and the zillions of people waiting for Ed Sheeran to come play his set on the Wavemasters stage.

Fistral had never, ever been this busy.

I was panicked and stressed, my mind racing in a jumble of headbutting thoughts. If I was going to go out into the water and show my best stuff, I had to stop the wheels from spinning. I needed one minute when I was totally calm.

I practiced some breathing techniques and then tried to channel my yoga-class teachers. Stuff anybody watching. I needed to A) chill out, and B) stretch my muscles so that I didn't injure myself.

I threw a few shapes on the sand, easing into a downward dog and then moving through a sun salutation.

Then I crouched into a ball, tipped on to my forearms and held my whole weight there in crow pose. I dipped forward, touching the top of my head to the ground. With my hands on either side and a little way back from my head, I pulled myself up slowly, one centimeter at a time into a tripod headstand.

I held that headstand for a minute and forever.

And, when I came down, I was ready to shred.

Chapter Forty-five

Anders was calling my name. He was standing between two guys: one with a long-lens camera and another with a clipboard. I recognized them both from Zeke's signing at the Billabong shop. Saskia and the Saunton girl, Lana, had just arrived, along with a few other girls who just seemed to want to hang out and watch the showdown.

Saskia was paler than usual. Maybe she didn't like the look of the conditions either. Lana didn't seem at all bothered. Without even saying hi to me, she started waxing her board. She was the stereotypical blond surfer chick, with perfect long straight hair that looked like the light from a hundred-watt bulb was beaming down on it. She didn't have the nicest face in the world though, and a sneer made her mouth ugly.

I didn't want to get in her way and I hoped she'd stay out of mine. There were plenty of waves. We shouldn't have to fight for them. Still, there was something about her that set my alarm off. I'd try to put some distance between us.

One of the newspaper guys said he wanted a dry-hair shot of us outside the Billabong store, so we all had to trudge back up the beach with our boards.

One of Lana's friends in the crowd handed her a Ziploc bag of make-up and hair products, and she went off to the bathroom to slap it all on. I looked around for Zeke, Kelly and my mom, but it was impossible to find them in the hordes and I didn't have my phone.

I followed Lana, as I was busting for a pee, and figured I could scan the beach from the balcony outside the public toilets.

Because of Wavemasters, there were way more hen and stag parties around than was normal for nine thirty on a Saturday morning, because people were getting to the beach early to nab the best spots to watch Ed Sheeran. I took my board into the ladies' room with me and left it leaning against the wall by the hand dryers. At nine-and-a-half-feet long, it would never fit in the tiny bathroom stall. Luckily Lana was there doing her make-up, so she'd shout out if someone tried to swipe it.

"OK to keep an eye on my board?" I asked.

She grunted in my direction and I gave her the nod.

When I came out thirty seconds later, Lana was gone, but my board was still there, so I grabbed it and walked back around the side of the building, still looking for Zeke, Kelly and my mom.

Nope. Nothing.

I swung around the back of the complex and over the draw-bridge to the store. With the big cameras snapping away and the video cameras rolling, the crowd was beginning to pay attention to the Billabong event and I could hear voices in the crowd rating us like we were cattle, while we posed and blinked in the bright sunshine.

We walked back down to the break again, and I finally saw Zeke, waving at me from some rocks at the water's edge. He was holding a video camera and standing among a group of men and women with long lenses. They were in the best position to catch all the action on film.

I waved back, and right at that moment Anders gave a signal and someone sounded a buzzer. The race was on.

The three of us legged it into the water, gripping our huge boards under our arms, and together we stroked out into the surf.

With Fistral full-on pumping though, and no calm channels, we had to turtle-roll through the impact zone at top speed, as the longboards were too sturdy and buoyant to duck-dive. It wasn't too tricky, as long as we hit the waves really fast and at exactly ninety degrees.

Once again, Saskia made it to the line-up first. The girl was fast. She stroked for the first wave and took off on a barreling right-hander. Stunning wave. Lana tried to drop in on her but didn't make it. So I'd been right about Lana. She was one of those Wild West, anything goes, *I'll do what I want and screw you* types.

But falling off the back of the wave had pushed Lana further out to sea and she wasn't in position to make the second wave of the set.

I was. I caught an immense ride. It was a really groomed, glassy wave, with not a drop of water out of place. It looked just like the opening credits of that American TV show *Hawaii Five-0*, where they roll to footage of a perfect blue, clean-breaking barrel. Up and riding, I tried to throw in a mixture of traditional and progressive longboard maneuvers, including some cutbacks and drop-knee turns, but the steepness of the wave face didn't make it easy. When the wave weakened, I stepped off the rail and hopped back into the water.

Second time out back, I was only just managing to paddle wide on the worst of the breakers when I saw that Lana was up and riding, just pretty standard moves: head-dips, switch stance and that was it. Nothing too flashy. Then she launched a hang-five that I didn't see coming at all. The rail bogged into the wave face though, and she tanked. Thank God. If she'd made that, we'd all have been toast and she'd have been swinging off to Sunset Beach with Anders on one side of her and Zeke on the other.

I was checking out a great-looking tepee of a wave when a clump of kelp bunched up around my ankle. I tried to shake it off my foot, but by then I'd messed up the timing and it was too late for me to take off. I flipped around and paddled further offshore and still hadn't made it fully into position when I saw Saskia take off on the next wave, a big one, and come pouring down the face, easily making the drop. There were all kinds of ballerina-ish footwork going on, so again the judges would have to score her high for excellent control. At the end of her ride there was no swan dive, just a graceful step into the sea.

I paddled for a wave and realized late it was too weak to offer much scoring potential so I slid down the back as I couldn't risk losing my place in the line-up. I thought of Zeke, and how his competition success came not just from physical surfing talent but from his smart wave-selection decisions. I would have to get better at that, because being able to spot the best wave in a set was a powerful skill that divided winners from losers.

As if on cue, I watched Saskia paddle into a tight little tube, so tight that I thought she wasn't coming out of the last pinching section; but a small gap opened up, the kind of exit that surf commentators called the "cat flap" or "doggy door," and Saskia was obviously calm and collected because she stayed low and conjured her way through without getting clipped by the chandelier section of the wave.

With a sinking feeling, I thought of Zeke recording everything from the rocks. I knew he'd see that Saskia was locking in good scores and that I was chasing her lead. It was completely gutting. Saskia had the edge over me in shortboarding, and in longboarding too, it seemed.

I decided then that if I was going to give it my best shot, I had to leave it all out there and hold nothing back; I'd try a move that I didn't think either Saskia or Lana would be able to do on their slightly shorter boards. Keeping my weight in my right foot as much as I could, I moved toward the nose of the board.

I was going to try for the hang-ten. It was a mega-difficult move, but probably the coolest thing you could do on a longboard, and a successful hang-ten with return along the stringer would attract major points off the judges. Quick as a flash, I was at the nose of the board, hanging my toes over the edge, when I felt my feet slip from under me and I was suddenly airborne.

I got worked, and rolled around on the seabed a little, but not as bad as I'd expected from that critical section of the wave.

What the hell had gone wrong?

I had never slipped like that before. It was like all the wax had evaporated from my board, which was impossible.

I pulled my board toward me using my leash and, yep, the wax was still right where I'd put it, in the exact same configuration of diamonds that I always used. In the lull of a bobbing wave, I put my face down to get a better look at the deck, and caught a reflection of the sun on the nose of my board. Something slick was sitting over the matte surface of the board wax there. I touched it, brought my fingers to my nose and smelled . . .

Flowers.

My board wax didn't smell of flowers; I always used the classic Mr. Zog's Sex Wax for cold-water surf conditions, and that smelled like coconut.

Nothing I owned smelled of flowers.

But the smell was familiar; I just couldn't quite put my finger on where I'd come across it. I turned around quickly so I wouldn't get slammed by a breaker, and I saw Lana wiping out.

That was it. Her hair reeked of flowers.

No way.

She had totally sabotaged my board.

Spread hair gel or something all over the nose of my board when we were in the toilets.

I dived down, grabbed a handful of sand and started raking it over the goo, hoping to get off as much as I could, but it didn't seem to be working.

Forget it. Move on.

In the final ten minutes I didn't try any more nose-riding. Instead, I stopped focusing on the other girls, got busy, caught as many waves as I could, crammed in a ton of strong rail cut-backs, trusted my gut instincts to identify the better waves and found my own surfing rhythm. I remembered what Zeke told me about his contest strategy: he'd stay calm, and when the heat was flat he'd plan out sequences of maneuvers, riding waves in his head that hadn't come yet. Confidence and a positive attitude were vital; Zeke said that to outperform your opponents, you never said die. You kept chipping away until the buzzer sounded, even when it looked like you were beat; especially then. You had to keep the pressure on the other competitors by chasing one decent wave after another until you found the sick ride that would land you the winning score.

With his words in my head and the last two minutes counting down, I knew I'd ridden some competitive waves but had to keep going, despite the fact that I was wrecked from paddling a line-up with so much current running through it and so out of breath I was practically gasping. With one minute left on the clock, I took off deep on a pristine head-high tube. I caught a glimpse of Saskia sitting on her board with her fists pressed against her eyes, gutted that I'd grabbed such a good wave in the last few seconds, then I got locked in the green room. I held a high line and came flying out of it. The buzzer sounded just as I'd stepped off my board, and I could only hope that last wave was enough.

Chapter Forty-six

It wasn't.

The best surfer in the world is the one having the most fun. Saskia had the most fun during the Billabong contest, no doubt. She'd managed to control her board, demonstrate clean footwork, and she had a smile on her face as she did it.

She'd done her thing, done it well, and she'd won. She was a more experienced surfer than I was, had a better eye for waves and a better execution of maneuvers.

A group of onlookers crowded around the judging tent, waiting for the scoring to be announced over the loudspeaker. Wes, Elijah, Garrett, Dave and Sephy were standing to one side, and they all looked pretty nervous. Elijah and Garrett still weren't really talking, but the fact that they were on the same patch of sand without fighting seemed like progress.

My mom, Aunt Zoe, Cara and Kelly had been down at the water's edge, and they raced up the beach with me, itching to check out the scores.

Zeke jumped down from the rocks where he'd been filming and ran past the crowds and straight up to the judging panel. As a Billabong team rider he wouldn't have to wait for the official announcement. A judge handed him a sheet of paper and I saw him go gray in the face when he saw how close the scores were, but he tried hard not to show how bummed he was that I'd crashed and burned at the final hurdle. I walked over to him and he handed me the paper.

We were scored on our best wave, and there was only a points difference of 0.40 in the scoring for me and Saskia, which was nothing and which hurt like hell, but there was no prize for second place.

For all of her shitty tactics, Lana was nowhere near. Her best wave was a 5.78. Mine was an 8.20 and Saskia's an 8.60. Lana didn't hang around. She made a beeline for the car park, and I watched her progress across the beach, her figure getting smaller and smaller until she was lost in the crowd.

Zeke put his arm around me but he seemed to have lost his powers of speech. I'd never seen him look so miserable before.

"Sorry for letting you down," I whispered.

He said, "You so didn't. Anyways, I've booked that hot-air balloon trip for sunset tonight. We'll eat some great food, spot some new surf breaks and shake this off."

I turned and kissed him, grateful to have something to look forward to, something to take my mind off the crushing disappointment.

Then my mom gave me a big cuddle and said, "Oh my God, Iris. I couldn't believe that was my little girl out there. You were wonderful. Your grandmother would have been so proud," which made me well up with tears.

"Thanks, Mom," I said, resting my head on her shoulder.

Sephy appeared, placed her palms together and said, "Namaste," which we said in yoga class and which I knew meant, "I bow to you." Then she took my hand and said, "Keep your face turned toward the sunshine, surfer girl, and let the shadows fall behind you," and right then, I knew "face turned toward the sunshine" would become my own personal mantra.

Dave, Elijah, Wes and Garrett came over, and took turns hugging me.

"Gutted for you, honey," Dave said. "But you're a damn good surfer and don't you forget it."

I looked at Wes, who said, "I know this majorly sucks, but there are other ways to get sponsorship."

"Those judges are idiots," Kelly said, giving me a kiss on the forehead. "Don't let them stop you."

Garrett grinned and said, "Yeah, screw Billabong. Go get sponsored by Quiksilver."

"We'll help," Elijah said. "We could record some footage of you surfing. Put a reel and a résumé together for you to send out to surf companies."

Garrett was obviously impressed with this idea, because for a second it looked like he was going to give Elijah a fist bump, but he must have thought better of it because instead of doing that, he relaxed his fist, dropped his hand and nodded at Elijah and murmured, "*Booyah*."

"Thanks, Elijah. That'd be great," I said.

"Such a shame you didn't win," Aunt Zoe said. "You were so good too. But, Iris, you have got to teach me how to surf. That looked incredible!"

Sephy piped up with, "I'll teach you. One mother to another. Trust me, girl, it's gonna blow your mind."

Cara was pawing at Zeke and he picked her up and put her on his shoulders, where she sat quietly stroking his hair.

Saskia was high as a kite, but she came over to commiserate with me.

"You know, there's a place open now, as Anders's personal assistant . . ."

"Yeah, good point," Zeke said, brightening a bit, and looking at my mom in a hopeful way.

"Anders is not gonna want me," I said, feeling totally useless. "I'd be terrible at it and it would be like torture, sitting around doing paperwork and making calls while you guys were off riding the best waves on the planet. At least here I can surf."

"But I can't stay here with you," Zeke said.

I saw Saskia check the look on Zeke's face and she turned to me. "What happened out there? The hang-ten thing? It looked like you had it perfect and then you were sailing through the air. I've never seen a wipeout like that before. It was like someone sucked your legs off the board."

"I don't know."

I couldn't say what had happened. They'd just think it was sour grapes.

"What was it, Iris?" Kelly said.

"The nose of my board."

Saskia was already picking up my board to look at it. I saw her face fall when she caught the smell. She rubbed her hand along the surface and picked up a few traces of something slippery.

"That is hair serum. Pure silicone."

She shot a look in the direction of the car park, where Lana was no doubt putting her foot to the floor, leaving Newquay for Saunton Sands.

"The cheating cow," Kelly said.

"Wait a minute—somebody sabotaged Iris's surfboard?" my mom said.

Aunt Zoe took Cara off Zeke's shoulders and cuddled her tight. "That is appalling," she said. "Iris, you were robbed."

Zeke was gripping my hands and saying, "Baby, listen: it's not over."

"This is a diabolical disgrace," my mom said, getting redder and more teacher-ish by the second.

And then Saskia did something that I'd never in a million years have expected. She marched straight up to Anders and the other judges, and dragged them back to me and Zeke.

"What is it? What's going on?" said Anders.

"If she'd managed to hang ten, what would that have scored her?"

"Hard to say, really, but that's a heavily weighted maneuver," one of the judges said.

"So more than an 8.60, right?"

"Yeah, sure," Anders said. "It would have scored somewhere between an 8.75 and a 10, depending on the execution."

Saskia took a deep breath and looked me straight in the eyes, even though she was talking to Anders.

"Iris won, then. The only reason she didn't make the hang-ten was because Miss Thing from Saunton Sands cheated her ass off and wrecked Iris's board with silicone so that Iris couldn't maintain proper traction."

I couldn't believe my ears. Saskia, who I'd thought was my biggest rival and who I'd treated like my sworn enemy, was offering me the opportunity of a lifetime. The thing she'd worked toward for two years.

Why?

OK, so what had happened was unfair, but surfing was like that. One heat could have all the good waves and your heat could be flat. Sometimes you got the perfect wave, because you were in the perfect spot through luck not skill. You literally took the rough with the smooth, and when it was rough you sucked it up and hoped you'd do better next time. It was just the nature of surfing.

My mom looked like she was on the point of bursting a blood vessel.

One of the judges turned to Saskia and said, "I feel bad for Iris here, but what's done is done, and we can't judge on what might have been. You're through, Saskia. Congratulations. You are the new face of Billabong UK."

"Not if I withdraw," Saskia said quietly.

What?

She was talking herself out of the ultimate prize. Maybe she didn't want it if she hadn't won it fair and square. Or maybe she cared so much about Zeke that she wanted him to be happy and she guessed that Zeke being happy meant me winning this thing.

But there was something else in Saskia's eyes. Generosity. I saw it then: the thing I'd never let myself see before. I'd been so busy being snippy about her clothes and her accent that I hadn't let myself see that behind all the surface glitz, Saskia was a cool girl with a heart of gold.

Talk about prejudice. I'd never even given her a chance, but now she was giving me everything. I knew, very clearly, that this could be the first step on the ladder of an amazing career and a life to match. As a Face of Billabong, I would have a backstage pass to the most epic waves on the planet, as well as a constant stream of the best boards and a chance to hang with some of the most radical surfers that had ever lived.

And best of all, I would be there experiencing it all with Zeke, the person who inspired me every single day.

"Are you formally withdrawing?" the judge asked Saskia.

She took a deep breath, and said, "Yes."

Anders talked to the other judges, and it all went very serious as they each checked out the nose of my surfboard. Then Anders had a quiet conversation with Saskia before turning back to me with a huge grin on his face.

"Well then, Iris, it's yours for the taking."

"Yeah?" I said, still not quite believing it. Kelly was hanging off my back, shrieking. Zeke was holding both my hands and dragging me up toward the stage, and my mom and Aunt Zoe had completely lost it and were hugging each other through floods of tears.

"Iris, this is it. You did it, baby," Zeke said, his hands shaking with excitement.

Over my head Kelly screeched, "Ed Sheeran's got the giant check!" I looked up at the stage, where I could just make out a slim ginger-haired guy holding a big white piece of cardboard.

"So are you gonna go for it, flower?" Anders asked me.

I looked at Saskia, who was nodding encouragement, and I looked at Zeke, whose eyes were shining with happiness. Then I thought of Nanna.

I said the only thing I could say:

"Hell yeah."

Acknowledgments

I would like to thank the following people for their assistance:

My wonderful family for helping me to the surface so many times when I was drowning in the impact zone of modern publishing. My agent Ben Illis for always believing in the writing. My editors Roisin Heycock and Talya Baker for excellent ideas and advice.

Tassy Swallow and Jaide Lowe for sharing the highs and lows of life as teenage pro-surfers. Likewise, the brilliant Oli and Emma Adams.

The environmental activist group Surfers for Cetaceans, including pro-surfers Chris del Moro and Dave Rastovich, as well as Justin Krumb and Howie Cooke, for their passion for surf culture and their efforts to protect the marine environment.

Rhys John, Max Hepworth-Povey and Christopher Hunter of Errant Surf for illuminating chats and fun in the water.

Big wave pro-surfer Chris Bertish for telling me how it felt to paddle the mighty Cribbar.

The Bra Boys of Maroubra for their insightful documentary and for making me think about surf brotherhood.

Sara and Jade at the Little Cake Shop for keeping me fed and watered while I wrote this book.

Fistral surf buddies Laura Ward and Francesco Rigolli for surf chat. Likewise Tina Beresford and Karl Michaelides. Thanks also to the other local surfers who gave their time to help me write this book and particularly the surfers of North Fistral, who have been dazzling me for more than a decade.

Sarah Clarke of Checkered Photography. Daniel Stapleford, Aimee Stapleford and Kristin Becker for invaluable help with research and all things yoga.

My colleagues, the Book Foxes of Vulpes Libris, and particularly the writers and reviewers Eve Harvey, Hilary Ely, Moira Briggs, Leena Heino and Kirsty McCluskey, as well as Paul Glass, Jon Cann, Laura Ward, Kate Neal and Beki Jenkins for kindly reading early drafts of this novel.

Screenwriter and novelist Rosy Barnes for always nagging me to write the big scenes.

About the Type

Text set in Perpetua Regular at 11 / 14.25 pt.

Perpetua is a book typeface designed by Eric Gill, released by Monotype in 1929, and modeled in the style of transitional serif fonts of the late eighteenth and early nineteenth century.

Typeset by Scribe Inc., Philadelphia, Pennsylvania